Pr:

CONFEDERACY OF FENIANS

"Imaginative, creative, and eminently well written, Jim Nealon's *Confederacy of Fenians* captures the essence of the struggle for independence and identity. Within the landscape of our past lie lessons that both inform and challenge. Nealon's fanciful rendering of a Confederate–British alliance during the American Civil War, leveraged through the quest for Irish freedom, stays true to the situations and personalities of our past but challenges his reader to wonder 'What if?' A first-class, well-researched and captivating read."

> —Greg Fields
> Author of *Through the Waters and the Wild*, 2021 New York Book Award Winner in Literary Fiction

"Nealon's beautifully written first novel will cause the reader to question his assumptions and what might have been (and give Irish patriots a smile). A must-read."

> —Ambassador (ret.) Thomas B. Robertson

"Clear your schedule before starting *Confederacy of Fenians*; you will not be able to put it down. Nealon's debut is a fascinating mix of historical characters woven into a gripping plot, making it a perfect book for fiction readers who love history, or history buffs who love fiction."

> —David P. Wagner
> Author of the Rick Montoya Italian Mystery Series

"Spoiler alert: this is a fun read, fast paced and enlightening. Jim Nealon may have launched a whole new genre in history, imagining the paths almost taken. In this case, Gettysburg students know how easily the outcome of that battle could have resulted in a Confederate victory there. Nealon creatively pulls on that thread and weaves together tales of Irish independence, the Underground Railroad, and the ensuing battles that might have shaped a different war between the states."

—John Dickson
Author of *History Shock*

"At a time when our country is rethinking the status of central figures in the Civil War, it is useful to have a novel that imagines an alternative vision of the war. And what an imagining it is. Nealon spins a remarkable yarn that is gripping from start to finish. If you like historical fiction, this is a must-read. I couldn't put it down."

—Paul Lauritzen
Professor Emeritus, John Carroll University

"For all who love history—for all who have wondered the great what-ifs of America's defining moments—James Nealon's intelligent and intriguing dive into alternative history is not to be missed. Drawing on a depth of knowledge about the American Civil War and its leading figures and movements, Nealon asks a bold question: would Irish soldiers fighting for the Union have forsaken their oaths for a greater calling—the achievement of their centuries-old struggle for independence from the English crown? Nealon's first foray into the realm of alt-historic fiction will leave you wanting only one thing: his next novel."

—Todd M. Johnson
Acclaimed Historic and Legal Fiction Author of *The Barrister and the Letter of Marque, The Deposit Slip, Critical Reaction,* and *Fatal Trust*

Confederacy of Fenians

By James D. Nealon

ISBN 978-1-64663-508-5

Published by

 köehlerbooks™

3705 Shore Drive
Virginia Beach, VA 23455
800–435–4811
www.koehlerbooks.com

CONFEDERACY OF FENIANS

JAMES D. NEALON

VIRGINIA BEACH
CAPE CHARLES

To Kristin, Rory, Katie, Maureen, and Liam.
Thanks for listening to all the stories. Or at least pretending to.

This is a work of historical fiction, not a history book. It's a story, a yarn. While most of the characters are real historical figures, and I've tried hard to portray their actions as true to character, I nonetheless present an alternative version of the Civil War, a (hopefully) gripping *what if.*

What if Lee had won at Gettysburg? What if the British had entered the war on the side of the Confederacy? And what if these events had motivated the Fenian Brotherhood, the shadowy, secret society of Irish revolutionaries based in New York, to turn coat in a ploy to secure Irish independence after the war? Yes, an alternate take on history, but all possible if the outcome at Gettysburg, which hung in the balance for three days, had been different.

Three of the five main characters play themselves, if you will: George McClellan and his wife Nelly; Jefferson Davis and his wife Varina; and General John Fox Burgoyne, son of "Gentleman Johnny" Burgoyne of Revolutionary War fame. More about him later. A fourth main character, John Patrick Lane, a leader of the Fenian conspiracy in the book, was actually my real-life ancestor. He really was a passionate proponent of Irish independence.

Among the supporting cast are the great figures of the Civil

War—Lincoln, Grant, Longstreet, Lee, Custer, Stuart, and others. Also, the leading figures of the Fenian movement, including John O'Mahony and Thomas Francis Meagher, commander of the fabled Irish Brigade.

British General John Fox Burgoyne was in life the son of "Gentleman Johnny" Burgoyne and a leading figure in the British military for sixty years. He attained the rank of field marshal upon his retirement in 1868. In this book I offer him the opportunity to avenge a stain on the family name.

Finally, Viola is a fictional character, a free Black woman fighting the Civil War in her own way. I'm told that authors should love all of their characters equally, but Viola is my favorite. And if there is any question about where I stand on the Union or slavery or the Confederacy or the role of women, she speaks for me.

Enjoy the yarn.

Jim Nealon
Exeter, New Hampshire
November 2021

BURGOYNE

Canada—US Border
October 1863

John Fox Burgoyne looked out over the New York countryside, staring across the border from Quebec for fifteen minutes, silently, and it had become awkward. He could sense his staff officers' impatience as they stole concerned looks at each other or stared at the ground. Small clouds of steam flared from their horses' nostrils in the crisp Canadian air, and their blooded horses, unaccustomed to inaction, pawed the hard dirt.

Behind Burgoyne, 15,000 British soldiers in columns of six stretched for two miles, shivering, and wondering as soldiers will what the hell was happening up ahead and why they'd been roused at 5 a.m. to stand in the road. Even Burgoyne's horse, which normally knew better than to question the general, cast a sideways glance as if to say, *"Shall we get on with it then?"* He received no reply.

A mile behind Burgoyne, Corporal Michael Stanton stood in line next to Corporal Robert Jenkins. Their company had come to a halt fifteen minutes previously, and both wondered if their war would begin and end in the tiny Quebec village of Saint Bernard de Lacolle.

Stanton turned to Jenkins and said, too loud, "Right enough, the general has cold feet, and no wonder, my feet are damned cold as well."

Jenkins coughed and stamped his feet. "I don't think it's the weather that's slowing Johnny down. More likely ghosts. It wasn't far from here that his old man's troubles began."

"This one's no London fop. All business and don't we know it."

"Still and all, I'm glad I'm just carrying this pack across the border and not the load he's carrying on his shoulders."

"Silence in the ranks," called their sergeant, though without his usual enthusiasm.

"Everyone is feeling the weight," whispered Jenkins.

At the head of the column, Burgoyne was in no hurry to invade the United States of America. This, as in all things, distinguished him from his famous father. *Gentleman Johnny Burgoyne,* he thought. His father had made his own crossing from Quebec to New York in 1777 full of the arrogance of the Empire and aware that his success in crushing rebellion would be a very good thing indeed for his career as a soldier certainly, but as a playwright and London social lion most assuredly. The humiliating surrender at Saratoga that autumn had stymied his military ambitions, but in fact his theatrical career had flourished.

The son was determined that history would not repeat itself. There would be no second Burgoyne disaster on the battlefields of North America. To the contrary, where the father was drama and theatrics and style, the son was an engineer, a planner, a logistician, and fond of cold steel. This time there would be no overambitious and predictably botched plans, and he would not be outmaneuvered by citizen soldiers. The experience of sixty years of soldiering, at New Orleans, on the Peninsula, and at Sevastopol had led him to this moment, and he would seize it.

"Gentleman Johnny indeed," he muttered.

"Sir?"

It was Major Thomas Packenham, his aide-de-camp.

"Major, prepare the column to move forward."

"Yes sir. Sergeant Major, colors and band to the front."

The order long anticipated, the color guard and the regimental band of the 92nd of Foot were already in place.

"Sir," said Major Packenham. "I was thinking *The World Turned Upside Down*."

Generally immune to irony and unacquainted with mirth, but with a highly developed sense of history, Burgoyne chuckled.

"Make it so, Major Packenham."

The band struck up the old barroom drinking song, made infamous by Lord Cornwallis as his soldiers stacked arms and abandoned their trenches at Yorktown. With the colors fluttering in the light breeze, John Fox Burgoyne nudged his impatient horse forward and led the British Army into the United States for the first time since 1815.

The world turned upside down? No, not this time, he thought. *The world put right again is more like it.*

"A bit of an anticlimax, eh Major?"

"Sir?"

"The border. A line on a map. No mountain range, no river, no guard posts, no entrenchments on either side. We're about to cross the border, invade a sovereign nation, and the only witnesses are those cows. An anticlimax."

"Yes sir."

Major Packenham listened in amazement as Burgoyne whistled quietly along with the band.

McCLELLAN

Washington, DC
October 1863

His desk seemed to fill half the room. It was solid, substantial, and functional. *Not unlike the man,* he mused. He sat in a deep, plush leather chair before it, bolt upright, back straight, feet flat on the ground. General George McClellan had been staring at his desk for the better part of an hour, deep in thought. Light streamed in through the windows, and a low fire burned in the fireplace, both adding their warmth to the wood and leather furnishings and insulating him from the chilly autumn morning.

McClellan raised his eyes and looked around. The room told a story of his professional life up to that point. It was the room of a man of substance and accomplishment. The size, the look, the smell, the decor, all lent a heavy air of achievement, quality, and prosperity. McClellan took quick stock of the various objects, each reminding him of how far he'd come and how much he'd already accomplished at just thirty-six. The sword he'd worn as a young officer in Mexico. Another, far fancier, inlaid with gold and delicately carved, which had been a gift from British officers in the Crimea. On the table were the books on cavalry tactics and use of the bayonet, both of which he'd authored before he was thirty. Slung over the back of a chair was the polished saddle which bore his name. The walls featured maps of bold military expeditions to the Red River and to Washington Territory, and paintings of magnificent steam engines from his time as a railroad executive. This inventory, undertaken a dozen times a day, took mere seconds and filled him with pride, but always ended with that feeling of emptiness, of unfinished business. The room contained few reminders of his greatest achievements, leading the Union Army to grand but poorly appreciated victories in western Virginia, on the Virginia Peninsula, before Richmond, and at Antietam. Unfinished business.

McClellan had always known it was his destiny to save the Union and crush the rebellion. That destiny had been thwarted, delayed, interrupted twice by the incompetent buffoon in the President's House. He became angry at the thought. Fired twice by Abraham Lincoln, both times on the verge of launching grand offensives that would have led to sweeping and decisive victories in the field. He knew it. His soldiers knew it. The public knew it. Only Lincoln couldn't see it. He could feel the heat rise in his face and his neck, and he began to perspire.

His brief tour of his study complete, the general's eyes returned to his desk. Side by side lay two telegrams. He had read each a dozen times already, and he read them again. One had originated just a couple of blocks away, at the Executive Mansion, and was signed *A. Lincoln. He could have sent a handwritten note, by God, or delivered the message himself. That would have been the proper and manly thing to do.* The other telegram, from New York, was signed by Governor Horatio Seymour, one of the country's most prominent Democratic Party politicians.

Each telegram, read separately, might offer McClellan the opportunity to fulfill his destiny. Together, they complicated his life, and perhaps the fate of the country, beyond measure.

Lincoln's telegram offered McClellan, again, the position at the head of all Union armies. At least that was the general's assumption. McClellan was respectfully requested to attend the president at 9:00 a.m. the following day on a matter of the greatest import for the nation. It couldn't mean anything else.

He studied the message with Talmudic attention, but Lincoln gave nothing away, offered no hint of apology for his previous treatment of McClellan. *Fair enough. There will be time and opportunity to take care of that, and revenge and vindication will be all the sweeter for the wait,* McClellan mused.

While the first telegram offered the prospect of setting history to rights, and tacitly recognized what the general and others already knew—that only McClellan could save the Union on the battlefield—the second telegram was a surprise. Seymour offered nothing less than the Democratic Party's nomination for president in the upcoming election of 1864, still a year in the future.

For the tenth time in the space of an hour, McClellan weighed the opportunities. Returning to the field and destroying the Rebel armies would assure his rightful place in history, at the very top of the heap. Washington. McClellan. Or perhaps McClellan. Washington.

But the Democrats were offering an even greater opportunity. The chance to crush Lincoln at the polls. They didn't specifically state that he could simultaneously be commander in chief and general of the armies. But why not? Napoleon had led the nation and the French Army. Couldn't McClellan, the Young Napoleon, do the same?

There was a light tap on the door and Nelly peeked in. Smiling, elegant, straight to the point. A soldier's wife.

"Are you coming down, George? Dinner's been ready this half hour. Perhaps you can do me the courtesy of joining me at the table and explaining why couriers have been coming and going all day and why you have that look in your eye."

And a sharp tongue, he thought, but smiling to himself. *Nothing gets past her.*

"I'll be right down. I need to draft a short message. Five minutes."

The door closed gently, and he heard the stairs creak as Nelly returned to the dining room. She was accustomed to waiting, and he was accustomed to making her wait.

An hour earlier it had seemed an impossible choice. But now it was clear. There was only one thing to be done. McClellan dipped his pen in the well and put it to paper. *Mr. President,* he began.

LANE

Boston, Massachusetts
October 1863

Sitting in a chair in his tailor shop, which was also his home,
John Patrick Lane awoke with a start for the third or fourth time in
the last half hour. For a moment he didn't know where he was. As this
happened to him frequently, he quickly went through his protocol,
starting with the windows. Right, two small-framed windows on
either side of the door, and another to the side. *That means I'm at
home in Boston.* The process took less than a second and he was at
ease.

The sense of not knowing where he was had started in the
army. He would wake up multiple times a night confused and lost.
He always hoped that he was home in Kilcrumper, near Fermoy
in County Cork, sleeping on the floor in front of the fire with his
brothers. But his protocol would kick in, and in an instant he'd know
that he was in fact in a tent, or sleeping on the ground, and that he
was in the Union Army. And his heart would sink.

His guest was late. Lane took the watch from his pocket, flipped it open, and saw that it was almost ten at night. The note had told him to expect his visitor at seven. But he was coming from New York, and it was raining, and he was in a line of work in which punctuality and predictability were not virtues.

Lane started to doze again, the rhythm of the rain on the roof better than any pill to lull him to sleep. It was a cold rain, too cold for the time of year, and Lane smiled as he drifted off. *I'm glad I didn't leave Cork in search of better weather.*

Lane had rehearsed his pitch a hundred times. He was more certain now that his proposed course of action was the correct one, but as the hour grew late he was less certain that his visitor would see it that way. The plan had come to him the instant that he'd learned that Great Britain had decided to support the Confederacy and had declared war on the United States.

Pounding on the door woke him with a start, and this time he knew exactly where he was. He rose, flattened the creases in his pants and jacket, and took three steps to the door.

Will I recognize him?

Sure, he'd seen the face, woodcuts of course, on the pages of *The Nation* and *The Boston Pilot.* The most famous Irishman in America, and the most notorious.

He opened the door and stared for an instant. No, he wouldn't have recognized him. No matter.

"Mr. O'Mahony, you're most welcome, come in out of the rain."

"God save all here."

The head of the Fenian Brotherhood in America strode in, clothes dripping, small pools of water following him, and he seemed to fill the small room. He doffed his coat and hat, handed them to Lane, and took a chair—Lane's chair—in front of the fire.

"Will you be having tea?" The question was asked in Irish.

O'Mahony's eyebrows lifted, and a slight smile curved on a rugged face not accustomed to an upward arch.

"I will, sure," he answered in Irish. "So, you have the old language?"

Lane recognized the accent as his own, the sweet cadence of Cork, the visitor's Irish pure and fluent with a trifle of the scholar.

"I do. And now that tailoring is a challenge," he gestured with the stump of his left arm, "I teach Irish to the likely lads in the neighborhood. It keeps the devil from the door."

"Hmph. Long waiting list is there? But I assume sedition also helps pay the bills."

Lane smiled, handed his visitor the tea, and took a seat facing him. *A good start. Common ground.* A short pause as tea was sipped, the warmth of the fire absorbed, and a quick but professional sizing up ensued.

O'Mahony broke the silence, and when he spoke, it was in English this time. "You've heard the news. Britain has finally come into the war on the side of the south. We've an opportunity to strike a blow. There are 200,000 Irishmen in the Union Army. And now they'll have their chance to kill the Saxon bastards as well as Johnny Reb. Burgoyne may have already crossed over from Canada."

Lane said nothing. *Let the man speak his mind first.*

O'Mahony went on. "And when the war is over, there will be 200,000 Irishmen, minus the poor bastards who are killed along the way, trained, armed, and ready to fight for Irish freedom. This chance will never come again. We've got to do better at signing the lads up to the Brotherhood and get ready for the day. That's where you can be helpful. A wounded veteran. An Irishman. A Gaelic scholar forsooth! You've credibility lad."

Now, thought Lane. He slipped back into Irish. "Sure, it's a grand opportunity. Win the war, save the Union, kill some Englishmen, and hope that when it's over we can muster a Fenian Army to cross the ocean and fight for our freedom. But what if there's a better way? What if we can seize this moment and secure Irish independence now, without firing a shot in Ireland?"

Lane expected an argument at best, derisive laughter and a wave of the hand at worst.

Instead, O'Mahony finished his tea and moved his chair a foot away from the fire. He was dry, warm, and comfortable. "So one-armed Union corporals are grand strategists, is it? Sure, it's a wonderful country."

Lane stiffened. *Here it comes,* he thought. He assumed O'Mahony was suspicious enough of a twenty-four-year-old corporal's ability to organize large scale-rebellion, and completely unprepared to be lectured on the organization's—his organization's—aims and strategy.

"Is there more tea at all? And is there something a wee bit stronger, seeing how we may be here awhile?"

Lane went to the cupboard and removed a bottle. Not normally a drinking man, now he wished he'd thought ahead and bought a bottle of the good stuff. He half-filled two glasses and handed one to his guest.

O'Mahony eyed the brown bottle. "Protestant whiskey, is it? No matter. All in the name of Irish unity. *Slainte.*"

Ten minutes passed. The whiskey, Protestant or not, slowly put them at ease, and there was nothing awkward about the silence. Lane took the measure of the older man. Not as young as the woodcuts suggested, and a bit thicker about the middle. Not handsome, certainly. But something about him projected great strength, resilience, and stability, and Lane couldn't help but feel the fellow was reading his thoughts. The eyes were a penetrating blue, and his hair long and swept back. Like a character in a Russian novel. All in all, probably a fair choice to lead a secret society of revolutionaries. At the very least, he looked the part.

Lane knew it was up to O'Mahony to break the silence, and he did.

"John, after you refill the glasses, why don't you tell me, in great detail, your grand plan for Irish freedom?"

DAVIS

Richmond, Virginia
October 1863

Jefferson Davis glanced at the clock. Fifteen minutes until his appointment with the general, whom he knew would be punctual. He returned to the documents on his desk. As his mind wandered, his eyes were drawn back to the clock, which stood seven feet tall and dominated one wall of his office in the Confederate White House. It was the nicest piece in the room, and the only one that lent an air of permanence, of weight, of a future. The rest of the furnishings looked like they'd been donated or purchased at auction, which in fact they had.

He sat behind the desk, piled high with paper, most of it dispatches from commanders in the field, much of it after action reports of battles and skirmishes long since fought. Davis read it all, or tried to, and he was now holding Robert E. Lee's report from Gettysburg. Davis remembered from experience that commanders wrote up their victories much faster than their defeats, and this particular dispatch had arrived in Richmond soon after the general's spectacular victory in

Pennsylvania. Davis had devoured every word at the time. The written record of the greatest victory on the continent since New Orleans. "I should read it again before our meeting," he said aloud to himself.

Gettysburg, Pennsylvania
July 10th, 1863
Sir: I have the honor to inform your Excellency that with the aid of a Benevolent Providence our armies have won a glorious victory . . .

Davis knew the template well. He'd written such reports himself, though never of a battle of this proportion or import. He also knew that he wouldn't learn much from the report. Lee was from the old school. *Benevolent Providence indeed.* Wasn't it Stuart's timely arrival that carried the day, along with Pickett's extraordinary frontal assault? *George Pickett.* Davis wondered if there were ever a more unlikely hero. *An Immortal. Last in his class at West Point. No matter. He'd learn what he needed to know from Lee.*

Davis had much to discuss with his famous general, especially now that the British Army had crossed from Canada into New York, or was about to, precise destination unknown. Davis had no direct communications with that army and assumed Lee didn't either.

He turned from Lee's dispatch to the letter from Prime Minister Palmerston, which had arrived via a blockade runner to the port of Charleston, then come by rail to Richmond. Coordinating with the British was not going to be easy.

Palmerston's letter was direct. *So much for British understatement,* thought Davis. It said that under the terms of Britain's declaration of war, the British government in London and their commanders in the field would set strategic objectives and choose when and where to engage Union forces. Davis found himself frowning, just as he had the first dozen times he'd read the letter. And now he had to explain to the hero of Gettysburg that he would hereafter take strategic direction from John Burgoyne.

Burgoyne. Davis remembered a pre-war conversation with George McClellan after his return from observing the Crimean War. McClellan admired professional soldiers, and Burgoyne had stood out, a careful, intentional commander whose calm countenance belied a certain ruthless nature of someone who fought to win. He would make few mistakes. *A fine choice indeed if we can align him with our strategy.*

Davis wondered about Lee, a man he'd known since Mexico but didn't really know. All courtly self-effacement in public, but Davis knew that in this army of preternaturally proud men, Lee was in a world of his own, and proud to the point of prickly. But presidents give orders and soldiers obey them, and that's how it would have to be with Bobby Lee.

The enormous clock struck the hour and the door opened. General Lee was shown in, and the door closed. They would meet alone. Hands shaken, formal greetings exchanged, and the two men sat across from each other in wooden chairs that didn't match. Lee, though fresh from the field, was impeccably dressed and sat straight and poker-faced. With his enormous head and torso, he towered over the president. Davis appreciated formality but Lee made even Davis feel slouched and sloppy.

"General, it's a pleasure to congratulate you in person for your victory."

"Thank you, Mr. President, but what general couldn't win the day with troops such as these? The men were magnificent, and I was well-served that day by my corps and division commanders. General Pickett's charge and subsequent rout of the Federal positions on Cemetery Ridge was the greatest feat of arms I've ever witnessed."

"I've read your dispatch but look forward to hearing more. General Lee, you're aware that General Burgoyne has apparently crossed from Canada into the United States?"

"Mr. President, I only know what I've read in the Washington newspapers, and what I heard in the streets of Richmond when I arrived this afternoon. But that being the case, I have some thoughts on how to use the British troops to support our efforts to bring the war to a swift and decisive end and secure our independence. I believe the Federal Army is demoralized and poorly led, and that Washington City may be ours for the taking. Perhaps we could spread this map out and I can show you what my staff and I have in mind."

"By all means, General. But let me show you a letter from Prime Minister Palmerston, which arrived earlier this week. As you'll see, Britain's declaration of war comes with conditions. Foremost among them is that they wish to take the strategic initiative. I suggest we find a way to engage directly with General Burgoyne and reach agreement on how to align our objectives and our disposition of forces."

Davis watched carefully as Lee read the letter, then read it again. Lee appeared to be deep in thought, sitting silently, the letter still in hand but his gaze far away. *Let him come to terms with it,* thought Davis. *Let him speak first.*

Lee placed the letter carefully on the table between them. He cleared his throat and spoke in a quiet voice.

"Mr. President, do I understand that you support the spirit of this letter, that the Confederate armies will cede the initiative to the British, and engage the enemy at their direction and in support of their efforts and war aims?"

It was Davis' turn to pause. He knew that the wrong choice of words could be disastrous.

"General Lee, I speak for a grateful nation when I say our continued success and very survival depend on you. I believe that there are enough Federal soldiers to go around, and that it will be our own army which will carry the day in the end. But keeping the British in the game, opening a second, northern front in this war, is the single greatest guarantee of our independence, your grand victory at Gettysburg notwithstanding. I believe that we can and should do whatever we can to keep the British Army in the field."

This time Lee did not pause. His brown eyes seemed to turn a brighter color, and Davis could see that his face had reddened. Lee rose and reached for Davis' hand. "If that's the case, Mr. President, then I can see that my service has come to an end. If I may, let me suggest that General Longstreet assume command of the Army of Northern Virginia. I don't believe it would be convenient to return to my command to say farewell to my staff and the army. I shall join Mary here in Richmond. It has been my great honor to serve my state and my country and to lead this army. I want to express my personal thanks to you for the confidence you have always shown in me."

This last statement was barely audible. Before Davis could recover from his shock, Lee had picked up his felt hat and gauntlets from the table by the door and left the room.

McCLELLAN

Washington, DC
October 1863

General George McClellan was punctual and precise by nature, and he arrived at the Executive Mansion precisely fifteen minutes after the appointed hour. The lone sentry, a sleepy and bored soldier, recognized McClellan and attempted to come to attention. *Another sign of the sad and demoralized state of the Union Army,* thought the general. *That will change soon enough.*

He was met by Lincoln's young secretary, John Hay, who made no mention of the hour, and led the general directly into the president's office.

Lincoln was standing, staring out the window with his back to the door when McClellan entered. The silhouette did justice to a Thomas Nast cartoon. He turned, smiled, and took long strides toward McClellan, bony hand outstretched in greeting. "General McClellan, thank you for coming on short notice."

McClellan stopped, arms at this side, and let the president approach. *No bear hug or embrace,* he thought. McClellan clasped the president's hand firmly but briefly, and Lincoln pointed to a small sofa in the center of the room. McClellan sat, back straight, his hat on his lap. He still hadn't said a word.

"I trust Nelly is well? My wife sends her greetings and promises to visit soon."

The high-pitched voice and the country accent grated. What others found folksy the general found coarse and common.

"Quite well, thank you, and Mrs. Lincoln is always welcome."

McClellan noted the change in the president's appearance since the last time they'd met. If possible, he seemed thinner, the face cavernous, the skin pale and unhealthy, the hair unkempt as if he hadn't slept and hadn't bothered to brush it this morning. His black coat and matching trousers were wrinkled. *Well, walking the halls at night, following the progress of incompetent generals, grabbing a few hours of sleep in a chair, isn't good for the health,* he thought.

"Do you know the story of the country doctor and the donkey, General?"

Great God Almighty. Not another ridiculous homespun tale, not at a time like this. McClellan felt the acidic taste in his throat, shifted in his chair, and looked at the president without listening. *I will not be a prop for his stories and fables, and I will not pretend to laugh at the childish punchlines.* He remembered previous meetings, including a particularly distasteful one in his tent after Antietam, trying to follow the thread of Lincoln's tale on that unpleasant occasion. He didn't remember the story, but he did remember that rather than congratulating him for his historic victory, Lincoln had made clear that he was disappointed that McClellan's bloodied and exhausted army hadn't followed Lee back to Virginia. He'd been fired, for the second time, soon after. His neck and jaw tightened as he sat even straighter.

Uncertain if Lincoln had finished his story, and not caring, McClellan said, "Mr. President, perhaps you can tell me why you wanted to see me this morning."

Lincoln stopped, seemed about to finish the story, tilted his head, seemed about to continue again, but said, "Well General, you are in a hurry this morning. That is gratifying to see."

McClellan reddened. *A reference to the slows?*

"As you are well aware, the British have declared war on us, and have taken up arms to support traitors and slaveholders. Even now a small British force under General Burgoyne is on American soil and is making its way south. More British troops are on the high seas, and we can expect the British Navy to challenge our blockade of Southern ports. We must act quickly and with great force. We have no option but to open a northern front against the British while continuing to defend Washington from Lee's army. This will take organization, skill, and audacity." He paused. "And I believe you are the officer most able to accomplish this for your country in her time of need."

As I thought, mused McClellan. *But don't make it easy for him.* The general counted to ten, then said, "Mr. President, this is not the first time I have been asked to save the Union. As you well know, and as the country knows, on previous occasions I was relieved of command after winning great victories, and when on the verge of ultimate success. Do I have your word that I will have a free hand, and be able to finish the job this time?"

It was Lincoln's turn to pause. The smile gone, Lincoln slumped in his chair, his knees higher than his head. The gap between his shoes and his trouser cuffs showed his pale, skinny legs. McClellan's hatred turned to embarrassment, and he felt like Lincoln was on the verge of a breakdown.

"Yes, General, you have my word. You will have overall command of all Union armies, and I expect you to be in the field. My recommendation is that you leave Meade in command of the Army of the Potomac but that you make your headquarters there. But these will be your decisions to make."

"Mr. President, there is no time to waste. I accept, and will put my affairs in order and join my command within days."

McClellan rose from the chair, gave Lincoln's hand another perfunctory shake, and let himself out of the office. *Easier than I expected,* thought the general. *Now, to deal with Governor Seymour.*

On the short walk back to his residence, McClellan noticed that some of the trees were shedding leaves.

LANE

Boston, Massachusetts
October 1863

John Lane was exhausted. The hours of cross examination from his guest had worn him out. A few glowing embers were all that remained of the fire, and the whiskey bottle sat empty on the table. Drinking half the bottle hadn't been part of his plan, and Lane promised himself that he'd never drink that much again. There was a good reason that he normally drank very little, and he always regretted breaking his rule.

John O'Mahony rose slowly out of his chair. Lane handed him his coat and hat, and the older man walked slowly toward the door. He, in contrast, appeared none the worse for the whiskey. Lane watched as, one hand on the knob, O'Mahony paused, turned, and said, "I expect to hear from you in two weeks' time. There's not a moment to lose." With that, the head of the Fenian Brotherhood disappeared into the Boston night.

Lane tried to clear his mind and make sense of the evening. O'Mahony had listened intently, leaning forward in his chair as Lane had outlined his plan to free Ireland from British rule. Then came the questions, hours of them. Would the Irish soldiers in the Union Army go for it? How to get the word out without raising suspicions? What about the officers?

As Lane reflected on the past few hours, a cold chill tingled his spine as he realized the chain of events that he might have just set in motion. For a moment he considered running after O'Mahony and telling him that, upon further consideration, he was certain that the plan could never work. It was all a mistake, and they should instead focus their efforts, as O'Mahony had planned, on striking a blow for Irish freedom in Ireland itself, and after this war was over.

Lane had rehearsed his speech well, and O'Mahony, to his credit, had let him speak at length without interruption. In retrospect it all sounded grand in the warmth and safety of a Boston parlor. But now that the Fenian Brotherhood, or at least its leader, had approved the plan, it seemed to Lane that it could never work, a plan as foolish as the debacle in Widow McCormack's Tipperary cabbage patch in 1848. While all of Europe had erupted in revolution in that turbulent year, in Ireland the grand plans had amounted to nothing more than that scuffle between forty would-be rebels and a small force of Royal Irish Constabulary. Lane shuddered at the prospect that he, too, would be a footnote to history, and a ridiculous one.

The greatest shock of all came when O'Mahony, just before leaving, wagged a thick finger and said, "No lad, I'm too well known myself to meet with Burgoyne. I've too many friends in the Union Army and among the politicos. They'd be on to us in a flash. You'll have to do it yourself. No one knows you and no one will suspect you. You'll have to meet with Burgoyne and convince him that this plan will shorten the war, guarantee victory, and that Home Rule for Ireland is a fair price for the British to pay for our help."

Meet with Burgoyne? Lane didn't even know where the British general was, beyond somewhere in the state of New York and presumably marching south. Pitching a crazy plan to O'Mahony was one thing. Convincing Burgoyne, and eventually the British prime minister, cabinet, and queen, seemed impossible by comparison.

Though it was nearing dawn, Lane decided he'd sleep. *I'll clean up in the morning*, he thought. He pulled the bed out of its place in the wall, sat, and removed his boots. *Sleep will be a blessing.* The rain had stopped, and the weather had changed. Now the moon, full or close to it, shone through the window in the pre-dawn darkness. Lane lay in bed and turned the plan over in his head one more time. The British had declared war on the United States in support of the Confederacy. There were 200,000 Irish soldiers in the Union Army, and as many or more who were of fighting age but hadn't enlisted. The Fenian Brotherhood, and by extension the Irish troops, would pledge their support to Britain and fight against the Union. By any military calculation, that should throw the balance in favor of the Confederacy and the British. All the British had to do was pledge Home Rule for Ireland at the conclusion of the war. And there it was, the dream of Wolfe Tone, Robert Emmett, Daniel O'Connell, and the Young Irelanders, achieved at a bold stroke without ever firing a shot in Ireland.

O'Mahony had questioned Lane for at least an hour on the terms of independence. "You keep saying 'Home Rule' rather than 'freedom' or 'independence.' What exactly are you talking about?"

"Words are important. The British will never agree to complete independence. But maybe restoration of an Irish Parliament with authority over domestic matters. We'd have to recognize the crown. I call it 'Home Rule.'"

"So now you're a grand strategist and an expert in constitutional government. I could never sell that to the lads in Dublin."

"It's no different than what O'Connell fought for thirty years ago. A million people gathered on the hillsides to hear him speak. Tell your friends in Dublin that it's a first step, a giant first step, toward complete independence."

Lane woke up twice, both times certain that he was back home in Kilcrumper, until a quick look at the windows proved that he was in his tiny place in Boston. As usual, his heart sank.

DAVIS

From the soft leather chair in the drawing room of his residence, Jefferson Davis stared into the fire. The season and the weather outside didn't really call for a fire, but Davis was always cold and the fire both warmed and soothed him. He was exhausted from another day of governing. He laughed out loud at the word *governing*, but there was no humor in it.

He'd long ago determined that his southern homeland would be a wonderful place but for Southerners. Now that he was president of the Confederate States of America it was truer than ever. Fractious, stubborn, independent, belligerent, and litigious. Lincoln had constitutional powers and institutions that enforced them. Davis laughed aloud again at being the chief executive of a nation based on the primacy of the states and the weakness of the central government. Lincoln governed. Davis begged and cajoled.

He should have taken a field commission. But when war broke out, he'd written that damn telegram to Governor Pettus: *Judge what*

Mississippi requires of me and place me accordingly. It felt right to say that. Statesmanlike. A man for the times. As a graduate of West Point, with combat experience in Mexico, and as a former secretary of war, Davis was certain that he would be offered an important field command, and Pettus had immediately put him in charge of all Mississippi state troops. But a month later he was acting president of the Confederacy.

He'd considered appointing himself a general officer, then resigning the presidency. Let Stephens worry about the post office, public works, currency, the tariff. Let Stephens broker the jealousy among the states, and explain to proud Southern officers why someone less worthy had received the commission that they coveted.

Davis turned to look at Varina sitting next to him. She was knitting socks for the soldiers as she often did.

"Something strikes you funny this evening. Perhaps you'd share the joke with me."

"I wish there were something funny to share."

"How was your meeting with General Lee? I understand Mary is ill again. The rheumatism may literally be the death of her. I must pay a call."

Davis looked back into the fire.

"When you visit, don't be surprised if you see the general wearing bedroom slippers and a house coat. He resigned his command yesterday after I showed him Palmerston's letter. Apparently, he expected the British Empire to fall in behind him. There will be hell to pay when the papers learn that I've permitted the Lion of Gettysburg to resign his command."

He looked back to Varina. "I didn't insist that he stay or run after him."

Davis knew that Varina, alone among the leading women of the Confederacy, was no fire-eater. In private, she supported neither secession nor slavery. She didn't engage in the hero worship of Robert E. Lee, Stonewall Jackson, J.E.B. Stuart, and the others. In fact, she had told Davis when the war began that she felt in her bones that it would not end well. For those reasons, and more, he confided in her when he could confide in no one else. She was the only person in his inner circle who gave him advice free of Southern affectation.

"Assuming that you accept his resignation, have you considered a replacement?"

"Lee himself suggested Longstreet."

Old Pete. Lee's warhorse. He didn't possess Lee's aggressive nature, his gift for maneuver, or his genius for high-risk tactics. But give him a stone wall to defend, or high ground, and he was the very devil. And he was mostly free of the histrionics which were an occupational affliction among Southern officers.

"I believe that Britain's entry into the war will change its essential nature. We no longer need to invade the north to win allies or to gain supplies. If we can defend Richmond, as I believe we can, and if General Burgoyne's invasion forces Lincoln to send troops north to stop him, as I believe it does, why the times may well call for a Longstreet rather than a Lee. Perhaps there is indeed a Benevolent Providence."

Davis watched Varina for a reaction. Now it was she who stared into the fire, the knitting needles resting in her lap. *If there were justice in the world,* he thought, *she'd be running the country and I'd be knitting socks.*

"Such a sad man. I know his wife but not well. They've lost children. But I believe Richmond couldn't be in safer hands."

BURGOYNE

Along the Hudson River, Upstate New York
October 1863

General Burgoyne leaned over a map stretched between two camp stools in his tent. The lantern cast odd shadows over the paper and made it increasingly difficult to read. No matter. His course was dead south, toward Albany, along the line of the Hudson. The place names were an odd mix. Names familiar to an Englishman, like Greenwich, Queensbury, Lake George. Then the red Indian names such as Adirondack, Schenectady, the Mohawk River. Why did they honor a race they seemed determined to exterminate? Not so very different than the Celtic and Saxon names in Britain, perhaps. His eyes were drawn to names that were more familiar than the others, names he'd heard all his life—Ticonderoga and Saratoga.

Burgoyne pulled his watch from its small pocket and held it to the lantern for the tenth time this half hour. Packenham should have returned by now. Burgoyne knew it was the thrill of a lifetime for a young, ambitious officer—reconnaissance in enemy territory— and that Packenham was having the time of his life. He recalled his own exploits, riding alone or with two or three others through the Louisiana swamps, in the hills above the Spanish coast. That was soldiering.

Burgoyne allowed his mind to wander back in time. He had little memory of his famous father who died when he was ten years old. And though he was born years after his father's defeat, he couldn't recall a moment when that humiliation didn't form part of his consciousness. For some reason, he thought of his mother, the actress Susan Caulfield. To the public she was his father's mistress, but to the general she was simply Mother. He knew from the time he could think that he was no artist, despite his mother's encouragement, and he had no interest in London society and the social intrigue that so inspired his father. He would be a soldier. And while he'd never allowed himself to put name to the thought until this moment, he knew that he would eventually erase that stain from the Burgoyne name.

A sentry's distant call and muffled voices brought Burgoyne back to the present and he knew that Packenham had returned. An aide appeared at the tent opening and asked if the general was free to see the major. He was.

Even by lantern light Burgoyne could see that Packenham was excited. His uniform was caked in dust, his shoulders were heaving, and he seemed to be barely suppressing a smile.

"Enjoy your day in the saddle, did you, Major?"

"Indeed, I did sir. Beautiful country. But empty. Small towns of little note. Farms. Few people about, and not a sign of troops, either regulars or militia. I rode as far as Pottersville. Here sir," Packenham said, pointing to a map. "The road is wide open."

"Were you seen, Major?"

The slightest hesitation. "I was. I encountered two young ladies in a buggy and seized the opportunity to question them at some length about the disposition of troops and the road to Albany."

Burgoyne looked up from the map. "Was the interrogation

successful? Did your prisoners break down under your unrelenting pressure?"

Packenham didn't take the bait. "They assured me that all the young men have long since joined the army and that there are no Federal troops between here and Albany. Sir, I also believe that if we increase our pace we can be in Albany in a week. And sir, I confiscated this from the young ladies." He handed Burgoyne a newspaper.

"Thank you Major, that will be all. See to your horse and get something to eat. I'd like to see a written report in the morning."

Slowing the march was more like it, he thought. *Packenham and the other officers are anxious to engage the enemy for the greater glory. Better to take our time, keep our lines of supply and communication with Montreal as short as possible, and force the Union troops to come as far north as possible and engage us on ground of our choosing. One swift kick might well be enough.*

Burgoyne held the newspaper, *The Albany Argus,* near the lantern and read the headlines:

British Forces Invade From Canada!
100,000 Strong Says Pinkerton!
Albany, New York City Threatened
Lincoln: We Will Meet the Threat

Burgoyne placed the newspaper on his camp bed. *Indeed, but where will you meet it, Mr. Lincoln?*

McClellan

General McClellan sat at his field desk, pen in hand. He had rejoined the Union Army earlier in the day, and there was much to be done. He was anxious to see his troops firsthand, talk to his officers, look men in the eye, observe drill, and see for himself what the debacle at Gettysburg had done to his beloved Army of the Potomac. But first things first. He had to deal with Governor Seymour and the business of the Democratic Party nomination for the presidency.

Headquarters, Army of the Potomac
near Manassas, Va
October 7, 1863
Governor:

I am in receipt of yours of the 22nd of last month, offering me your Party's nomination for President in the national elections scheduled for next autumn. While grateful for the confidence so expressed and mindful of the historic opportunity, I nonetheless must fall back on my duty as a soldier first. Earlier this week President Lincoln requested that I assume command of all Union Armies in the field with the express purpose of meeting the grave threats to our nation, now presented by General Lee's victory at Gettysburg and the presence of an allied British Army now invading from the north. It is the President's feeling that the times call for organization and strategic vision that have been lacking at the highest levels of this government and this army. It is my determination to quash the rebellion, as we were so close to doing after the grand victory at Antietam, and drive the British invaders back to Canada. I must therefore defer any decisions of a strictly political nature until such time as this war is won. It is my hope that we can remain in contact during the coming months as both military and political exigencies reach their respective conclusions.

I remain & c.,

Geo. B. McClellan, General in Chief.

McClellan placed the pen in the well, relaxed, and read the letter to himself. *Just the right tone,* he thought, putting the nation above personal ambition, but leaving a door open as well. *Seymour is nobody's fool and will understand.*

The letter complete, McClellan looked up from the desk to a map pinned on the wall of his tent. *Just like old times,* he thought, camped between Washington City and Richmond, with Robert E. Lee and his army athwart the road to the Southern capital. What had Lee been thinking after Gettysburg? He could have swung south in the wake of the rout and threatened Washington, but instead had decided not to pursue Meade. He'd taken his time returning to Virginia, gathering supplies, Stuart sowing panic with raids and feints, and had finally taken up old positions near Fredericksburg, on the line of the Rappahannock. Daring the Union forces to march south again. But Lee had accomplished his goal; his victory had brought the British into the war and entirely changed the strategic calculus. Now he could afford to sit and wait for McClellan to attack.

But there would be no grand On-to-Richmond march now. McClellan's gaze drifted north on the map to New York State. His immediate challenge was to dispatch sufficient forces to meet Burgoyne, and whatever was coming behind him, while protecting Washington City from Lee. Or Longstreet, if the explosive and inexplicable rumors coming from Richmond were true. Maybe now it's Bobby Lee who knows what it's like to be fired on the verge of victory. *Could Davis be that stupid?* Not the Jefferson Davis who had been his mentor ten years ago.

McClellan's eyes returned to Virginia. But how to divide his forces? If Pinkerton was correct, Lee had more than 100,000 men in the field, and Burgoyne would not have dared invade with fewer than 50,000. McClellan needed to strike Burgoyne now before he was reinforced from Britain. But he needed to keep enough men south of the Potomac to protect the capital.

That's why he needed to take the measure of his army. Meade's strategy at Gettysburg had been sound, but why had seasoned troops, well entrenched on high ground, collapsed, and run in the face of Pickett's attack? Poor leadership, the plague of the Army of the Potomac. He, McClellan, had trained and inspired them, but at the end of the day it was leadership that won or lost the day. *Well, leadership will cease to be a problem beginning today.*

The moment called for bold and swift action. In the back of his mind, McClellan saw an opportunity to banish forever his reputation for "the slows," Lincoln's insult that still burned. A plan had taken shape in his mind, an audacious plan, and he knew just the officer to undertake it and make it succeed.

"Captain Wilson, send for General Custer."

LANE

Brattleboro, Vermont
October 1863

It was the second time John Lane had been on a train. The first time, earlier this year, he'd been in uniform returning home to Boston from a hospital in Baltimore, his left arm, what was left of it, tightly bandaged.

He remembered everything about the Battle of Fredericksburg, at least his small part in it, except getting wounded. He remembered the terror—not dread or anxiety—as they assembled at the bottom of Marye's Heights. Colonel Bliss had made a fine speech, or so Lane was told later. He couldn't hear a thing above the roar of battle. The 7th Rhode Island advanced under fire, in decent order, and paused once to fire into the invisible enemy far up the hill and hunkered down in a sunken road. Lane recalled firing into the smoke, no enemy soldiers in sight.

Finally, one hundred yards from the top, with soldiers falling all around him, Lane thought they might carry the hill. Some of the men had been cheering, driving up the hill in a battle frenzy. Others, like Lane, had hung back behind the first wave, committed to doing their duty but not anxious to be the first to crest the hill and meet the enemy face-to-face. Lane found himself thinking that this was nothing like the battles he'd read about. This was sanctioned murder amid chaos. The next thing he remembered was lying on the ground clutching his wrist and watching blood flow from where his hand should have been. It didn't hurt, not yet, and Lane ripped his blanket from around his neck and wrapped it around his arm, from elbow to wrist, to stop the blood.

And there he lay on the cold ground, surrounded by the dead, the wounded, and the terrified. Their attack had fallen short, and bullets buzzed inches above his head. For John Lane, time had stood still. He recalled now, while riding the train, that they had mustered at the bottom of the Heights around noon, so he must have been wounded before one o'clock. It was dark and freezing when the word was passed for the regiment to reform at the bottom. Lane couldn't see his watch, but had thought by the darkness that it must be past seven. Thirsty and weak, Lane had been able to walk down from the Heights on his own, picking over bodies as the bullets whistling overhead added to his misery.

At the bottom of the hill, Lane had literally bumped into his sergeant, a Galway man, who told him that Company B was reforming in the rear. Lane showed him the bloody stump of his arm, and the sergeant simply waved him on. "Keep walking 'til you find a field hospital laddie. They won't be hard to find. You'll not be the only customer."

The surgeon who had examined Lane the next morning congratulated him on his million-dollar wound. "Your war is over son." An orderly wound white cloth around the bloody stump and added, "You're lucky it was freezing cold last night. You might have bled to death otherwise." Lane pondered the meaning of *luck* and decided that, all in all, the surgeon and the orderly were right.

As the train slowed, Lane snapped out of his daydream.

The conductor passed through the car repeating, "Brattleboro, Brattleboro Vermont." *Halfway to Albany, more or less,* thought Lane.

It could hardly be called a plan, but after his meeting with O'Mahony, Lane knew he had to find Burgoyne.

The next morning, he walked the mile from his home on Genesee Street in the South End to the Boston Public Library on Boylston Street. He sat in the magnificent reading room, a place he came to often, staring at a map of the eastern United States. He drew a line south from Montreal, and another line west from Boston. They intersected at Albany, so Albany was where Lane would begin his search for the British Army.

Lane knew finding an army shouldn't be difficult. However, gaining an audience with its commanding general and convincing him to commit to Irish freedom in exchange for promises of assistance from an invisible Irish Army was another matter entirely. *Plan indeed.*

DAVIS

Richmond, Virginia
October 1863

Jefferson Davis was frowning, brow furrowed, gaze distant. It was a look that came easily to him. He didn't like hosting meetings in which the outcome was in doubt, and he was about to host such a meeting.

A quick look at his enormous clock and Davis noted that his guest was late. But he was coming from the field, and there had been rain, and you never knew about the roads in autumn.

A knock at the office door, and an aide announced, "General Longstreet."

Davis rose from his chair and greeted the general warmly.

"General Longstreet. Pete. Thank you for coming and congratulations on the grand victory at Gettysburg. Your Corps delivered the blow. Please sit."

Longstreet scowled as he took his seat. "As you might guess, Mr. President, I advised General Lee against the assault on Cemetery Ridge. I recommended that we wheel south and threaten

Washington. But the general was determined. And against all odds George—General Pickett—took that hill and damn near destroyed an entire corps. If we had followed up, you and I would be having this meeting in Mr. Lincoln's office."

That's Pete. Never bask in success when you can blame someone for failure, thought Davis. It was Davis' decision to let Meade escape, and to bring Lee's army back to its current location between Washington City and Richmond, and Longstreet knew it. *I'm the strategist,* thought Davis, *and you sir, follow orders. This isn't a war of conquest. It's a battle for survival.*

Davis examined his old friend and found him unchanged. Dressed for the field, comfortable, direct, bordering on sullen. But unfettered by the manners and style that weighed so heavily on many of his comrades, including Robert E. Lee.

"General, I'm sure you know why I asked you to come this morning. General Lee has decided, on his own accord, to, uh, to end his service as commander of the Army of Northern Virginia. He has recommended that you succeed him, and I can think of no man more able to do so than you. I would like to offer you command of the Army, and I would implore you to accept."

Longstreet, legs crossed, had seemingly been staring out the window as Davis spoke. He seemed in no hurry to answer, and in fact it wasn't clear to Davis that he'd been listening.

"General."

"Mr. President, the only man who can replace General Lee, in terms of audacity and tactical genius, and in terms of inspiring the men, is General Jackson. I understand he has nearly recovered from the wound he received at Chancellorsville. And, if I may, we both know what the public reaction will be if I'm named as Lee's replacement. You won't have that problem with Jackson. The public can't get enough of him. Maybe if I had a nickname other than 'Pete.' And if not Jackson, George Pickett. The man of the hour. How he got his men up that damn hill I can't explain."

Davis pondered. *Longstreet and Pickett. Dear friends.* But Pickett last in his class at West Point, Longstreet three from the bottom. *Is there an inverse relationship between academic and martial success? A question for another time.* Well, General Lee would certainly never joke in a situation like this.

Davis had made up his mind. If the times ever called for another invasion of the north, Jackson might be the man. Pickett? Never. But for defending Richmond and the territorial integrity of the Confederacy, Longstreet was by far the best choice. *There's no point in being president if you can't give orders.*

"General, we all look forward to General Jackson's full recovery, which will indeed excite the public. And I am certain you will make full use of his considerable talents upon his return to the Army. And perhaps General Pickett is ready for command of a corps. But General, I will this afternoon sign the order designating you general in chief of the Army of Northern Virginia. You will have full authority to choose your corps and division commanders. I very much look forward to our close consultation and cooperation on matters regarding the strategic deployment of troops. And General, would you please read this letter from Prime Minister Palmerston, which lays out the terms under which Britain has joined our cause."

Longstreet was still staring out the window as Davis offered the letter.

BURGOYNE

Along the Hudson River, Upstate New York
October 1863

The letter from Prime Minister Palmerston was barely two
weeks old. The Royal Navy had delivered it to Montreal, then it had
come overland. The courier had carried nothing more. No letters
from home. Not surprising, given that the prime minister's letter
would have been dispatched in great haste and via military courier.
The Royal Mail would deliver his wife's letters, should she choose
to write, via steamship to Halifax, and then find its way to the army
in due course. Burgoyne was long accustomed to being without
news of family for months. The steamship had cut the time for a
trans-Atlantic crossing by more than half. *A mixed blessing to a field
commander,* Burgoyne thought. *On the one hand, it permits faster
and closer coordination with London. On the other hand, it permits
faster and closer coordination with London.* The general smiled at his
own joke. *This war will be won or lost here, not in London.*

Seated in his tent, Burgoyne read the letter again. Palmerston's
instructions were clear as far as they went. Proceed south down the

line of the Hudson and threaten New York City. Draw the Union Army away from Washington City. Avoid a general engagement until such time as he was reinforced. Force the Union to divide their army or choose to defend either Washington or New York. Expect the first troops to leave England in a week, which meant they were already on the water. Within two months Burgoyne would have more than 100,000 soldiers to augment his force of 15,000.

You shall retain overall command of all British forces in the field. Establish contact and communications with President Davis by any means possible. He has agreed that British war aims will be paramount as long as Southern independence is recognized, Burgoyne read.

British war aims. Palmerston did not elaborate. In their only conversation, before Burgoyne departed London for America, Palmerston had gone on at some length about the decision to intervene on the side of the Confederacy. It was clear that he, and many others, had never truly gotten over the loss of the colonies. But more importantly, Palmerston saw the United States as an emerging colossus, a country of enormous size, unlimited resources, unchecked ambition, and religious zeal for expansion. The Southern rebellion offered a once-in-our-lifetimes opportunity to cut the United States back down to size and halt, or at least delay, its emergence as a serious competitor to the British Empire. Palmerston hadn't mentioned slavery in their conversation, nor did his letter.

Burgoyne pondered that nothing less than the global balance of power depended on his ability to maneuver his 15,000 men made soft and lazy by years of garrison duty in Canada. His challenge was to threaten, posture, sow fear and panic, and force the Union to react to him, all the while avoiding a fight until he could do so at full strength.

Thus far Burgoyne had taken his time on his march south, intentionally giving the Union time to dispatch a force to meet him. He could threaten New York City in a couple of days' quick march, but he preferred to lure the Federal Army as far north as possible and shorten the distance from Montreal for the troops that would reinforce him. He, not the Union Army, would choose the field of battle.

No stranger to campaigning in cold weather, the snow flurries that were visible through the open flap of his tent nonetheless reminded him that North American winters came early and hard. His troops were fine for now, but soon enough they'd need to prepare themselves for the harsh realities of making war in winter. That argued for moving south, but his orders, and his own judgment, were clear. *Stay north, draw the Union out, divide their strength.*

Establishing contact with President Davis was another matter. With Southern ports still blockaded, and with no telegraph communication between the Northern states and the Confederate government, he would have to depend on couriers, who would run a great risk in trying to cross the lines. Burgoyne wondered if Packenham were game for more soldiering and summoned the young officer.

"Major Packenham, do you have a moment? I should like to know if you are disposed to another adventure on horseback."

McCLELLAN

Near Manassas, Virginia
October 1863

Pounding hooves and barking dogs announced the arrival of Brigadier General George Custer. McClellan pulled his watch from its pocket. *He must have ridden like the devil to get here so quickly.*

Boots pounded on the wooden platform that supported McClellan's tent. An aide, pushed aside by the boy general, announced, too late, "sir, General Custer" as Custer snapped to attention, executed a crisp salute, and stood at ease, speaking without being prompted. "Sir, welcome home. The army is delighted. Sir, what's afoot and how can I be of service?"

Custer had not aged, but he was all of twenty-three years old. The face was the same as the young lieutenant, fresh from West Point, who'd done yeoman staff work for McClellan on the Peninsula. The hair was short, the mustache drooping, but the chin was clean. *He probably can't grow anything there,* mused McClellan. The uniform was new and clearly of his own design, a wide collar, oversized buttons, white gauntlets, polished boots, and a red neckerchief. The felt hat, held under his left arm, was pinned up on one side and sported a black plume. No one in the Army of the Potomac embraced war like George Custer, and nobody so thoroughly enjoyed himself in its practice. He was having the time of his young life.

"General, thank you for coming at this late hour. There will be changes in this Army, starting immediately, and men of enterprise and resourcefulness are much in demand. I have been entrusted by President Lincoln with nothing less than saving the Union. There is much to be done. Washington City must be protected."

Custer's shoulders slumped. "Important work to be sure, General, protecting Washington. I have no doubt that the infantry and field artillery are equal to that crucial task. I pray that the cavalry might take the fight to the enemy, sir."

"I wasn't aware that you were a believer, General, but perhaps your prayers will be answered on this one occasion. As you are aware, General Burgoyne has crossed into New York and is even now driving south with an enormous army. Pinkerton assures me he wouldn't have invaded with fewer than 50,000 men. Perhaps many more. He will be followed by regulars from Britain who may even now be on the sea. We must mount a force sufficient to defeat them, but that will take time. In the meantime, we must strike a blow . . . slow them down to give us sufficient time to put our army in the field."

Now Custer was leaning forward on the camp stool, hands gripping the legs on either side, and staring intently at McClellan.

"Captain Wilson will deliver written orders to your headquarters in the morning, but let me explain what I have in mind." He unpinned the large map from the tent and spread it across two stools.

"You will take the First and Third Divisions of the Cavalry Corps by rail from Washington City to New York. You will leave the cars just north of the city and proceed northward along the line of the Hudson until you find the enemy. You will have sufficient force and mobility to harass, confuse, and detain him until such time as I arrive with this army. At that time, we will give battle and save this Union from the predicament that successive failures of leadership have created."

Custer could barely contain himself. "Sir, as you are aware, I'm outranked by Pleasonton, that is, by Generals Pleasonton, Buford, Kilpatrick. Even Merritt."

"Not anymore, General. You are as of this moment breveted Major General. And I have important plans for Pleasonton and the others. There will be no disagreement about who commands your troops."

Custer shot to his feet and stood, rocking back and forth from his toes to the balls of his feet. "Then I haven't a moment to lose, sir. I will have my men in Washington, ready to board the cars, by the day after tomorrow."

McClellan studied his young protégé in the lantern light. "General, to be clear, I need you to delay Burgoyne. Keep him away from New York City. Harass his supply lines and communications. By all means, engage his cavalry screen. Make him believe you have ten times the force that you actually have. But do not bring on a general engagement. The moment for that will be when the Army of the Potomac in all its glory has arrived. Is this all clear?"

Custer smiled. "Yes sir. Harass and delay. No general engagement. I look forward to seeing you up north, sir." And he was gone as quickly as he had appeared.

McClellan thought back to Mexico, where he had also chafed under authority and had been sure he knew better than his superiors. *We'll need to get started as soon as possible,* he thought.

LANE

Albany, New York
October 1863

John Lane sat in a chair reading in his boarding house in Albany. He was mindful of the light coming through the single window. He would wait until dark before venturing out in search of information. He was vaguely aware that the chair was perhaps the least comfortable piece of furniture he'd ever encountered. The tall straight back forced him to lean slightly forward and cut into his shoulders. The seat, made of wicker or some such material, had long since begun to unravel, and the thin cushion didn't prevent his rear from sinking through. *The perfect conveyance for preventing idleness,* he thought. He'd considered reading in the bed, but his mother had taught him long ago that beds are for sleeping at night, and not for passing the time in daylight hours.

If he didn't know the book by heart, it wasn't for lack of trying. It had been a gift from his father on his twelfth birthday, the first book he owned, and the first and last birthday gift he'd ever received. Lane had read *History of the Irish Rebellion* a dozen times. It had passed the time on the sea voyage from Liverpool to Boston, and he'd read it by lantern light during the war. The other soldiers in his company carried bibles. This was his bible.

It was this book, as much as anything, that had brought Lane to membership in the Fenian Brotherhood, a secret, oath-bound society dedicated to freeing Ireland from British rule. Now, *ironically,* he thought, to hatching a plan to commit treason against his adopted country, the United States of America.

He placed the book on his lap. *Seven hundred years under the British thumb. Unable to practice our religion. Our land confiscated. Our Parliament dissolved. Banned from the professions.* But occasional outbreaks of rebellion, under the old Gaelic aristocracy in the sixteenth and seventeenth centuries. So close in 1798, with uprisings all over the country, if only the French had committed more troops. Then semi-comical risings, not worthy of the name, in 1803 and 1848.

Lane thought of O'Mahony. *This time it's a horse of a different color.* These were hard-bitten men, not romantic dreamers. They weren't recruiting poets and students this time. They wanted soldiers. They imagined a huge armada of ships, filled with Irish veterans of the Union Army, bound for Ireland. Hard men, armed to the teeth, the British garrison forces no match for them. A triumphal march into Dublin, raising a green flag over Dublin Castle, for centuries the seat of British rule in Ireland.

Lane laughed bitterly to himself. Poetic, romantic nonsense. Another grand plan, just like 1798 and 1848, that would come to nothing. *My plan makes more sense.* That vast host of Irish veterans, instead of sailing to Ireland, would help the British and their Confederate allies defeat the Union, and in return the British would grant Home Rule for Ireland. It all came down to a single calculation; it was in Britain's interest that the United States, a rising power with vast potential, see her territory and population cut in half, and that she be boxed in, north and south, by hostile powers. Home rule for

Ireland would be a small price to pay indeed for putting a lid on the rise of America as a competitor.

It had grown dark outside. Lane placed the book on the small table next to the chair, stood, and put on his coat. *If I were back in Ireland,* he mused, *or Boston for that matter, and I needed information, I'd find a public house. Right. So off to get a drink and find the British Army.*

DAVIS

Richmond, Virginia
October 1863

Jefferson Davis sat in silence, the pendulum of the huge clock in his office providing the only sound. Before him sat a young man dressed in workman's clothing but of soldierly bearing. Davis was surrounded by aides, all soldiers, mostly very young men, and all seething with jealousy as they listened to the visitor's tale.

Major Thomas Packenham, General Burgoyne's aide-de-camp, was describing his four-day journey from Pottersville, New York to Richmond. He had traveled by buggy, apparently driven by a young woman, by train, on horseback, and on foot. Davis tried to calculate the distance. *At least 400, maybe 500 miles.* Packenham seemed extraordinarily pleased with himself in a way that only a young Englishman can.

Packenham's daring journey was interesting. But the letter he had delivered from General John Burgoyne was crucially important as the first communication between the British Army in the field and the government of the Confederate States of America. Davis read aloud the letter a second time.

Pottersville, New York
October 7, 1863
My Dear Sir:

It is with satisfaction that I report that advance elements of the British Army under my command have entered the United States and are currently encamped in the vicinity of the village of Pottersville in the state of New York. It is my intention to threaten the state capital of Albany and the City of New York and to draw Union forces as far northward as possible in an effort to stop us. I trust that by dividing his army, our common foe shall weaken the defenses of Washington City and offer an opportunity for forces of your Confederacy to threaten the enemy capital. It is my hope that we may in this way prevail on both the northern and southern fronts and so bring an early end to hostilities and thus guarantee southern independence. I shall count on your army moving on Washington at the first opportunity. It would be convenient to know the date on which your forces could begin their movement to threaten Washington City. The bearer of this letter has my complete confidence and may be entrusted with your reply.
I remain Sir & c.,
John Fox Burgoyne, General Commanding.

Just what General Lee feared, thought Davis. *Orders from the British regarding disposition of our armies.* Burgoyne was not wrong, of course, Davis reasoned. Threatening Washington and New York would force Lincoln's hand. The loss of either city could mean the end of the war, especially with elections coming in a year's time. Still, Davis preferred to sit tight in Virginia, protect Richmond, and force McClellan to make his dilatory way north to fight the British.

McClellan has his gifts, but speed and decisiveness are not among them, thought Davis. How that decision must have stuck in Lincoln's craw. The rumors, and Confederate spies, had all said it would be

Grant, but he was still tied up along the Mississippi with no end in sight to his siege at Vicksburg.

Davis stared out the window, arms folded, oblivious to the chatter between his staff and Packenham. The notion of attacking Washington did not sit well. If the Northern papers were to be believed, the Confederates could probably sue for peace now just with the threat that the British pose. Davis saw no way to negotiate with the British regarding strategy if every message between them takes four days to deliver, assuming that the courier doesn't get caught. *Burgoyne knows that and assumes we'll have no choice but to do as he says,* Davis reasoned. *Moving on Washington. Longstreet won't like it. Perhaps it was a mistake not to beg Lee to stay.*

"Major, you will dine with us this evening, and of course you shall stay with my family in our residence. One of my officers should be able to provide you with proper attire. I will, of course, begin immediately to prepare a response to General Burgoyne. Tell me, Major, your general, is he the negotiating sort?"

Packenham smiled. "I wouldn't say so, sir. More the type of officer born to command. He's quite at home giving orders. I would say, sir, that he's given to setting a course of action and seeing it through."

"Just as I assumed Major. Captain Slidell, could you kindly see to a suit of clothes for the major? Perhaps a gray uniform would suit him for an evening. And Major, when would you be sufficiently rested to return north?"

Packenham smiled again. "I should think tomorrow morning, early, would do, Mr. President."

BURGOYNE

Near Glens Falls, New York
October 1863

John Burgoyne sat on a camp stool in his headquarters tent, reading the letter from Jefferson Davis. Major Packenham, still dressed in civilian clothes, stood at ease. Without looking up, Burgoyne said, "Please sit down Major. Once I've read this, I'll want to hear from you. I want to know what I should be reading between these lines. I want to hear all about Mr. Davis."

Packenham remained standing. "Yes sir."

Burgoyne understood. It wouldn't do for a junior officer to sit with the general, like friends in a London gentlemen's club.

The general read the letter.

Richmond, Virginia
Confederate States of America
October 11, 1863
General Burgoyne:
    I am in receipt of yours of the 8th inst. and am anxious that

we should coordinate our efforts to maximum effect. To that end, I should like to explain the current strategic situation in the eastern theater and make some recommendations for action.

First, that the Army of Northern Virginia under General Longstreet, currently encamped between this city and the Federal capital, shall commence operations to threaten Washington. These actions will begin no later than the first day of November. Our army's advance, coming as it does in the wake of our victory at Gettysburg, should force General McClellan, now in command of all Federal armies, to concentrate forces to meet the threat. I believe that the loss of their capital could prove fatal to their cause.

Second, that British forces threaten Albany and New York City, forcing McClellan to send a substantial portion of his army northward to meet that threat. It is our understanding, based on newspaper reports and information gathered from friendly sources, that a small Union force is already on its way north as a vanguard. I would like to suggest that engaging and defeating that force before McClellan can reinforce it would support our efforts in both the military and political realms.

Finally, it is my judgment that the sooner we can divide the enemy's army and the sooner we can force him to commit on two fronts, the better. For the time being, General Grant and the Western Army are mired in a siege on the Mississippi River and in no condition to come to the support of McClellan. But that situation may change at any time.

I look forward to close cooperation in support of our mutual aims.

I remain & c.,

Jefferson Davis, President

Burgoyne frowned as he absorbed the message. Yes, a party of 6th Dragoons had returned from reconnaissance just an hour ago, reporting that Union forces had arrived by train north of New York City two days ago, and were headed north along the Hudson. Cavalry, it appears. Davis' *suggestion* of meeting and defeating that force before McClellan could reinforce it was sound. The newspapers suggest that the officer in charge, a General Custer, is ambitious and aggressive. *Good news indeed. Let his ambition and aggression bring him northward and to the field of our choosing.* The men were tired of a slow march, seemingly without purpose, and idleness did an army no good. Action was just the thing to boost their morale.

"Major, may I suggest that you get something to eat, burn those ridiculous clothes, get some rest, and prepare yourself for more adventure. I should like that you find me a battlefield."

McCLELLAN

Near Manassas, Virginia
November 1863

George McClellan was everywhere. Accompanied by a small coterie of staff officers, he visited each corps commander, rode past regimental camps to wild cheers, spoke to common soldiers, and he reviewed troops, including a Grand Review in which 25,000 soldiers marched in tight formations past his reviewing stand. Among those in attendance to see the martial display, and the zenith to which McClellan had trained and inspired his men, were senators, congressmen, ladies and gentlemen of Washington society, and members of the presidential cabinet. Those not in attendance included President Lincoln, who had not been invited.

McClellan knew that it was important that the men *saw* him, knew he had returned, knew that this time they would not be stopped when on the verge of victory by politicians. That couldn't be accomplished in a day, or through a written proclamation, as some generals seemed to believe. It took time, training, drill, discipline. Lincoln called this *the slows*. McClellan called it *preparation*. He knew that if an army did not believe in its commander, and didn't believe that it could win, that it was doomed to failure.

McClellan was indeed everywhere, but for the moment he was sitting on a tree stump outside his tent. He'd been in the saddle all day and he had liked what he'd seen. Not only had the men recovered from the humiliating loss at Gettysburg, but they were eager to be back in the field and prove that, properly led, they were capable of anything. *They'll soon have their chance,* he mused.

Sitting with McClellan was George Meade, hatchet-faced, surly, and quarrelsome, but at least not given to idle chatter. He sat quietly on his own stump, whittling something of indeterminate shape. Meade was still in command of the Army of the Potomac despite the debacle at Gettysburg. The press had called for his head and Lincoln, that reliever of generals, was inclined to fire him. Partly for that reason, and partly because Meade would fight, McClellan had kept him on. *I don't need him to strategize,* McClellan reasoned. *I just need him to fight.* McClellan glanced at Meade, looking for a sign. Had Gettysburg taken the starch out of him? Did he need to go, like McDowell, Burnside, Pope? *No. Like me, he has something to prove, and I'll give him that chance.*

Fight. There was going to be a fight, in fact two of them. One to prevent the rebels from taking Washington City, and the other, up north, to repel the British invasion.

McClellan's plan was simple. He had no choice but to divide his forces, and he would lead the bulk of the army north to fight Burgoyne. Defeating the British invaders would be a spectacular achievement and would capture the attention of the press and the public. The political ramifications were obvious, especially in Governor Seymour's home state. Defending Washington would be less glamorous, and he would leave that to Meade. If Meade's smaller force wasn't up to the job, and if Lincoln and the cabinet were forced to flee in haste, well, these things happen in time of war. McClellan was pleased that he'd sent Nelly to live with his family in Philadelphia.

Moving his army north, already underway, but slowly so as not to rouse suspicion in Richmond, was a tremendous feat of logistics, but no different than the amphibious movement to the peninsula in 1862. A simple matter of mathematics—so many men, so many horses, so many wagons, and so much equipment requires a certain number of ships and a certain number of days. General Meigs could move the army to New York in his sleep.

McClellan's aide, Captain Wilson, ran from the communications tent, paper in his hand. "Sir, excuse the interruption, a telegram from General Custer."

"Thank you, Captain. And Captain. Please assemble the corps commanders at seven this evening for a council of war."

McClellan read the brief telegram, then handed it to Meade.

Poughkeepsie, NY

Sir: Arrived NY without incident. 10,000 men and horse on march north. Reliable informants put enemy north of Albany. Harass and delay. Await yr arrival. Custer

Meade handed the paper back to McClellan. "General, you'll get a full report at your council this evening from General Meigs, but I believe we've already put two corps on the boats to New York. We should have a force sufficient to meet Burgoyne in place in a week. Let's hope young Custer is still harassing and delaying when we get there."

"Yes. And let's hope Pete Longstreet isn't in a hurry to visit the sights in Washington City. This particular dance requires time and careful choreography."

LANE

Near Ballston, New York
November 1863

John Lane was pleased to be off the train and on his feet.
He was walking north, having taken the train that morning from
Albany to Ballston. Now he was headed toward Saratoga Springs
with every hope of finding the British Army coming in the other
direction. What he'd do when he found them, and how he'd get an
audience with General Burgoyne, had dominated his thinking ever
since he'd learned of the army's whereabouts. He didn't yet have
answers to those questions.

It had taken Lane three nights of open-handed largesse in the
tavern of the City Hotel to meet someone who knew the British
Army's location. Every working man in Albany was delighted to drink
for free at Lane's expense, but none knew more than the newspaper
reports, and most knew much less. *But the Lord does indeed work in
mysterious ways*, he thought. When he finally found someone who
had seen the British, and just the day before, the circumstances were
beyond invention.

Seated at the bar of the tavern, Lane looked up to see a one-armed man take the stool next to him. Each eyed the other's stump at the same moment, and their eyes met.

"Aye. Fredericksburg."

"The same," said Lane. "7th Rhode Island, Marye's Heights. My first and last battle."

The man got the bartender's attention. "Two whiskeys. Ah, the Heights. 77th New York. I'd seen a thing or two before Fredericksburg. The peninsula and Antietam. Hard to believe Old Abe is rolling the dice with McClellan again. Third time's the charm maybe."

The bartender delivered the whiskey. They raised their glasses and the newcomer said *slainte* before draining the liquid in a gulp and slamming the glass back on the bar. "Two more."

Lane couldn't believe his ears. "You're from Cork."

The man smiled. "Isn't everyone? Kilbolane."

It was Lane's turn to smile. "I'm from near Fermoy myself. But I've people in Kilbolane. Do you know the Ahearns at all?"

The man looked up in exaggerated thought. "The horse thief Ahearns or the buggering Ahearns?"

Lane laughed. "So, you do know them. Well, I'd shake your hand but it's a bit awkward. Let's take the thought for the deed and have another one."

They drank in silence at first, Lane trying to slow the pace, the newcomer, Dennis Dinneen, taking his time to warm to the conversation.

"You live in Albany?" asked Lane.

"Not at all. I have a farm in Wilton, north of Saratoga Springs. Two mornings ago, I went out to feed the chickens and found the British Army camped on my farm. The sight of the bloody redcoats took me back, I can tell you. I'm on my way now to find this General Custer and apprise him of the situation. And you?"

Lane had rehearsed a story. "I've a brother in Glens Falls and we haven't seen each other these ten years. I'm going to see him and his wife and kids, whom I've never met."

"Well, take the train and stay off the road."

How many one-armed Corkmen veterans of Fredericksburg do you suppose there are in Albany? Lane wondered.

His mission weighed heavily, yet Lane couldn't help but enjoy a walk in the country. The air was crisp and windless, and the sky deep blue. The countryside reminded him of home. The Blackwater wasn't the mighty Hudson, and the fields and pastures were much bigger here. Still, if he closed his eyes, he could imagine he was walking from Fermoy to Castlelyons to visit his cousins.

Lane heard the creaking sounds of a wagon behind him, then the voice of the driver extolling the horse to keep moving. Lane moved aside to let the wagon pass.

"Whoa there. Whoa there." The wagon stopped, and Lane found himself staring at the driver, a woman of about his age, dressed in men's clothing. She was Black.

"Where you headed?"

"Glens Falls," he said, sticking to his story.

The driver laughed. "You should be there next week at your pace. Hop on. I'm going as far as Saratoga Springs, maybe a little farther, and I like having a body to talk to. Viola."

"Begging your pardon?"

"*Viola.* My name is Viola. I assume you have a name, or should I call you the mysterious stranger with the foreign accent?"

Lane's plan hadn't anticipated an alias. "John Lane. Em, pleased to meet you."

Viola smiled. "I'll bet you are." The wagon lurched forward.

Seated next to the driver on the wooden bench, Lane looked behind him. The bed of the wagon overflowed with bulging burlap bags.

"What's in the bags?"

"Potatoes. There's a hungry army up ahead and they'll buy all the potatoes I can bring them. This is my third trip in a week. I've bought every potato in Fulton and Saratoga counties, or everyone I could find."

Lane looked at the woman and reflected for a moment. "You're feeding the British Army? Who are aiding the Confederates!"

"I'm feeding the hungry. And that would include myself and my children. Are you a preacher? An abolitionist? Or just a man who can't afford a horse who judges hardworking people?"

Lane appreciated a spirited discussion as much as the next man, but he checked himself. Plenty of time later to ponder the irony of a Black woman abetting the Confederate cause.

"So, you've done this before? Sold food to the British? You know where to find them?"

"Yes. And now you do too." She nodded ahead, where an enormous dust cloud, preceded by four dragoons in red coats riding out to meet them, announced the arrival of Burgoyne's army.

"I hope you're stronger than you look. Those bags weigh fifty pounds each and the soldiers don't like unloading them. I'll give you three cents a bag. Is that stump going to be a problem?"

DAVIS

Longstreet's Headquarters
Near Warrenton, Virginia
November 1863

General James Longstreet was leaning forward on his camp stool drawing figures in the dirt with a stick. His uniform collar was unbuttoned, but his patriarchal beard hid his neck from view.

Next to him, Jefferson Davis sat upright on his stool, impatience crossing his face. He had the aspect of a man who believed he'd made a convincing argument but been rebuffed. *I'll try again*, thought Davis. *I'd like Pete to come around on his own, but if I have to make it a direct order, so be it.*

"General, I believe we can agree that Southern independence is at hand, if only we can seize the moment. As you know, Custer is somewhere in New York, and may have already engaged with Burgoyne. McClellan is on his way to reinforce Custer and a general engagement is inevitable. We have every reason to believe that McClellan will find a way to lose. He has divided his force and left Washington City exposed. Now is the time to strike Meade and threaten the capital. In the wake of Gettysburg, and with Northern sentiment turning so thoroughly against the war, I don't see how Lincoln doesn't sue for peace. And for us, peace means independence."

Longstreet could be frustrating beyond all measure. He didn't appear to be listening to his president. *Yes, we're old friends, but being president means something,* Davis thought.

"Mr. President, why don't we give General Burgoyne an opportunity to do some fighting. Presumably that's why he's come all this way. If he can defeat McClellan, we don't have to attack Washington. We occupy splendid ground here in Virginia and for the first time in two years, Richmond is not under imminent threat from a Federal Army. If Burgoyne can defeat McClellan, then a feint toward Washington should be enough to convince Lincoln that he can't preserve the Union. He'll have no choice but to recognize the Confederacy. And it won't cost us a single soldier."

Davis pulled Palmerston's letter from his pocket. The Prime Minister had been clear. He expected the Confederate Army to attack Washington while Burgoyne engaged Union troops up north. It made sense.

"General, I gave my word to the British that this army would move on Washington by early November. We're behind schedule. Kindly make plans for offensive action against the Army of the Potomac and, if possible, the capture of Washington City. History has offered this moment, and by God, we will seize it. You will have written orders in the morning. They will state the broad objectives which I've just given you. I will leave the details to you and your staff. General, we are going to win this war, now."

Davis stood, and Longstreet slowly got to his feet. The men shook hands, exchanging no further words, and Davis nodded to his staff. They mounted their waiting horses and rode away at a trot toward the rail station at Warrenton Junction.

By God, if I had command of this army, I'd be drinking whiskey in Willard's Hotel in a week's time, Davis fumed. *I have generals who are too proud to take orders; I have generals who don't want to fight;*

I have generals who fight duels with each other; and occasionally I have generals who inspire their men to unthinkable acts of courage and glory. He thought of George Pickett. That most unlikely hero. *I will inquire as to the state of General Jackson's health. Let's hope his wound hasn't made him contemplative, as Dick Ewell's did since losing his leg at Manassas. I believe General Longstreet is going to need him.*

BURGOYNE

Near Milton, New York
November 1863

General Burgoyne had very reluctantly granted an interview to the young American, who turned out to be no American at all. Burgoyne had spent enough time in Ireland to know the accent when he heard it.

The dragoons who brought John Lane to Burgoyne's headquarters tent, near the tiny hamlet of Milton, told an unlikely tale, bordering on the preposterous. Lane pretended to be an informant, claiming that the Federal cavalry was looking for the British Army to intercept them. Burgoyne remained skeptical, trying to overlook the fact that his potential informant was, according to the dragoons, a one-armed potato merchant apparently in the employ of a Black woman. *What a country*, thought Burgoyne.

The general sat when Lane was ushered into the tent, a dragoon holding each of his arms. Burgoyne quickly sized him up and determined that he posed no threat. "That will be all, sergeant. Wait outside."

The visitor held his cap in his hand, not knowing whether to sit or remain standing. *Good*, thought, Burgoyne, *keep him off balance.*

"Your name?"

"John Lane."

"You're Irish?"

"Born there. I served in the Union Army." He held up his stump.

"You're here to offer information on the Union forces that are pursuing us?"

"No sir. I'm here to offer you something better."

"I see. And that would be what precisely?"

"I'm here representing the Fenian Brotherhood. There are 200,000 Irish soldiers under arms for the Union. When the Fenian Brotherhood gives the word, those soldiers will switch sides and fight alongside you and the Confederacy."

Burgoyne looked at the man's face. Soft, more a scholar than a soldier. Lane appeared nervous, but not out of his mind. His offer was certainly not what the British general expected to hear. "And why on earth would they do such a thing?"

"They would do it in return for Britain's promise of Home Rule for Ireland at the conclusion of this war."

Burgoyne was silent, his mind on the imminence of battle.

I've got Union cavalry to contend with. Major Packenham should be back already with his report on General Custer's whereabouts. He probably ran into another young lady in a buggy. I don't have time for this. Still, the notion of a widespread uprising within the Federal Army was intriguing. The combined political and military effects of such a thing would be fatal to the Union.

"Pardon me. If Her Majesty promises to grant Home Rule to Ireland at the conclusion of hostilities, 200,000 Irishmen in the Union Army will switch sides and fight for Britain? I should think that this war offers Irishmen a rare opportunity to kill redcoats, and that they'd find that hard to resist."

The visitor was silent.

"Whom do you represent?"

"I speak for John O'Mahony, the head of the Fenian Brotherhood in the United States."

Burgoyne heard the pounding of hooves and Packenham's voice. "I need to see the general immediately." The major burst into the tent and saluted, ignoring Lane.

"Sir, I've seen the enemy troops. They were encamped and I counted at least fifteen regimental flags. All cavalry as far as I could tell. I would estimate 7,500 men."

"Very good Major. Kindly show me on the map."

Packenham walked over to the map pinned on the side of the tent. After a moment's hesitation, he pointed. "Just here sir," he said, placing his right index finger on a point just east of Saratoga.

Burgoyne winced and hoped Packenham hadn't noticed. "How far from here, Major?"

"Fifteen miles, sir. A brisk hour's gallop."

Turning to Lane, the general said, "Don't go away Irishman. We shall pick up this conversation once I've dealt with your ambitious and aggressive General Custer. I'll wager you thought you were done with army life."

McCLELLAN

General George McClellan gazed out the window of the luxury sleeper car. He'd decided to take the train rather than accompany the troops by sea. This way he could be there when they arrived, and hopefully confer with Custer before setting out with the main force in pursuit of the British.

His time with the railroads before the war had spoiled him. A private car was the only way to travel. His staff was seated together in the car ahead.

Seated beside him, Nelly read from a book. On a whim, McClellan had stopped the train in Philadelphia and convinced his wife to come as far as New York City. She could stay with friends and be close by when the general defeated Burgoyne and the British Army. Perhaps, if all goes well, he thought, they might pay a call together on New York Governor Seymour.

"What are you reading?"

"*Great Expectations.*"

McClellan smiled. *How appropriate.* "That Dickens fellow? His books are a thousand pages long and it turns out everyone is somebody's long-lost uncle."

Nelly looked up. "Yes. Perhaps I should read again your manual on bayonet tactics. That would be much more entertaining. Have you a copy with you?"

McClellan smiled again. "You've read it before? I had no idea."

"Mr. Dickens has a way with the language, and I find him quite funny. You know people waited on the docks in New York for the ships to bring the next installment of his stories."

"Yes. He's a wealthy man as a result. I wonder if General Burgoyne is acquainted with him. With Burgoyne's pedigree they probably travel in the same circles. Gentlemen's clubs, the theater, and partridge shooting perhaps. In any case I prefer the French and German writers."

"Yes, so light and entertaining. Especially the Germans."

"Perhaps while you're in New York you should offer your services to Mr. Greeley. I'm sure the *Tribune* could use a literary critic."

"Perhaps I shall."

"You know I met Burgoyne in the Crimea. I wonder if he remembers me."

Nelly looked out the window at the New Jersey countryside. Farms and more farms. "I'm quite certain he knows who you are now. What have you heard from General Custer?"

"Nothing, since a telegram he sent soon after he arrived in New York. I expect he has found the British by now, and there should be a message waiting when we get to the city. I'm anxious to take the field. Custer is a fine officer, but patience is not among his manifold virtues. He will certainly harass Burgoyne, but he'll be hard-pressed to resist a general engagement if one is offered. I should have 75,000 additional men north of New York City in a matter of days and then we shall see about giving battle."

Nelly looked at her book but didn't read. "Are you concerned about Washington City? You left General Meade with a much-reduced force to defend it. One might almost think you wanted it to fall."

McClellan looked at her sharply. "I designed the defenses of Washington myself, as you know, and they are very strong. Sixty-eight forts ringing the city. Longstreet is not a man who enjoys a frontal assault on an entrenched position. I believe I have time to deal with Burgoyne, then return south and relieve Meade before too much damage is done."

He added, in a quieter tone, "And that will be that. I believe that the country's political future will become clear at that point."

The train slowed, and an aide entered McClellan's sleeper from the adjacent car. "Sir, they are flagging us to stop in Trenton. It probably means there are dispatches."

"Thank you, Captain Wilson."

As the doors opened, a soldier carrying a leather satchel jumped up the steps, walked briskly to the rear of the car, reached into the bag, and handed Wilson an envelope. The captain ripped it open, glanced at it, and turned to the general.

"Sir, a message from General Custer."

McClellan read it, looked out the window for a moment, read it again, then handed the message to his wife.

"Let's get the train moving again Captain. *Great Expectations* indeed."

LANE

Near Milton, New York
November 1863

John Lane was sitting on the cold ground beside a campfire flanked by two British soldiers sitting on camp stools. He wasn't clear whether he was a prisoner or whether General Burgoyne had simply requested that he stay in camp until such time as they could finish their conversation. Either way, he wasn't going anywhere.

With the news that Custer's troops had been spotted a mere fifteen miles away, Lane witnessed the British camp come alive, orders bellowing, tents struck, wagons quickly loaded, and regiments formed in line of march. Ninety minutes after the courier had arrived, the camp was empty save for Lane and a small contingent guarding the supplies left behind. It was all too familiar to John Lane who realized he didn't miss it at all.

The two soldiers were heating water for tea and engaged in army banter. Lane listened, and noted that one was clearly Irish, though certainly not a Corkman. He thought it might be a western accent.

"Will you have some tea?" the soldier asked.

"I will sure," replied Lane in Irish.

"We've none of that here" was the sharp reply, in English. "What color is this uniform, lad?"

Lane sat quietly, then asked, "What drove you to join the British Army?"

"Probably the same thing that drove you to America. I didn't fancy starving to death."

Fair enough, thought Lane.

"You're from the west."

"I am. Mayo. Crossmolina. The name's Staunton," the corporal said.

"What do you grow there?"

"Rocks mostly, some thistles. Potatoes in a good year, but there were precious few of those starting in '46. Black '47 was worse. I was sixteen and walked to Castlebar and joined the regiment. Sixteen years a soldier."

"And a corporal's stripes for his troubles. There's no telling how far he'll advance, given time. In another thirty years he could be Sergeant Michael Staunton." His comrade, Robert Jenkins, laughed.

The Irish soldier handed Lane tea in a tin cup. No milk and no sugar, but it was steaming hot and most welcome all the same.

Lane considered, again, his brief conversation with Burgoyne. The general hadn't thrown him out. He'd listened, asked questions. *His interest is obviously piqued. He'll want to know how he can be sure that I can deliver. That won't be easy since I certainly don't know if I can deliver.*

Lane heard a familiar creaking sound from the road, and looked up as Viola drove by in her wagon. Spotting Lane at the same time, she brought the wagon to a halt with a practiced "whoa."

"You want a ride back to Albany?"

Lane looked at the soldiers, then back to Viola. "I've business here."

Viola looked surprised, hesitating a moment before saying, "Fine.

I'll be back tomorrow with another load. If you're finished with your business, I can take you back." She clicked her tongue a couple of times and the wagon started forward with a slight jerk.

She didn't mention the brother in Glens Falls, thought Lane.

Corporal Staunton eyed Lane with a smile. "You've unusual friends. Or is she your wife?"

Lane pondered a moment. *Well. Do I have a brother in Glens Falls, or business in Albany?* "We're business partners. We buy and sell potatoes."

The soldier laughed. "Sure, you've traveled a long way to stay in the family business. You couldn't find anything better to do in America than sell praties?"

Lane held up his stump. "I tried soldiering. On the one hand, I was good at it. But on the other hand . . ."

Both soldiers laughed.

Lane knew from experience that in the next hours he would hear the distant sounds of battle. He sipped his tea and wondered what in God's name he was going to say to convince Burgoyne upon his return.

DAVIS

Near Lewinsville, Virginia
November 1863

It was exhilarating for Jefferson Davis to be back in the saddle.
He was a wartime president, and by God he was going to see this
war for himself. He'd spent considerable time in the field with the
troops and his generals the year before, when McClellan threatened
Richmond. Then it had been a short ride, too short, from the
Confederate White House to the front. From the battlefield he could
see the church steeples of the city. This was different. He had taken
the train from Richmond to Fairfax Station, and now he was riding
through the northern Virginia countryside with Pete Longstreet, his
staff officers, and an escort from the 9th Virginia Cavalry.

Where Davis was drinking in every sight and sound, Longstreet
looked angry and out of sorts. Which he no doubt was. No general
wants the president at his side on the eve of battle. It won't do to play
soldier. *I'll ride to the rear when the shooting starts,* mused Davis, *but
for now I'm going to make sure Old Peter understands exactly what's
expected.*

They rode past a white frame church. Five or six houses lined the road with farm fields running off behind them.

"Does this crossroads have a name?" Davis asked. Longstreet grunted. "Colonel Sorrel, does this clump of houses earn a name on your map?"

"Lewinsville, sir. I reckon we're five miles from the Chain Bridge."

Lewinsville. Davis had lived in Washington City for years as a senator and as secretary of war, and he'd never heard of it.

"General, are you surprised we've met no resistance since leaving Warrenton?"

"No sir. Meade has pulled back to the defenses of Washington. Since McClellan took most of the Army of the Potomac north, Meade had no choice but to tighten his ranks and shorten his supply and communication lines. He's stretched thin. But they've had over two years to build up the ring of forts around the city, and they're formidable. We have a couple of options. Lay siege, which is damn near impossible since we'd have to surround the whole city. We don't have the numbers for that. Or to try to punch through. Of course, there's a third way. We can threaten, harass, raid, and generally create mayhem and scare hell out of the Yankee government and press. That's what General Stuart was born to do. And if the British do their part, why I expect Lincoln would have no choice but to offer terms."

We've been over this a dozen times, thought Davis. *And Pete knows it. Our agreement with the British requires that we attack Washington City, and attack we shall.*

Longstreet read his thoughts. "Stuart should have crossed the river early this morning, at White's Ferry. He'll have his hands full with the batteries that guard the approaches to the city, but he'll manage. He should be in position by tomorrow morning. His orders are to make as much fuss and racket as he can and draw the brunt of Meade's attention. As you know, I've sent Jackson forward to clear the way to Chain Bridge. There are two Federal forts that protect the bridge, Forts Marcy and Ethan Allen. I suspect Jackson will bypass and isolate them rather than waste time attacking them. If he can secure the bridge, he'll enter the city and meet up with Stuart."

"And Pickett's corps?"

"Pickett will wait until we've crossed the Chain Bridge. Meade will have to move all the troops he has throughout the city to meet us. At that time, General Pickett will try to cross the Long Bridge. If he can cross, we should have 70,000 men loose in Washington City in two days' time. Should we burn the President's House, or wait for the British to do that?"

Davis didn't laugh at the joke. "The thought has crossed my mind." It was a bold plan, and nobody could say Longstreet hadn't gotten the message. Davis found himself thinking it might be too bold. Maybe they really should demonstrate and threaten for a few days, wait for news from Burgoyne, and see if Lincoln wants to talk.

"How do you find General Jackson?"

A long silence. Davis knew that Lee had been the glue that held the prickly Southern generals together. Longstreet and Jackson were as different as can be. The one stolid, dependable, easy to read. The other mercurial, odd, but gifted and driven by a higher authority.

"General Jackson seems delighted to be back with his men. And they are certainly glad to have him back. I believe he is anxious to deliver a blow, prove that his wounds and time away haven't changed him. Taking the bridge should be just the tonic to set him up. If anything, he's quieter. And more trusting in Divine Providence. Whatever that may be."

Davis hesitated, then asked. "Is he comfortable serving under your command?"

Longstreet laughed, a harsh sound that started in the chest and slowly found its way to the throat. "I didn't ask."

A low rumble, like distant thunder, sounded. There wasn't a cloud in the sky. Longstreet took his watch from his pocket, flipped it open, and said, "General Stuart is ahead of his own ambitious schedule. Colonel Sorrel, kindly ride ahead and inform General Jackson that

Stuart is engaged. And would he keep me and, uh, President Davis apprised of his progress in clearing the approaches to the Chain Bridge."

Davis was fairly standing in his stirrups, red-faced, straining to hear, and looked for all the world as if he were about to yell *Charge!* and gallop ahead.

Longstreet spoke. "Mr. President, as you make your way to the rear, rest assured that my staff will keep you up to the minute on our progress."

BURGOYNE

Bemis Heights, near Saratoga, New York
November 1863

John Fox Burgoyne sat his horse atop Bemis Heights, with a clear view of the Hudson and the surrounding countryside up to ten miles distant. Below, in the narrow gap between the Heights and the River, his 6th dragoons were in full retreat, vastly outnumbered by what looked like a full brigade of Federal horsemen. They were heading north, in good order, no rout. Staring through field glasses, he was learning what he needed to know. That the Federals were here, in brigade strength at least, and full of fight. *Well and good.*

Burgoyne was of course aware that Bemis Heights formed part of the Saratoga battlefield in 1777, most of which lay to the north toward the village of Schuylerville. He was keenly aware that his father had stood on this hill, perhaps on this very spot, and had surveyed the disposition of his own troops. He didn't particularly believe in ghosts, but he felt a presence, a weight, in any case. *Does something linger from that far off time? Most likely not. But what is it that weighs upon me so?* As good a day as any to clean the slate.

Far to the north, through the glasses, he could see the dust cloud which marked his infantry, making their way toward the fight. If the dragoons did their job properly, they would lead Custer's brigade of horses right into the British Army. Mounted soldiers would be no match for veteran infantry, especially when so greatly outnumbered.

"Major Packenham, be so kind as to ride like the wind, apprise General Mountjoy of the situation, and have him prepare for action. You may tell him that he should expect a brigade of Union cavalry in his front within the hour. And Major?"

"Sir?"

"Avoid young women in buggies. Leave that for another time."

Packenham was away, digging his spurs into his horse's flanks and whipping with the end of his reins.

Burgoyne smiled. *He reminds me of myself, my young self. Quite unnecessary but a fine effect. I envy his enthusiasm.*

Burgoyne lifted the glasses back to his eyes and stiffened. Still in retreat from Custer's advancing cavalry, his dragoons were about to enter a wooded area that spread on both sides of the dirt road. At the far edge of the woods, hidden from the road, he could see blue-clad soldiers holding horses. That meant that dismounted cavalry were in the woods, no doubt waiting in ambush for his dragoons. There was not a thing he could do but watch.

He didn't have long to wait. From his vantage point he saw smoke rising over the road, and confusion, and heard the faint but distinctive crackle of small arms. Red-uniformed horsemen were riding in every direction, in small groups, while a small force seemed to have dismounted. Or perhaps they'd been shot from their horses.

It was over in fifteen minutes. He could see that a sizeable force of his men, possibly a hundred, had regrouped and were riding north toward the dust cloud that preceded his infantry. Many more redcoats lay on the ground. And perhaps as many seemed to be prisoners and were dismounted, walking among the blue soldiers on horseback.

The Union troops and their prisoners marched southward, from whence they'd come, no doubt to reunite with Custer and his main force.

Bastards!

"Captain Wilkerson, follow behind Major Packenham. Please advise General Mountjoy that there are wounded and dead to attend to on the road in the woods."

"Where will you make headquarters, sir?"

"Below. Saratoga."

McCLELLAN

Albany, New York
November 1863

General McClellan had left his wife in New York City and
continued by rail to Albany. The Army of the Potomac would
disembark from their transport ships in New York harbor. As
many as possible would travel north by train, and the rest would
have to march. *General Meigs has his work cut out for him,* thought
McClellan. He knew that Meigs was probably the most capable
officer in the entire Union Army. He chafed at not commanding
troops in the field, but was too valuable as quartermaster general.
Significant elements of the army should be in Albany by tomorrow, he
mused, but he wouldn't have his entire force together for at least ten
days. Decisions would have to be made. Much depended on Custer's
report.

McClellan was met at the station by Custer himself, with a large
entourage of staff. Behind the soldiers was a growing mass of adoring
citizens, mostly young women and small boys, anxious to be in the
presence of the hero of the hour. The boy general was beaming.

"Welcome General. I trust you had a comfortable journey? Mrs. McClellan is well?"

"Quite well, thank you, and sends her regards. I'd like to see the battlefield. I suggest we talk while we ride."

They mounted their horses and set off through the city, crossing the Hudson and heading north. Very soon they were riding through the New York countryside, the sun shining but the air cold. They could see their breath and that of their horses.

"We'll go to Bemis Heights, which is two hours of brisk riding from here. From there we'll be able to see the battlefield, and I can describe in detail what transpired. We will also be able to see Burgoyne's army from there. He is camped to the north, near Saratoga. My cavalry is south of there, spread between the Hudson and Saratoga Lake. If Burgoyne moves south, we'll know it immediately."

"Tell me about your encounter."

Custer smiled. Was he always smiling? "We rode north from New York City as ordered. The Reserve Brigade, mostly regular cavalry under General Merritt, was in the lead, a couple of miles ahead of my main force. Merritt's scouts saw a party of British dragoons heading south, so he set an ambush in the woods. He sent two companies of the 5th regulars forward to lure them in. The dragoons gave chase. Merritt then brought up the remainder of the brigade, and the dragoons were forced to turn tail and retreat. But they did so in good order. They had about four hundred men to Merritt's thousand. As the dragoons retreated through the woods, dismounted troopers sprung the ambush, and it was over in minutes. I'd estimate that two hundred or so got away. The rest were killed or wounded or taken prisoner. We've got over a hundred of them under guard in camp. What would you like me to do with them?"

McClellan didn't hesitate. "They can walk under guard to Albany. The provost guard can take them from there. Put them on the cars to the nearest prisoner camp where they can join their rebel allies for the duration of the war. There will be no prisoner exchange when it comes to the British."

They rode on, nothing more pleasant than to be in the saddle in the wake of victory. They dismounted twice to rest the horses, walking silently for ten minutes each time, McClellan deep in thought. *What next?* Custer had given Burgoyne a bloody nose, but nothing more. If Pinkerton was correct, he had at least 50,000 troops with more on the way from Britain. Timing was everything, he knew. Should he wait to consolidate his entire force in ten days? Or strike now, as soon as the advance elements of his army arrived by rail? Everything he'd learned and seen argued in favor of waiting. Nothing was more important than careful planning and precise execution. Still, there was an opportunity. Burgoyne's supply and communications lines were extended, and he was operating in enemy territory.

"General, how many troops would you estimate that Burgoyne has?"

"Sir, you'll see from Bemis Heights. Assuming it's his whole force in camp there, and he hasn't left troops north and out of sight, I'd say he has about 15,000 men."

McClellan was shocked, and skeptical. "Pinkerton and his operatives have repeatedly estimated Burgoyne's force at 50,000 or more."

Custer slyly smiled again. *An annoying habit,* thought McClellan. "Sir, unless they sleep stacked on top of one another, ten per two-man tent, that's not possible. You'll soon see for yourself. I'm confident in the 15,000 estimate. I was sorely tempted to take them on myself." Custer glanced over at McClellan, smiling still.

"Yes, in contradiction of a direct order. I appreciate your restraint."

They reached Bemis Heights in late afternoon, the autumn sun nearing the horizon. Through his field glasses McClellan could clearly see tents, and if he focused and concentrated, he could

make out soldiers and horses as well. As an engineer, he was an
expert in estimating the size of an army encampment, and Custer
was right. There were probably 15,000 troops on the plain below.
20,000 at most. *Where are the rest?* Was Burgoyne inviting him to
attack, with 30,000 additional troops, or more, lying in wait over the
horizon? McClellan would have 30,000 men in and around Albany
by tomorrow evening, in addition to Custer's troopers. A puzzle.
And an opportunity.

LANE

Near Saratoga, New York
November 1863

John Lane had been brought to Burgoyne's camp in an army wagon, accompanied by his two British guards. It had taken hours and he was cold and hungry. The soldiers seemed immune to any discomfort or hardship and were in no rush to complete the journey. Lane remembered well. Any time spent not fighting and not marching was considered luxurious and to be prolonged and enjoyed.

Safely delivered, he was now waiting, another strong memory of army life, especially camp life. Waiting to drill, waiting to eat, waiting for orders, waiting to be dismissed. And now waiting to meet with a commanding general who had just been dealt a stinging and probably shocking defeat. Burgoyne would be in a nasty mood. But perhaps that was Lane's opportunity.

An officer appeared, and told the soldiers, "Look sharp and follow me with the prisoner."

Prisoner. No doubt the recent battle had changed everyone's thinking regarding Union soldiers, even a one-armed former soldier.

The small procession made its way through a maze of army tents, wagons, campfires, and guards, and stopped in front of a white tent that was larger than the others, and which had guards and staff officers milling about outside.

"Wait here." The officer entered the tent.

John Lane had spent enough time in army camps to sense the mood, and it was tense. He stood with his guards and attracted little attention from the staff officers. Corporal Staunton, the Mayoman, whispered, "What business does an Irish potato merchant have with the general?"

"He's deeply interested in the proper preparation of the potato to provide maximum sustenance to his troops. I've been contracted to provide instruction."

The guard stared at Lane, unsure what to say.

After ten or fifteen minutes, an aide appeared at the tent flap and waved Lane in, alone, the guards remaining outside. Burgoyne was standing between two other officers, obviously of high rank, and they were all poring over a map stretched between two camp stools.

"The prisoner, sir."

Burgoyne looked up, eyed Lane suspiciously, then a look of recollection came over him.

"Just so. The Fenian. Gentlemen, this man claims he represents the Fenian Brotherhood. And that he can deliver 200,000 Irish soldiers from the Union Army to support our cause. All the crown has to do is promise Irish Home Rule in return. Does that fairly summarize your case, Mister . . . ?"

"Lane. John Patrick Lane. Late of the 7th Rhode Island Infantry, and now, yes, representing the Fenian Brotherhood. And yes, that's the proposition, fair enough."

"Yes, Mr. Lane. Now sir, assuming the crown agrees to your, em, proposal, which is presumptuous indeed, what proof do we have that you can deliver what you promise?"

"The Brotherhood has men in all the Irish regiments, as well as every other regiment that has more than a few of us. My own regiment was half Irish, and my company was almost entirely so. Immigrant men from Boston and Providence. My sergeant was the Fenian representative. We knew what we were about. Gaining experience for the day we'd sail back to Ireland and throw you lot out. My plan will save us all, you and us both, a world of trouble." Lane was fairly shaking as he spoke. He couldn't believe that he, the corporal, and an Irishman, was raising his voice to a general in the British Army. And he was surprised at the emotion that welled inside of him.

Burgoyne stared at Lane a long while, then looked at his fellow officers, each in turn. He turned back to Lane. "Suppose you tell me precisely what you have in mind. What does Home Rule mean?"

Lane looked at each of the officers. Probably a hundred years or more of military experience among them, defending and expanding the Empire. No doubt some of them had served in Ireland, maintaining order and enforcing British law.

"An Irish Parliament, like the one that existed before the Act of Union in 1801. Authority over domestic matters."

"And the crown?"

"The Queen remains the Queen of Great Britain and Ireland."

One of Burgoyne's officers interrupted. "I thought you Fenian lot were Republicans. A bunch of damned Jacobins!"

"Thank you, General Mountjoy. Mr. Lane?"

"Certainly, the Fenian movement represents the cause of Irish freedom, and the ultimate goal would remain a republic. But I am certain that Home Rule would be seen as a positive and necessary step. I can assure you that the organization would accept it." *Can you really?* he asked himself.

"When might your Fenians be ready to, em, commence operations, Mr. Lane?"

"Just as soon as you can confirm that our offer has been accepted. As soon as the prime minister has given his word."

Burgoyne was staring at the map again. "I suppose I have little to lose. If you are unable to deliver on your promise, Her Majesty needn't deliver on hers. Mr. Lane, if I decide to propose your plan to the prime minister, it will be at least a month before I could expect an answer."

From prisoner to Mr. Lane. Progress. "Then I suggest you lose no time in writing to the prime minister."

Burgoyne gazed hard at Lane. "How shall we communicate?"

Lane smiled. "I assume this army has an endless need for potatoes."

DAVIS

Richmond, Virginia
November 1863

Jefferson Davis was pacing in the parlor of his Richmond residence, a fire burning in the fireplace, and another deep inside of him. Varina, as always, was knitting in her chair. Davis disliked the room and in fact disliked the house. Come to think of it, he disliked Richmond, and disliked being president of the Confederacy. His mood was dark.

"You might sit down. You're working yourself into a state."

"I am long since in a state and make no mistake." Davis had hoped, dearly hoped, that by now Washington City would have fallen to Longstreet's army, and that a victorious Burgoyne would be marching south with his British troops. He had hoped that Lincoln would be suing for peace.

"I saw Mary Lee this morning. I paid a call. She was gracious but poorly. She had trouble pouring tea for the rheumatism."

"Was the general in evidence?"

"I heard footsteps upstairs. It could have been the help. Mary said the general is well and is writing. No further information."

"Writing. If Southern generals aren't dueling, they're writing. I hope the general takes his time with whatever he's writing."

"The newspapers are upset with your General Longstreet. They're certain that General Lee would have taken Washington City by now."

"Just as they were certain that invading the north was a mistake, that I should have kept the army home to protect Richmond. Until we were victorious at Gettysburg. Then it turned out it had been their plan all along. And I didn't fire him. General Lee. He resigned."

"What news from General Longstreet?"

"His initial enthusiasm to take Washington City has waned. His attempts to cross the Potomac at Chain and Long Bridges were frustrated. Stuart likewise ran afoul of Federal infantry. But Longstreet claims that it's just a matter of time. He holds the high ground on the Maryland Palisades, and in Virginia on Arlington Heights. His big guns are raining shells on Washington City. Stuart is being Stuart and playing havoc with their supply lines and cutting telegraph wires. Lincoln and the cabinet have fled to Philadelphia."

"So, Washington is under siege?"

"Technically no, since our troops haven't surrounded the city completely. We don't have sufficient forces to do so, and won't unless the British can fight their way southward to join our army. But Washington City is cut off on three sides. Half the northern newspapers are screaming for McClellan to return and drive off the invaders. The other half are imploring Lincoln to recognize Southern independence and end the war."

"And what news from your new British friends?"

Davis shot a glance at Varina, and scowled. "I have precious few friends in this world, it seems. The only information I have is through the Northern papers. Apparently, young General Custer thrashed the British somewhere along the Hudson, but it doesn't seem to have been a general engagement. I expect that Burgoyne will lick his wounds, bide his time, await reinforcements, and keep McClellan busy up north. That should at least give Pete the time he needs to capture Washington City."

"So, you've worked yourself into a state for nothing. Longstreet has things in hand along the Potomac, and McClellan is occupied in New York. Meanwhile, we enjoy our independence, in spite of rampant inflation, scarcity of food, empty shops, and the vitriol of the press. And the fact that all the men are away for the harvest."

Davis laughed and finally sat. "You certainly have a way." Varina tried to hand him the day's *Richmond Daily Dispatch*. Davis laughed again. "I'd rather you handed me those knitting needles. I don't need to read the papers to know what people are saying. I have you to tell me that the shops are empty. I shall sit by your side and stare into the fire."

As they sat together, Davis pondered Varina's words. Perhaps things really weren't so bad. Washington under threat of capture and constant bombardment. McClellan far away, tied up, and facing a formidable foe. Vicksburg somehow holding out against all odds. *For us, survival is success. So for now, we're successful.*

BURGOYNE

Near Saratoga, New York
November 1863

Burgoyne sat alone in his tent, John Lane and Burgoyne's officers having been sent away.

I should dismiss this scheme out of hand, he thought. *If I write to Palmerston, proposing Home Rule for Ireland, he could print the letter in the papers, and it would be my ruin. On top of a second defeat at Saratoga.*

Saratoga. He'd spent his professional life atoning for his father's original sin, and now this debacle at the hands of a flamboyant twenty-three-year-old. There was only one thing to do. Await reinforcements, offer battle, and crush McClellan. At Saratoga. Once and for all.

But what if Lane was correct. What if there really was a shadowy brotherhood, 200,000 strong, awaiting word to do the bidding of their Fenian masters? If a third of McClellan's army is Irish, imagine the impact.

I've nothing to lose. If Lane can't deliver, the crown owes the Irish nothing. If he does deliver, Home Rule for Ireland, under the crown, is a small price to pay for striking such a blow to the United States of America.

"Sir?"

It was Packenham, peeking in the tent flap.

"Yes, Major, what is it?"

Packenham stepped in and handed Burgoyne a leather envelope, embossed with the crown. "A message from Montreal, sir."

Burgoyne opened the envelope, pulled out the letter, read it, and handed it to Packenham. "The first troops have arrived from home. This dispatch is four days old. The first reinforcements should be here in a week, perhaps sooner if General Gordon is brisk about it."

"Shall we head north, consolidate our forces, and force General McClellan to give chase?"

"We shall not. We shall await General Gordon here and beg McClellan to attack us, here." At Saratoga.

"Yes sir." Packenham looked deflated.

"Major, we shall write a letter. To the Prime Minister."

"Yes sir. If I may sir." Packenham placed a camp stool in front of Burgoyne's small field desk, placed paper in front of him, took pen in hand, and dipped it in the inkwell. He waited.

Burgoyne was deep in thought. Palmerston knew Ireland well. He had an estate there. Mayo? Sligo? In the far west. He underwrote emigration schemes for his tenants during the famine. God knows some of them are probably in the Union Army. Probably Fenians. He would understand. He knew these people. The queen would be a different matter. *I must emphasize that the status of the crown doesn't change.*

"Sir?"

"Quite Major. Today's date, then 'Saratoga, New York.' No, make that today's date, then 'Along the Hudson River. My Dearest Prime Minister:'"

McCLELLAN

Near Bemis Heights, New York
December 1863

George McClellan didn't like being outnumbered. Decisive victories had eluded him before, especially at the gates of Richmond, because his army had been badly outnumbered by the Confederate troops. Lincoln didn't believe it. Some of the newspapers questioned it. But it was a fact. Pinkerton had shown him the numbers.

He had always sworn that if he ever got another chance, the chance he so richly deserved, that when the time came, he would face the enemy with overwhelming force and achieve the final victory.

So, he was extremely uncomfortable with the plan that he had agreed to, the plan that Custer had hatched and placed before him. It was bold and decisive; McClellan would grant him that. But Custer was just twenty-three years old and had never known defeat. *He seems to believe that it's all a great game.*

Poring over maps with his corps commanders, with Custer present as commander of his cavalry, McClellan had pondered his next move. Every bone in his body urged him to wait to consolidate his entire force—just a few more days—then move on Burgoyne. With luck, British reinforcements would not yet have arrived.

Custer, speaking up in front of men twice his age, and who outranked him, suggested another plan entirely. The boy general proposed that he, of course, lead his cavalry north to intercept British reinforcements before they could get to Burgoyne. McClellan, taking the troops he had on hand, which outnumbered the British, though not by a lot, would attack and destroy Burgoyne. McClellan could then move north and join Custer in dealing finally and decisively with the British reinforcements.

The plan was sound and prevented Burgoyne from consolidating his forces. But McClellan liked better odds, more lopsided numbers, especially since he would be on the attack.

I'll say this for Custer, his enthusiasm is contagious.

As he made sweeping gestures over the map, the corps commanders and staff officers nodded, smiled, looked at each other approvingly, and it was clear that he had brought them all over to his plan. *I could disapprove,* McClellan thought, *but the others would always remember that Custer had favored bold action and that I had urged caution.*

After the meeting, Custer presented himself for final orders before setting out with his troopers. McClellan found himself speaking to Custer in a way that he, McClellan, hated to be spoken to.

"General, your orders are clear. I've written them out, but I'll say again. Your job is to slow the British down. Delay their arrival, by days if possible. Harass, annoy, attack supply trains, skirmish with their cavalry, but under no circumstances bring on a general engagement. Once I've dealt with Burgoyne I will come to your aid, and we shall destroy them in turn. Is that clear?"

Smiling, as always, Custer replied, "Clear as this bright December morning, sir. Harass. Annoy. Delay. No general engagement. Await your arrival. Looks like snow sir. I haven't seen a real snowfall since West Point. That should work in our favor, slowing them down."

With that, Custer mounted and wheeled his horse, which snorted and reared, as if on cue. Custer doffed his plumed hat, holding it aloft as he cantered to the head of his column of mounted men.

God help me, thought McClellan. *Could that really be for my benefit? That boy will learn humility one day, but I hope it isn't this week. I need him to carry out his plan and buy me time.*

McClellan was atop Bemis Heights with his Corps Commanders and staff, each gazing through field glasses at the British Army encamped below them.

"They've dug in since yesterday and placed artillery. It looks like they've decided to fight there," said General Gouverneur Warren, commander of II Corps.

General John Sedgwick smiled as he watched the army below. "Yes. It seems the father wasn't the only Burgoyne with a flair for the theatrical. 'Gentleman Johnny' would be proud of the son. The mother as well, for that matter. Saratoga. Betting that two Burgoynes can't meet defeat in the same place. At the hands of the rustics. I'll take that bet."

McClellan was silent, then finally turned to Captain Wilson. "Captain, I need a precise estimate of when we can expect our troops to arrive by ship." Then to his officers, "Gentlemen, we shall discuss in detail when we return to camp, but please have your men formed up a half hour before dawn, the day after tomorrow. We shall provide General Burgoyne with his own memories of Saratoga."

LANE

On the Albany Road, New York
December 1863

The weather had turned markedly colder, and Lane wasn't dressed for it. It was a gray day, too dark for mid-afternoon, and a stiffening breeze from the northwest smelled of snow.

Lane had spent two nights in the British camp, sleeping in a tent with his British minders. He didn't call them guards because he wasn't a prisoner, not really. He had awakened each night, freezing, unsure of where he was, but with the smells and noises, his first thought both nights was that he was back in the army. He lay awake both nights wondering how he was going to deliver on the momentous promise he had made to General Burgoyne.

He had taken his leave from the two British soldiers, the Mayoman still curious if he were really a potato merchant, and how he'd gotten an audience with the general. He was walking south, back toward Albany, where he would take the train from Albany to New York City, find John O'Mahony, explain that the game was on, and await word from London.

He'd been walking for close to an hour when he heard a now-familiar creaking noise behind him. He turned and saw, as he expected, Viola driving her horse and wagon in his direction.

"Whoa there, whoa. Not you, I'm talking to my horse. You need a ride now, or you still have *business* with the general?"

"My business is concluded, thank you. And yes, I would gladly accept a ride to Albany." Lane climbed aboard and sat next to the woman. Glancing behind he could see that the bed of the wagon was full of empty sacks.

"I'm not going all the way to Albany. My farm is north of town. But you'll be close. How was your brother in Glens Falls?" This last was accompanied by a sharp glance from Viola.

"Em, I didn't see my brother on this trip. My business takes me back to Albany. I'll see him next time."

"You a spy or something? Am I going to get in trouble for giving you a ride? You know how easy it is for a Black woman to get into trouble for no reason at all? You don't have a brother in Glens Falls."

Lane sat quietly, bouncing with the wagon over the hard-packed dirt road. Snow flurries started to fall, but they melted as they hit the ground.

"I've a number of brothers and a sister as well, and where they live is my concern. I'm not a spy. I'm a messenger of sorts. If we get stopped and questioned, I suggest that we agree that my brother does indeed live in Glens Falls and that I was helping you today with your deliveries. Potatoes."

"Hmmph. Depends on who stops us. You're prepared to explain that I'm not a runaway and that you're not helping me escape?"

The snow was coming down hard now, the wind had picked up, and it was in fact miserable atop the wagon. The temperature was dropping, and the snow was now sticking to the ground.

"Are you a runaway slave?"

"Hah. How long has your family been in America? My family's been here a couple hundred years. Of course, doesn't mean I can vote. No. I was born here in New York. Free. My people are from Virginia."

"No women can vote."

"That's right. But here in New York even a Black man can't vote unless he owns significant property. Almost none qualify."

"Sure you're not the only one with problems. I live in Boston. There are signs in the shop windows. *No Irish Need Apply.* The Irish are at the bottom of the heap."

"Haha!" Her laughter was derisive, dismissive.

"You have no idea. You think you're at the bottom of the heap? There's a whole other heap you don't even know about."

"How far is your farm?"

"On a good day, two hours from here. In this weather, I can't say." Viola shook the reins, encouraging her horse to pick up the pace, but he was immune to her charms.

They rode in silence, the snow starting to accumulate on the wagon, on their clothing, and on the road. The horse could apparently sense the road, but Lane couldn't see it except when it was framed by trees or shrubbery.

"I'm still unclear why you're selling potatoes to the British. They're fighting for Southern independence. That will guarantee the continuation of slavery."

"And your *business* with the general? Seems to me like you're doing the same thing. And you a soldier. And an Irishman. I thought the Irish hated the British. You must be a spy."

They rode silently for a long time, the snow coming harder now.

"You're not going to make it to Albany tonight."

DAVIS

Richmond, Virginia
December 1863

The messenger had asked to see President Davis alone. *A remarkable young man,* thought Davis. His second roundtrip, alone, from New York to Richmond. Obviously upper class, educated, fine manners. But bold and daring and resourceful as well. *Not unlike the fellows I grew up with,* he thought. Young men dedicated to riding fast horses and hunting make for poor scholars but excellent soldiers. *He'll never forget these times if he survives them.*

"Major Packenham, please come in. I trust you had a pleasant journey?"

"Most enjoyable, thank you, sir. I left snow behind, so your Southern weather is most welcome."

"I find it chilly myself, but we've had no snow thus far. Did you have any trouble crossing the lines?"

"No sir. As you know, Union forces are concentrated within Washington City. I didn't see a single soldier from either side until I crossed the Potomac. I was in greater danger from your own soldiers than from Federal troops."

"Major, how did you, uh, get here?"

Packenham flashed a full, self-satisfied smile. "Various conveyances, sir. A couple of farm wagons in the early going. Then mostly by rail. The Northern trains are quite comfortable. Once in Maryland I, em, borrowed a horse from a farmer. It turned out to be more suited to plowing than to riding so I borrowed another. A fine animal."

"Mmm. Have you a written message from General Burgoyne?"

"The general thought it imprudent to commit his message to paper. In case of, em, capture, sir."

"I understand. Please proceed."

"Sir. General Burgoyne wanted you to know that there was a skirmish fought near Saratoga. General Custer and Federal cavalry, in force, ambushed a regiment of dragoons, inflicting some casualties."

"So I understand from the Northern newspapers."

Davis could see that the major had no intention of dwelling on the embarrassing incident at Saratoga.

"General Burgoyne has received word that British reinforcements have arrived in Montreal, under General Gordon, and they are, or soon will be, marching south to join with the general."

"How many reinforcements, Major?"

"Probably 30,000, sir. Once his forces are united, General Burgoyne expects to fight General McClellan in the vicinity of Saratoga."

"I see. Has he considered attacking McClellan before the Union can consolidate all their troops?"

"He has sir. But he believes that his position near Saratoga is strong, and he prefers to fight on the defensive. And sir. There's something more."

Davis didn't speak, but stared at the major, hands clasped on his lap, eyebrows raised.

"Sir, the general was insistent that this be for your ears only. General Burgoyne has been in contact with a representative of the

Fenian Brotherhood. They claim that, in return for a promise of Irish Home Rule following the end of the war, they will deliver 200,000 Irishmen currently serving in the Union Army to our side."

Davis stared at Packenham. "I'm sorry, Major. The Fenian Brotherhood? Irish revolutionaries?"

"Just so, sir. There are 200,000 Irishmen under arms in the Union Army. It's an open secret that they are training to fight for Irish freedom once this war is over. Their plan, em, their proposition is that in return for Britain promising Irish Home Rule after this war, they will switch sides and fight with us."

Davis remembered Mexico. What did they call themselves? The St. Patrick Brigade? Irish immigrants, escaped slaves, US Army deserters. A ragtag group, but they fought like tigers. On the Mexican side. Against the United States. At Charubusco and elsewhere. The Americans had hung those they'd captured.

"We have Irish units of our own. The Louisiana Tigers. There's a Tennessee Regiment. General Cleburne. I wish I had a dozen like him. So, what happens next?"

"General Burgoyne has written to the prime minister. He hopes for an answer in a month's time."

Davis pondered. Ridiculous on its face. But imagine if whole regiments lay down their arms or switched sides. They had whole brigades manned by Irish. It could be the last straw for the Union and hasten the end of the war.

"Thank you, Major. As the general requests, I shall keep this news to myself. Now, I'd like to explain the situation regarding Washington City. I believe General Longstreet will soon launch a second assault and try to force a crossing of the Potomac. Like General Burgoyne, I will be more comfortable explaining this to you rather than committing it to paper."

BURGOYNE

Near Saratoga, New York
December 1863

Burgoyne was no stranger to snow. He'd seen plenty at home in England, though seldom like this. And of course on the continent and in the Crimea. It made soldiers cold, and cold soldiers were lazy soldiers. They let down their guards and seek shelter. Now was no time to have lazy troops.

Burgoyne had doubled the guard and sent squads of dragoons out on patrol to ensure that McClellan wasn't planning his own Washington-style surprise attack in a snowstorm. There would be no Trentons. And where was Gordon? As if in answer, he heard hoofbeats, muffled by the snow, and voices outside the tent. An aide, snow covering the shoulders of his overcoat, peeked in to announce, "Courier from General Gordon, sir." Without waiting, a breathless young officer, who looked like he'd had a very cold and very hard time of it indeed, walked through the flap and came to attention.

"Captain Hutchinson, sir. General Gordon presents his compliments. He wishes to report that he is a long day's march from here and hopes to arrive *th'morra forenicht* or early the next morning. He's got enemy cavalry in division strength in front of him and has to fight for every *sleekit loupin* inch of ground. The wee bastards. Beg your pardon, sir." The captain's Scots burr was almost unintelligible, but Burgoyne got the gist.

"Thank you, Captain. English will do just fine here. We'll get you some hot food and some tea just as soon as you show me on this map precisely where General Gordon is fighting the *sleekit loupin* bastards."

Captain Hutchinson, perhaps not as sheepish as he might be in the presence of the general, didn't look up. He squinted in the lantern light and pointed. *"Richt aboot 'ere,* sir. Right here."

Between Forts Edward and Miller. About twenty miles, guessed Burgoyne. A day's march in decent weather for a likely man like Gordon, but the snow and Custer will slow him down. The general doubted he would see Gordon by tomorrow.

"Captain, what has been the nature of the fighting between General Gordon's troops and the enemy cavalry?"

"Just a wee rammy here and there, sir, not a general engagement. The enemy cavalry are capable, sir, and they hit and run, harass our wagons, fell trees across the road and the like. Nothing General Gordon can't handle, but it slows him down and he's *gey crabbit,* sir. Em, mad as a hatter. Fit to be tied. Bloody angry."

"Yes, I understand, Captain. How bad are the roads?"

"Bloody impossible, General. It's not so much the roads as the visibility. I was riding blind most of the time. It's a miracle I found you at all. I almost rode right into your sentries, asleep as they were, the bloody *sassenach* bastards, begging your pardon, General."

"That will be all, Captain. Major, have someone see to his horse and get him something to eat. A haggis would no doubt do."

Burgoyne looked again at the map, deep in thought. He could wait for Gordon, at least another thirty-six hours, and hope that

McClellan didn't attack until he arrived. Or he could launch a surprise attack before McClellan was fully reinforced.

"Major, when you've seen to the captain's comfort, kindly request that Generals Mountjoy and Trevelyan come to see me. We've much to discuss."

McCLELLAN

South of Bemis Heights, New York
December 1863

Not ten miles away, George McClellan dismounted his horse, handed the reins to an orderly, brushed snow from his coat, and turned his felt hat upside down to rid it of snow as well. He stomped his boots on the wooden platform and entered his tent through the flap. It was just as cold inside as out. The oil lantern gave off precious little light and less warmth.

McClellan had visited each of his corps commanders and most of the division commanders. He wanted the men to see him, to know that despite the snowstorm, he was active, engaged, leading. It wouldn't do to hunker down. Burgoyne could try to exploit the weather by launching an attack at any time.

McClellan hadn't heard from Custer, but that wasn't surprising. His orders were clear, and the fact that Custer was still in the field was proof enough that he was doing his job harassing the British as ordered. The snow should slow the British down, but it would also delay the Union troops coming up from New York City.

If Sykes can get here with his men before Burgoyne is reinforced, he thought, *that's an opportunity.* It was hard for McClellan to believe that the British invaded with only 15,000 troops, but there they sat. If Sykes arrived tomorrow, he could attack the following morning and have a three-to-one advantage.

I need to deal with Burgoyne before he's reinforced. Then go north and strike the troops that Custer is harassing, McClellan concluded. It could all be over in a matter of days. Then, the British threat dealt with, he could return to Washington City and save the capital from Longstreet's legions. And that will be that. The future will be clear and certain.

Burgoyne. McClellan remembered him from Crimea. An engineer, like himself. Thoughtful, intentional, thorough. But aloof. He hadn't paid much attention to the young American officer, sent to Crimea to observe and report. *I doubt he remembers me.* Not a man prone to make mistakes. Respected by the other British officers, though not loved. What a burden he has carried, and now, encamped on the very battlefield that his father lost all those years ago. *It must weigh. He'll want to put those ghosts to rest once and for all. That's my opportunity.*

McClellan walked outside and stood next to the fire that his staff was gathered around. He would much prefer no campfires, with the enemy within spitting distance, but it was too cold, and he needed to take care of his men. There would be a big fight very soon, maybe the decisive fight of the war, and he needed every single man ready to fight. Leadership made all the difference. Lincoln didn't understand. *Pope, Burnside, Hooker.* McClellan felt anger rising, but he checked himself. There would be plenty of time to settle accounts in due course.

"Captain, talk to the quartermaster and see if he can increase rations tomorrow. The men will need the extra sustenance soon enough."

"Right away, sir."

"And Captain." This in a whisper, pulling him away from the fire, "Have we heard from the woman?"

Captain Wilson looked around, assuring himself that no one was within earshot. "No sir. Not since her last report two days ago, when she returned from the British camp. I suspect the storm is keeping her at home."

"I need to know General Burgoyne's intentions. Get a message to her."

"Yes sir. I'll go myself."

LANE

Near Albany, New York
December 1863

The wagon had left the main road to Albany a half mile back.
John Lane could see nothing beyond the swirling snow in front of
him. He could barely see the horse six feet ahead. Viola said, "Whoa
there, whoa," and the horse and wagon came to a halt. Viola hopped
down.

"We're here."

"We're where?"

"Home. Get down. You can come in and get warm, but then
you'll have to sleep in the barn."

Lane slid down and followed Viola. She rapped sharply on the
door, and a moment later it was opened by a woman who looked like
an older version of her. "Thank goodness. I was worried sick. You'll
catch your death. Who's this?"

"A traveler. He would have frozen to death. He'll sleep in the
barn. How are the children?"

Her mother, for that's who the older woman was, gave her a long, sharp look before replying. "They're both fine. They ate supper and they're in bed. I need to talk to you. Now."

The farmhouse, such as it was, seemed to have two rooms. The room they were in—large, with a fireplace, table and chairs, a large cupboard—and a second room where Viola and her mother now repaired. Lane assumed that the children were in there as well, asleep.

Lane looked around. *Bare but comfortable. Not unlike the houses back home,* he thought. He heard someone sneeze, twice, muffled. Had it come from the other room? It almost sounded like it had come from below. Lane strained but heard nothing more.

Viola and her mother emerged from the other room. "I'll show you the barn. I'll bring you something to eat as soon as I've fixed something. You'll have to leave in the morning. It's five miles to Albany. Less than a two hour walk in good weather."

Lane was going to reply, but he glanced at Viola's mother, glaring, hands on hips, and forgot what he was going to say.

"These are the only blankets I can spare. Don't build a fire in the barn. It's full of hay. If you cover yourself with blankets and hay you should be fine."

He followed Viola toward the door and heard another muffled sneeze, then another. Lane looked at Viola, then at her mother.

"Let's go." The door was open, snow blew in, and Viola was walking toward the barn. Lane closed the door behind him and followed.

The barn was small and was indeed full of hay. There were also burlap bags filled with potatoes.

"I heard someone sneeze. When you were in the other room and as we were about to leave. Do you have a husband? Do you have a cellar?"

"It sounds like you really are a spy. You'd best mind your own business. I'll bring you some food shortly." And she was gone.

Lane made himself as comfortable as he could, which wasn't comfortable at all. He piled hay in a corner, sat on it, and wrapped himself with the blankets. The barn cut the wind but didn't do anything for the frigid temperature.

Fifteen minutes later, Lane heard hoofbeats, then a knock on the door of the house. It opened, and he could see Viola framed in the light from the doorway. The rider went in. It looked for all the world like a soldier dressed in blue. Five minutes later, the door re-opened, and Lane could see that it was indeed a Union officer. He remounted and was gone.

Soon after Viola came to the barn carrying a dish covered in a towel. "It's not much but it's hot. Beans and pork. More beans than pork. And potatoes."

"Who was your visitor? Anything to do with the person hiding in your cellar?"

"I'm guessing the snow will stop after midnight. I think you'll have clear weather for your walk to Albany in the morning."

DAVIS

Near Langley, Virginia
December 1863

Jefferson Davis was in his naturally sullen state. He had taken the train early in the morning from Richmond to Fairfax Station, and was now on horseback on the Chain Bridge Road en route to see General Longstreet. The news was disappointing to say the least.

It was that in-between season in northern Virginia. The trees were bare, but the ground was still soft. The temperature was chilly—Davis was always chilly—but comfortable enough for a ride through the countryside. You could almost forget that there was a war and that the opposing troops faced each other barely five miles away.

Davis wondered, for the hundredth time, if it had been a mistake to let General Lee resign command of the Army of Northern Virginia. Longstreet was the perfect choice to defend Richmond. But he didn't seem to be in a hurry to take Washington City. He was a rock on the defensive. He was turning out to be a rock, an immovable boulder, in terms of offensive operations as well.

Longstreet's wire had landed with a thud. Union forces, in the pre-dawn hours, two days ago, had forced a crossing of the Long

Bridge and surprised Pickett's forces, entrenched on the Virginia side. Pickett himself, and many of his senior officers, had been away at the home of family friends south of Alexandria. *A fish fry. And a woman.* Davis scowled.

Longstreet would have to deal with the hero of Gettysburg. Federal forces had driven Pickett's men from their trenches, half asleep, running for their lives, many leaving their weapons behind. Jackson, whose men were upriver at the Virginia end of the Chain Bridge, six miles distant, had moved with great speed and skill and had stopped the rout at Arlington Courthouse. The provost marshal was still bringing Pickett's men back to the line. *Embarrassing and unacceptable. Longstreet will have to deal with it, but it has set back our timetable and I've no stomach for explaining it to Burgoyne. We should have taken Washington City a week ago.*

"General Longstreet and his staff, sir."

Ahead Davis could see Old Pete approaching on horseback, surrounded by a half dozen staff officers and with a cavalry escort. *He doesn't look happy. He thinks I'm going to take him to the woodshed and I've a mind to.*

"General. Good to see you."

"Mr. President. This is as good a place to stop and talk as any. Moxley, where are we?"

Colonel Sorrel replied, "Langley, sir. We're a mile or so above the Chain Bridge."

Five houses and a church, thought Davis. *It hardly deserves a name.* Both parties dismounted, and Davis and Longstreet walked together, in silence, until they were alone.

Longstreet spoke first. "Bad business the other day. George was caught with his pants down. Almost literally. It's not the first time he's had better things to do than lead his men. I've spoken to him. He's devastated. He expects you're going to relieve him."

There was a large rock under an enormous oak tree, now barren of leaves. Davis sat while Longstreet stood.

"I'm not going to relieve him. You are. I'd trade places with you any day. I'd give anything for a field command. But you're going to have to tell him."

As always, Longstreet paused before he replied. "Yep. We've been friends a long time. He has a heart of gold. And what he did at Gettysburg they'll talk about for a thousand years. Win or lose this war, cadets at West Point will study that charge. But you're right. He has to go. I'll tell him. Wouldn't surprise me if he asks to re-enlist as a private."

"That would be fine. I'm sure General Bragg could use a veteran private. In Tennessee."

Longstreet grunted, akin to a laugh for him. "I know you're frustrated. Think you should be dining off Mrs. Lincoln's china by now. Working your way through the president's wine cellar. But it's just a matter of time. Stuart continues to disrupt their supplies and communications. We're lobbing dozens of shells a day into Washington City, and most people have left. Richmond isn't under threat for the first time in two years. Meade is just holding on. The attack across the Long Bridge was just meant to buy time."

Davis listened. Across the dirt road, a group of six or seven children stared at the soldiers. A little girl, probably ten years old, waved. Davis smiled.

"If we can take Washington City, this war is all but over. You can go home to your family. And I can stop worrying about the lack of goods in the Richmond shops and the price of postage stamps. I need you to force your way into the city."

Longstreet grunted. *Was that assent?*

"Pete, I want General Stuart to replace General Pickett. The times call for General Stuart's, uh, combative nature."

"I consider General Stuart to be the finest cavalry officer this continent has ever produced. I need him."

"And you shall have him. Commanding Pickett's men. Fitz Lee will be an outstanding commander of the Cavalry Corps. How is Jackson?"

"If he were anyone else, I'd say full of piss and vinegar. Raring to fight. It being General Jackson, I'll say he's moved by the spirit. Guided by the light. He saved Pickett's bacon day before yesterday. And mine for that matter. You needn't worry about our *Stonewall*. I'd take a dozen of them."

"General . . . Pete. Let's end this. Take Washington City."

"I'll see what I can do."

BURGOYNE

North of Quaker Springs, New York
December 1863

John Burgoyne was astride his horse, at the head of his battered army. As always, first casualty reports had proven wrong, especially the numbers of missing in action. As the day had worn on, scattered units reported in, and he had a fuller picture of the butcher bill. The snow had stopped during the night and the day was crystal clear, cold but windless, the snow beneath his horse's hooves a soft powder.

McClellan had attacked just before dawn. The sentries had raised the alarm but only when the Union troops were upon them. The attack had come from the south, as expected, but also from the east. McClellan's troops had crossed then recrossed the Hudson to hit Burgoyne from the one place he assumed he was perfectly safe. If there'd been more light, the Federals might have captured Burgoyne himself, who's tent was a mere hundred yards from the river.

After the initial shock, the British lines had stiffened. Their officers, many coatless and hatless, had been awakened from their sleep by the first shouts and shots, rallying their men. As the dawn broke it was easier to see, and some order was restored to the British lines. Still, McClellan's clear advantage in numbers began to tell. He threw blue wave after blue wave at the red defenders, and by mid-morning it was clear to Burgoyne that there was no strategic advantage to standing and fighting. He ordered a fighting retreat, though that turned out to be unnecessary. As the British abandoned the field, in good order, McClellan did not pursue.

Burgoyne was composing his after-action report in his head. *Saratoga, New York. British forces under General Burgyone were driven from the field . . .* The London newspapers would have a field day.

Enough of that. His job now was to find Gordon, regroup, and go on the offensive. Burgoyne had no choice but to head north. Damned Custer had proven a nuisance indeed. But with luck, Burgoyne would squeeze Custer between Gordon and Burgoyne's army and force the Yankee boy general to retire. Then Burgoyne could go back for McClellan.

McClellan. I remember him from Crimea. Very impressed with himself. Bookish, well-read. A great believer in the art of war. Well, I certainly didn't expect him to attack, and to attack from the river. It never pays to underestimate your enemy. But why doesn't he pursue? The northern newspapers always hinted that McClellan was shy. *But he wasn't shy this morning.*

Though his troops had been surprised, and there would be punishment in due course, they had fought well. Some of the men had been on garrison duty for years and had never heard a shot fired in anger. They would want revenge.

"Captain, we've heard nothing from Major Packenham since he went south?"

"No sir. But he'll find us. We'll be easy to follow in the snow."

"And Captain, we have dragoons out in strength? We can't afford for their Mr. Custer to surprise us."

"Yes sir. It's General Custer who will likely be surprised to see us."

McCLELLAN

Near Saratoga, New York
December 1863

George McClellan, accompanied by his staff officers, rode at a
canter past the men of Warren's Corps. An enormous cheer erupted
and moved down the line of soldiers in a wave as McClellan rode
past, hat in the air, as tall as he could make himself in the saddle.

God there is nothing like it, he thought. To lead men in battle, to
victory, the very fate of the republic hanging in the balance. *Some
men are made for these moments.*

General Warren rode out to meet him. "Sir, with Custer up
north, we only have a few regiments of cavalry to pursue Burgoyne.
But they can harass his supply train. I can have my Corps on the road
in an hour. We can drive those bastards back to Canada. I've a mind
to cross the border and drive them all to the north pole."

"Thank you, General. Your men were splendid today. There's no
limit to what such men can accomplish when they are well led. No
General, we'll let Burgoyne run. Sykes should be up later today with
the rest of the Army of the Potomac, and I expect to see Custer as

well, once he's heard about our victory. When the army is reunited, then we'll go looking for Burgoyne. I want to hear Custer's report. We don't know how many troops are reinforcing the British. I like to know what I'm up against."

Warren looked at McClellan, then at the staff officers. There was no meeting of eyes, no reaction. *What an opportunity*, Warren thought. *If we move quickly, we can destroy Burgoyne before he has a chance to meet up with his reinforcements.*

"Sir, I'd be delighted to go after the British. We gave them a bloody nose, but I think we can knock them out of the fight."

McClellan rode on, buoyed by the cheers of his men. *I'll write to Nelly*, he mused. *She'll read about this in the papers, but I want her to hear it from me. I'll suggest that she pay a call on Governor Seymour's wife in Albany. The press will be delighted.*

Back at his tent, McClellan called for his aide, Captain Wilson. "The woman's information was most useful. She has a surprisingly accurate eye for the disposition of troops. I want her to continue to supply the British forces with food. I'll want to know how many reinforcements Burgoyne has. And I'll want to know exactly where they encamp. How much do we pay her?"

"Nothing. She won't accept any money."

McClellan looked at Wilson and considered why someone would risk her life for nothing. *No matter. I'm pleased that she does.*

"Captain, we should draft an immediate telegram for President Lincoln, then follow it with a detailed report on the battle, which we can send by courier. I should like the telegram to be very clear in conveying the magnitude of our victory today."

LANE

New York, New York
December 1863

John Lane was finding train travel commonplace. He was on his way from Albany to New York City to see John O'Mahony, the head of the Fenian Brotherhood in America. There was much to discuss. Burgoyne, though somewhat skeptical, had promised to present the plan for Irish Home Rule to Prime Minister Palmerston for eventual approval by the Crown. They'd expect an answer in a month.

Lane had been up with the sun. It was too cold in the barn. He'd gone outside and was thinking of rapping on Viola's farmhouse door. He was hungry. In the dim light of dawn Lane saw footprints, several sets of them, that ran from the door into the fields behind the house. He remembered the sneezing he'd heard the night before.

Viola had come out then, dressed for the weather.

"Going to follow those footprints?"

Viola stopped. "I'm going out to buy more potatoes. That's a hungry army. I expect there will be a fight soon and I'll have to find them afterwards. They buy everything I bring them."

Lane stared at her, trying to make sense of it all.

"I expect you'll want to get started toward Albany. It's five miles to town. Take you two hours in this weather."

"What did the soldier want last night, and who were you hiding in the cellar?"

"You don't hear me asking what business you had with the general, or why you're making up stories about a brother in Glen Falls. I recommend we both mind our own business."

"When I come back from New York City . . ." *Damn it. I shouldn't have told her that. A fine spy I am indeed.* "I'll need to know where the British Army is camped. I'll need to talk to General Burgoyne again. I'll come back here, and you can show me."

Now it was Viola's turn to stare. "Why is an Irishman, and a former Union soldier, helping the British army?"

"I asked you the same question."

"And I told you. Feeding the hungry. Myself and my children. That's all."

"That's clearly not all. What did the soldier want last night?"

"He wanted to know if I had any more potatoes. The Blue Army needs to eat as well."

"Who were you hiding in your cellar?"

"Travelers. They needed a place to stay during the storm."

"And they needed to hide in the basement and be up and moving before dawn?"

"I need to get moving."

In the far distance, they could hear what sounded like thunder. Lane recognized it immediately. The sound of the big guns.

"There's your fight, sure enough. I wonder who is attacking whom. Maybe you know."

"They'll be needing food when they're done fighting. I've got a lot of ground to cover. Enjoy your walk."

The five-mile trek through snow did, indeed, take Lane about two hours, as Viola predicted. He was now warm and happy to be out of the weather and riding comfortably on a train to New York City.

Lane looked out the window of the train car. It was a beautiful day indeed, the rooves of the farmhouses and barns covered in snow, and the trees heavy with it. His mind was vexed as he couldn't stop thinking about Viola. What was she up to? Could he trust her? Why would a free Black woman sell food to the British, which was akin to aiding the Confederacy? What did the soldier want last night?

Lane knew that blowing Viola's cover, whatever lay beneath it, would blow his own. But there were too many questions.

The train entered the city. Lane took the paper from this pocket, and looked at the address: *22 Duane Street, in Manhattan.* "Get off at the Chambers Street station. It's a short walk," O'Mahony had told him. Lane had only been to New York once, just passing through. On the train from the hospital in Baltimore back home to Boston. He hadn't been interested at the time, had barely looked out the window. He had been wondering how he, the now one-armed tailor, would make his living.

"Chambers Street station," called the conductor as he passed through the car. Lane was looking out the window and could see the cupola of an enormous building a few blocks away.

"That's the grand city hall of New York, so it is," said the conductor. *The Irish are everywhere,* thought Lane.

DAVIS

Jefferson Davis had taken the extraordinary step of calling a council of war, a meeting of his field commanders to decide a course of action. It wasn't how he liked to manage the war. But the stakes were enormous, and time was short. He had asked Longstreet to bring his corps commanders, Jackson and Stuart, as well as the new chief of cavalry, Fitzhugh Lee, to Richmond, and they were standing in his office poring over an enormous map spread across a table.

"Gentlemen, I am quite aware, especially given recent events, that none of you want to be away from your commands while they are facing the enemy. I will have you back on the cars to Fairfax Station and Alexandria by mid-afternoon at the latest. We need to break the deadlock in front of Washington City."

"What news from Burgoyne, Mr. President?" asked Fitzhugh Lee.

Davis scowled, picked up a newspaper and handed it to Lee. "I get my intelligence from the *Evening Star*. You'll see their report that McClellan inflicted heavy losses on Burgoyne at Saratoga, in New

York. Apparently, Burgoyne took flight, and apparently, McClellan did not pursue him. If this is true, it makes it all the more imperative that we take Washington City, and quickly."

Longstreet spoke up. "McClellan can leave Burgoyne to lick his wounds and come back to defend the city."

"Mr. President, General Longstreet, if I may." It was Jackson, who had been silent throughout the meeting.

"Please, General, go ahead."

"Sir. I believe that Washington can be taken, but not by forcing the bridges from Virginia."

Longstreet stiffened. *It's the first time he's hearing this,* thought Davis.

"I believe if we move with all dispatch, we can capture Washington before General McClellan returns to defend it. I propose the following: That General Stuart make a great show of trying to cross both the Chain and Long bridges into Washington to draw the enemy's forces and fire. Then, that General Lee and his cavalry ride around the city to the north from their current position to the west of it. I will take my Corps across the Potomac at Alexandria, and proceed northward to meet General Lee east of the city. Precisely here." Jackson put the index finger of his good hand on the map at Bladensburg. "We will then attack via the Bladensburg Road, which will bring us to the doorstep of the Capitol itself."

Davis looked up. "How fitting. Following the same route that British forces followed when they burned the city in 1814."

"Who says history doesn't repeat itself?" said Stuart with a grin.

Davis stared at the map. "General Longstreet?"

As was his custom, Longstreet was silent for a long while, staring out the window. Stuart fidgeted, the man of constant action, not one for councils of war. Fitz Lee, new to it all, felt the awkward silence. Jackson was serene, relaxed, certain that the Lord would guide him. His eyes were closed much of the time. Tired? Silent prayer?

"General?" Davis prodded Longstreet.

"It could work. There is no doubt that Meade believes we'll try to force a crossing at the bridges again. He has concentrated his forces there. But the entire city is ringed with forts and batteries. The key is surprise. General Stuart's charade will have to be very convincing, and I suggest that Generals Lee and Jackson move their troops by night. The roads around Washington are good and there is little chance of getting lost."

"Mr. President, another thought," said Stuart, not accustomed to infantry operations, and seeing now what was expected of him. "Sir, what's to stop Meade from sensing that Fitz and General Jackson have abandoned their positions and then coming across the bridges in force and marching on Richmond? My Corps will be the only troops standing between Washington and Richmond."

Davis hesitated. Stuart was right, and under normal circumstances he would err on the side of extreme caution in defending Richmond. But now he could see clearly that this was indeed the Confederacy's opportunity to win the war outright and guarantee their independence. If they hesitated, the moment could be lost forever.

"If that happens, we'll mobilize the shopkeepers, old men and schoolboys. But for now, let's be sure that your demonstration at the bridges is well executed, and that Generals Lee and Jackson can move without being observed."

"Mr. President," Jackson again. "Might we take a moment and pray together, and ask Divine Providence to watch over and guide our brave men in the coming action?"

Longstreet looked at his boots. Stuart suppressed a grin. Lee looked at Davis. "By all means, General. Perhaps you would lead us in prayer."

BURGOYNE

Near Bacon Hill, New York
December 1863

Burgoyne had found General Gordon and his troops camped in the vicinity of Bacon Hill, still ten miles or more from Saratoga. Gordon had brought 30,000 reinforcements, but better still, he brought news. General Campbell, with another 20,000 men, was only a couple days behind him. Palmerston had been true to his word. Burgoyne would soon have 65,000 men, crack troops, under his command. More than a match for conscripts and citizen soldiers.

They were seated on cracker boxes beside a campfire, alone. Their staffs hovered out of earshot. It was cold, but it was much more tolerable around the fire than in a field tent.

General Gordon, a Highland Scot, was angry at the world in the best of times. He was fit to be tied now. "We should have linked up with you days ago, sir. The bloody weather and the damn blue-coated cavalry have *aboot* driven me mad, sir. We've had to fight our way southward for the last week. The enemy is capable, sir. And the roads. I thought this was a civilized country."

Burgoyne smiled, though he wasn't amused. "I find it quite civilized up here compared to Louisiana." He remembered fording swamps. Alligators. Snakes. Backwoods people who didn't speak English. It seemed like another world. But they'd underestimated their enemy then and paid dearly for it. It wouldn't happen this time. "Let's not dwell on the past week, General. It seems their Mr. Custer has left us in peace for the time being. No doubt linking back up with McClellan, who will be consolidating his army."

"Shall we wait for them here, sir? They've bloodied our noses, beg your pardon, sir, maybe they think they can finish us off. Send us back whence we came. This is fine ground here, sir. If I can feed my men, I can defend this ground for a long time indeed."

"No, General. We'll bring the fight to them this time. We're not here to defend ground. We're here to take it. I doubt McClellan is aware just how many men we now have. I rather like our odds."

"What do you have in mind, sir, if I might ask?"

"Once General Campbell is up, we'll finalize the plan in great detail. For now, I can tell you this. Your troops and mine shall proceed south, as McClellan expects, and attack his position from the north. As he concentrates his forces to meet the threat, General Campbell will strike from the west and southwest, and we shall squeeze General McClellan between us."

Gordon gazed into the fire. A fighting general, a thirty-year veteran, and Burgoyne could see that his mind was making quick work of the logistics, the march, the timing, and the odds.

"I think if we get the timing right, we can drive the bloody bluecoats into their frozen bloody Hudson River. My men are tired of playing hit-and-run with their bloody cavalry. They're fairly itching for a fair, stand-up fight, sir."

"I'd expect no less, General. Have your Scots druids had positive *auguries*?"

Gordon smiled. *Who knew the general has a bloody sense of humor,* he thought.

"Aye, they have, and they're preparing to create a druid mist over the battlefield, sir. These Yankees won't know what hit them. Then the pipers, then we finish them with the claymores."

"Just so, General. Packenham?"

"Sir?" Major Packenham, returned from Virginia only hours ago, and now regaling the staff with his adventures, fairly ran over to where the generals were sitting.

"Major, you've had a couple of hours to rest. Might I trouble you to ride to General Campbell, apprise him to prepare three days rations, come up on the double quick, and be prepared to go into action immediately? I should like him to be here at his earliest convenience."

"Double quick, three days rations, prepared to fight." Looking at General Gordon, Packenham asked, "Sir, do we know precisely where I might find General Campbell?"

"Aye laddie, between here and Montreal. Tall fella. Mustaches. Red coat."

Packenham grinned widely. "Just so, sir." He saluted, wheeled, and hurried away.

"Ach, I'd trade places with that lad. That's real soldiering. That's why I joined, what I imagined as a lad in Cock Bridge I'd be doing. Not signing orders for blankets and beans."

Burgoyne looked at Gordon, then back at the fire. *We all joined for our own reasons.* The words wouldn't come; he wouldn't let the words come. But deep in his heart, Burgoyne knew that his own reason lay ten miles to the south.

"General, I should think you'll have a chance to do some real soldiering in the next forty-eight hours. Cock Bridge, was it? I've never had the pleasure."

McCLELLAN

Albany, New York
December 1863

George McClellan was staring at his wife. She looked up, smiled, reddened, and looked back down at her book.

"More of Mr. Dickens?"

She smiled again. "Yes. *Little Dorrit.*"

"Surely you've read that before? I seem to recall."

"Yes, and I'm reading it again. Sad and funny at the same time. The Office of Circumlocution. That's funny."

They were in the sitting room of their suite at the City Hotel in Albany. After his victory at Saratoga, McClellan had wired his wife. *A famous victory. Burgoyne has fled the field. Advise you pay a call to Mrs. Seymour in Albany.*

Nelly had wired back. *Train arrives in Albany tomorrow, 10:30 a.m. Meet me. Advise we call on Governor and Mrs. together.*

McClellan continued staring. *She has the political instincts of a first lady.*

Nelly had offered a brilliant idea and Seymour loved it. An

impromptu press conference. The governor standing beside the man of the hour. Flanked by their wives. Two days before, Seymour had contemplated moving the capital temporarily to New York City for fear of capture. Now, he could declare that thanks to General McClellan, the enemy was in retreat and Albany was safe. He would also raise his own profile.

After the press conference, the two men and their wives had met in the privacy of Seymour's office.

"This should just about clinch it, General. I believe we might want to make an announcement soon."

McClellan had shaken his head. "One step at a time, Governor. Burgoyne is in retreat, but he'll be back, reinforced. The decisive battle is yet to be won. Then, once we've settled with the British, we shall return to Washington City and deal with General Longstreet. All things in their time, Governor."

Looking directly at Seymour, Nelly said, "Governor, I had assumed that you aspired to the presidency yourself."

McClellan shot his wife a glance. Mrs. Seymour, all ringlets, rouge and bustle, looked like she would come out of her chair.

Seymour smiled. "One man of the hour at a time, Mrs. McClellan. I shall be delighted to do my best to deliver the great state of New York. This is a time to rise above personal ambitions. We must defeat Mr. Lincoln and we must put an end to this war. Your husband is the man for the job."

McClellan had studied the governor. Smartly dressed, long side whiskers, receding hair that was probably once red. *What is it about red hair and politics? Washington, Jefferson, Hamilton, Jackson, Van Buren, Seymour.* A polished politician. Gracious. And no doubt his personal ambition would not rise above being named director of the New York Customs House, perhaps the most lucrative government job in the country.

"Well said, sir. Though we must end the war on the battlefield," McClellan had replied.

Seymour had nodded. A clear reference to the Peace Democrats who wanted to end the war at all costs. That would never do.

"I believe your victory, and the victory to come, will put an end to the peace-at-all-costs talk. Yes, the war must be won on the battlefield, as you say, and the man who delivers that win will be rewarded by a grateful nation."

Later, in the hotel sitting room, Nelly felt McClellan's eyes on her. She looked up from her book. "Something is on your mind. Say it."

"Whatever on earth possessed you to ask Seymour if he aspired to the presidency himself?"

Nelly laughed. "I'm like your cavalry escort, George. I'm protecting your flank. I thought it was important to hear Governor Seymour say out loud that he wouldn't seek the nomination. Get it all out in the open. You are wise in the ways of war, George. But politics is a different kind of warfare, and Seymour is a field marshal when it comes to politics."

McClellan stared at his wife. *She will indeed be a remarkable first lady.* "We are a team to be reckoned with. Unlike the buffoon in the White House and his crazy wife. She claims to speak to the dead."

Nelly let the comment pass. "What do you have in mind for General Burgoyne, George?" she asked.

"Do you believe Little Dorrit and Arthur are a good match?"

"George!" Nelly beamed. "When do you find time to read Mr. Dickens?"

LANE

New York, New York
December 1863

After leaving the train station, John Lane had asked a policeman, an Irishman it turned out, how to find 22 Duane Street. He didn't know any of the landmarks the policeman mentioned—City Hall, the Courthouse, St. Andrew's Church—but he understood when he pointed him in the right direction. He asked another policeman, also Irish, standing at the corner of Chambers and Elk, and two minutes later he found himself in front of the modest building. Lane took the paper from his pocket, confirmed the address, and started up the stairs.

A man was walking out as he was walking in, and Lane asked if he knew where to find Mr. O'Mahony's office. Jerking his thumb behind him, he said, "Up the stairs. Follow the cigar smoke."

Lane climbed the stairs and saw a hallway with a series of closed doors. None had a sign of any sort. He went up to the first door and knocked. He could hear voices inside. He knocked again.

"Come in, then, it's open."

He turned the knob, pushed open the door, and saw John O'Mahony seated around a table, along with four other men.

O'Mahony looked up and nodded in recognition. "Gentlemen, that will be all. I've another meeting, as you can see."

The others, all bearded men in their forties and fifties, gathered papers, donned coats and hats, and filed out of the office with curious looks at Lane. None said a word. Lane smiled to himself. *A secret society.*

"Well John, come in and take a load off. Your wire was cryptic. You have some news?" O'Mahony motioned to one of the recently vacated chairs, and Lane sat.

"I do."

"You've seen Burgoyne?"

"I have."

"You pitched the plan?"

"I did."

"Jaysus lad, don't make me beg you. Will you tell me what happened?"

"I found Burgoyne north of Albany, as we expected. I got lucky. I met a woman who sells foodstuffs, potatoes, would you believe it, to his army. That got me into their camp."

"I see. Well done. And you lived to talk about it, so he must have listened."

"He did indeed. I believe he thinks it's an unlikely notion, but that he has nothing to lose. If we are able to deliver Irishmen to fight against the Union, it could help them immensely. If we're unable to deliver, they lose nothing. The crown simply doesn't grant Home Rule to Ireland."

"So he said yes?"

"He said he'd write to Palmerston, who of course would have to consult with the queen. He expected that, if all went well, he'd hear back in a month's time. Three weeks or so from now."

O'Mahony stared at Lane, looking through him. He was deep in thought.

"John, we've promised the British that 200,000 Irish soldiers in the Union Army are just waiting for our signal to turn coat and fight for the British, and for the South. We have to be ready to deliver on our promise."

Lane thought about his own time as a soldier. He'd joined the Brotherhood because his sergeant, a Galway man, had told him to. In his own company of almost one hundred men, at least half were Irish and at least half of those had joined the Fenians. The sergeant would on rare occasions have a man read a letter from the Brotherhood, probably written by O'Mahony himself, and he would put out a tin cup and solicit donations. Occasionally a man would drop a penny or two in the cup. Lane never had.

O'Mahony was talking but Lane wasn't listening. He was thinking that it had all been so . . . *what's the word? Aspirational.* It had sounded grand, that after the war, the Celtic host, hardened in battle, well-armed, would take ship for Erin's shores and roll over their British masters. But three weeks' time? He thought about the Widow McCormack's cabbage patch, and the other comic-opera rebellions from Irish history.

"John?"

"Right. I suggest we start with the most reliable units. The Irish Brigade, for example. Irish officers, mostly Irish troops. And Mr. O'Mahony, I suggest that this time they will need to hear directly from you. The lads, and certainly the officers, know who you are. You'll be able to explain the stakes much better than I can. If we can get the Irish Brigade to come over, others will follow."

"Yes. We have our most reliable contacts in the Brigade. They are indeed the most likely units to get, em, enthused for our project. I'd like to get Meagher to come with me. The men still love him."

Lane nodded. Thomas Francis Meagher. *Meagher of the Sword.* The most famous Irish soldier in the Union Army, though Lane knew that he'd resigned his commission. He had been commander of the Irish Brigade until after the Battle of Chancellorsville. He'd resigned in a dispute with his superiors. The bloody Irish. Happy to fight the enemy. Delighted to fight each other. But if anyone could convince Irish soldiers to fight for Irish freedom, it was Meagher.

"A fine idea. You should contact him. There's not a moment to be lost. I'll make my way back to Albany and re-establish contact with General Burgoyne. I'll let you know by wire just as soon as I have an answer."

O'Mahony looked at Lane. "This is moving faster than I imagined. See what you've set in motion lad. This is the moment when we always lose our nerve, when someone betrays us, when it all goes to hell. This time it has to be different. We'll never have another chance like this again."

Lane looked around the room. The table, the chairs, a desk piled high with newspapers. Nothing on the walls. A coat rack with O'Mahony's coat and hat. The headquarters of the secret society that would end 700 years of British rule in Ireland. The office was cold and drafty, but Lane found that he was sweating profusely, and his good hand was shaking.

"Do you have a place to stay tonight? Sure, you're welcome to hang your hat here in the office. The floor is softer than it looks. Are you thirsty? I suggest we go round the corner and further the discussion at the aptly-named King's Arms."

Lane stood and waited as O'Mahony gathered his hat and coat. *What have I gotten myself into?*

DAVIS

Richmond, Virginia
December 1863

Jefferson Davis was sitting behind his desk in his office in
Richmond. It was late. A single oil lamp burned, casting long shadows
across the large room. The door to the office was cracked open, and
he could hear the hum of activity as his staff processed the reports
that were coming in from the front. Davis, out of all character, had
his feet on his desk and his hands joined behind his head. His eyes
were closed but he wasn't asleep. He was exhausted, but exhilarated.

He had spent the day reading the wires as they came in from
Alexandria and Fairfax Station. Old Pete had obeyed orders and
attacked Washington City. Jackson's plan unfolded during the course
of the day, but all Davis could do was read staccato accounts that
came in over the telegraph wires, with a two-hour delay.

Davis had been up before dawn, knowing that the attack must
have begun, but also knowing that he wouldn't get the first reports—
always wrong—until later.

At eight in the morning a staff officer had rushed in. "First
message from General Longstreet, sir."

Davis, pacing, had fairly ripped the message from his aide.

Genl Stuart has launched demonstration on Va side of Long and Chain bridges. Federals responding in force. Couriers report both Jackson and Lee began advancing at midnight. Longstreet.

There were long periods of maddening silence. Davis knew that Longstreet, on Arlington Heights, sent his messages by courier to Alexandria or Fairfax. From there, telegraph operators sent the messages to the War Department in Richmond where they were transcribed and rushed to Davis.

It was past eleven in the morning when Davis received the next update. *Couriers report Jackson and Lee forces converged this hour east of city at Bladensburg Road. Little resistance. Longstreet.*

That would have been hours ago. The fate of Washington City was probably already decided. Davis admired Longstreet's quiet, unflappable style, but he wished that Pete would report more often, even if there was nothing to report.

Finally, at about five o'clock, a steady stream of messages began to arrive from Washington City itself. The first one brought Davis to tears. *Washington City in the hands of Confederate troops. Longstreet.*

What did it mean? Had Meade surrendered? Abandoned the city?

Twenty minutes later, Davis read, *Genl Meade has disengaged and fled in good order northward. Will not pursue at this time. Will consolidate possession of Washington City and await orders. Longstreet.*

With his eyes closed, Davis tried to imagine how the day had unfolded. Stuart, with his flair for the theatrical, making a loud and convincing ruckus, threatening to cross the bridges. Meade forced to rush troops there from elsewhere in the city to meet the threat. Jackson and Fitz Lee, making night marches, converging at dawn east of the city, and marching in mostly unopposed. Meade, realizing too late what had happened, and badly outnumbered, fleeing northward with his army intact, probably headed for Philadelphia where Lincoln and the Federal government had set themselves up. Davis thought of Mexico, and how seldom military plans work as they are written. Jackson. *Maybe there is a Divine Providence.*

"Sir? We've made arrangements for you to take the cars to Washington City at first light tomorrow morning."

Now what, thought Davis. *We've taken Washington, but can we hold it?* That would depend on Burgoyne. If he can deal McClellan a blow, Lincoln will have no choice but to negotiate. Independence would be all but assured. *I need Burgoyne to move quickly.*

Davis knew that his troops at Vicksburg couldn't hold out forever, and when it fell, as it must, Grant would be freed to move eastward. If McClellan defeats Burgoyne, The Union general would head south again with a mind to retake Washington.

"Sir?"

"Yes, Major. Cars at first light. I shall try to convince Mrs. Davis to come with me. It's been years since she's been in the White House."

BURGOYNE

Near Bacon Hill, New York
December 1863

Major Packenham had found General Campbell as ordered and informed him that the commanding general requested his presence, and that of his 20,000 men, as soon as possible. And be ready to fight.

Burgoyne was on horseback, making the rounds of his troops in camp as they waited for Campbell to arrive. Packenham smiled as he imitated Campbell's Scots' accent for Burgoyne. "Ready to fight, is it? Twenty-seven years in this uniform, wars on three continents, six wounds, and I should be ready to fight?"

Burgoyne tolerated the insubordination. They were alone, and Packenham had certainly earned his fun. "I trust that means the general is making all haste?"

"General Campbell said I could inform the commanding general that 'I'm a mile ahead of my bloody dust,' sir."

Burgoyne laughed. "I knew Campbell in Crimea. A fighter. Like all the Scots. What would this army do without them?"

Ahead, a wagon loomed into view, headed toward them on the road. As it passed, the Black woman driving nodded at Burgoyne.

"Who is that woman?"

"She sells food to the army, sir. Potatoes, I believe," the major said. "I'm told she has proven most reliable and charges a fair price."

"Is she someone's servant?"

"I don't believe so, sir. In the North, there are free Black people. I'm told that slavery didn't pay in the North, so it was outlawed over time. Now Northerners believe they're morally superior to their Southern countrymen. Former countrymen."

"Just so."

They reined in their horses and dismounted when they reached General Gordon's camp. An aide took the horses away, and Gordon appeared from his tent.

"Welcome, sir. I believe the sun will soon disappear behind that hill. Would you join me in a wee cup?"

"Scots whiskey, General?"

"No luck, sir. But it seems they make red wine here about. Some of my dragoons came upon some and I'm giving it a professional appraisal now."

"I see. And your conclusion?"

"Too early to tell, sir. Too early to tell. It's red and it's wet, so that's a start."

Packenham stood by in amazement as General Gordon poured General Burgoyne a glass of wine from a clear bottle. The liquid was a deep purple, like grape juice.

"Hmph. Perhaps the Americans should stick to rum and their bourbon and leave wine to the French. But any port in a storm, eh General? To your health."

Burgoyne stared into his glass. Gordon refilled it. Burgoyne didn't argue.

A long pause. When Burgoyne spoke, the banter had left him. His face was dark, his brow furrowed, his neck taut.

"General, when we strike McClellan, I want to hit him like a hammer. I want to destroy him. I want to drive him into the Hudson

River. I don't expect any prisoners. I want those people to understand who they are fighting and what the consequences are. Do I make myself clear, General?" Burgoyne drained the glass in one motion.

Gordon had listened intently and was on the edge of his camp stool. Slowly the edges of his mouth turned up, and his blue eyes were on fire. "Indeed, sir. I have just the fellas to drive your point home to General McClellan."

McCLELLAN

Near Saratoga, New York
December 1863

George McClellan was back in camp, sitting at the small field desk in his tent. It had been a long day, first saying goodbye to Nelly, then riding north to the camp near Saratoga. More inspections, observing drill, speaking to officers and common soldiers. Leadership.

The trip to Albany had been important. A face-to-face meeting with Seymour. They had an understanding. McClellan would win the war in the field. Seymour would ensure that he received the Democratic Party's nomination for president. The Peace Democrats would be sidelined. They were in agreement that the war must be won, then Lincoln defeated at the polls.

It had been wonderful to see Nelly. *She is at home in that world and will be a tremendous asset.* He thought about her, about the life they had built, the long absences, the deep affection and understanding.

"Sir, they're assembled." It was Captain Wilson, informing McClellan that his corps commanders and staff were gathered. The air was brisk, the sun bright. They would hold their council of war outside.

"General Sykes, welcome. General Custer, welcome back. Gentlemen. As you know, we have dealt the British two defeats in recent days. But their army is still in the field, and we must deliver a decisive blow. General Custer, could you tell us what you learned about the enemy reinforcements?"

Indeed he could. Custer, dressed in his spectacular uniform, seemed to rise off the ground and gain in stature. *My God, but he can puff himself up,* thought McClellan.

"Gentlemen, the cavalry has been busy. We first engaged General Gordon—for it is General Angus Gordon leading these troops— here." He pointed to a spot fifty miles to the north. "We played Old Harry with his supply train, engaged his cavalry screen, felled trees across the road, and generally did what we could to slow him down. He was only able to manage ten miles or so a day. He's now been joined by General Burgoyne and the rest of their army, and they are encamped here," Custer said, pointing to Bacon Hill.

"Thank you, General. How many men does Gordon have?"

"Judging by their supply train, counting tents and campfires, I estimate that he has 25,000 men under all arms. That includes a couple of regiments of dragoons, and some artillery."

McClellan did the quick math. *We'll outnumber them two to one. More.*

Sykes spoke. "General Custer, did you see any sign of further reinforcements? Any troops following behind Gordon?"

"No, sir, not at all. I was able to ride completely around Gordon's command, and I can assure you that there is nobody behind him."

McClellan was silent, staring at the map.

"Gentlemen, we shall wait here for General Burgoyne. I recommend that we make use of our time in fortifying our position here. He will attack us. With the news from Washington City, he will believe that he can end the war right here. If he can defeat this army, with Washington in secessionist hands, President Lincoln will have no choice but to sue for peace. Gentlemen, the war will be won or lost here, and I intend that it be won."

McClellan had seen the skepticism on their faces. He knew they expected him to attack Burgoyne, to follow up on the victory at Saratoga and seize the strategic opportunity. But McClellan knew that Burgoyne would be drawn back to Saratoga, and that he would feel forced to attack despite being outnumbered.

"Sir?" It was Captain Wilson.

"Yes, Captain?"

"The woman is here."

"The woman?"

"Yes sir. The uh, messenger. The informant. The, uh, spy."

"Ah, yes. Bring her in, Captain."

Wilson held open the flap of McClellan's tent for Viola.

LANE

North of Albany, New York
December 1863

John Lane was on the now familiar road from Albany, heading north out of town. He had slept on the floor of John O'Mahony's office the night before. Not as comfortable as advertised. He'd then retraced his steps to the Chambers Street Rail Station and taken the train to Albany. It was now early evening, and it was growing colder as the sun set. At least it wasn't snowing, though there was still snow on the ground from the storm earlier in the week.

The meeting with O'Mahony had gone about as he'd expected. The Fenian leader was committed to the plan, but Lane sensed that O'Mahony was leaning on him, expecting him to lead. *Shouldn't it be the other way around?* O'Mahony had committed to bringing Meagher into the picture and using his personal influence with the Irish Brigade. That was something. But it was still up to Lane to work with Burgoyne and get things started.

Burgoyne. He would go see him again, tell him that he'd briefed O'Mahony, and ask if there was any news from London, even though he knew it was too soon.

Lane turned off the main road, and in ten minutes, he was at Viola's front door. She would know where Burgoyne was camped, and she could take him there, under the cover that he was working with her. Avoid suspicion on the road. There would be lots of Union troops about.

He knocked on the door, and it was quickly opened. A young boy looked up. "Who are you?"

"Isaiah, get away from the door! I've told you to never answer the door. Never."

Viola pulled the boy out of the doorway, looked at Lane, and said, "What are you doing here?"

"It's nice to see you again as well. I need your help. Two things. I need you to take me to see our mutual friend the next time you make a delivery."

"No. What's the second thing?"

"I need a place to sleep."

"No and no."

"I can sleep in your cellar. Like the others."

"Come inside before someone sees you."

"Why is it a problem if someone sees me? We're business partners, remember?"

Lane walked into the house. Seated at the table, eating their supper, were Viola's mother and a young girl, younger than the boy who had answered the door.

"I'm John Lane. It's a pleasure to meet you all."

The woman said nothing. The girl smiled. The boy, standing next to his mother said, "My name is Isaiah. What happened to your arm? Are you a soldier?"

"No, but I used to be. I got hurt in the war. Now I work with your mother."

"Mr. Lane, you are welcome to sit down and have something to eat. Quickly. Then you'll have to go. You can't stay here. I'll be making another food delivery day after tomorrow, and I can take you along. But you have to find another place to stay. For everyone's sake"

"Thank you. I'm famished." Lane sat down next to the little girl. Viola's mother, who hadn't said a word, brought him a bowl of steaming stew. He bowed his head, said grace in a low voice, blessed himself, and took a spoonful. "Just the thing on a cold day. Thank you."

He ate in silence. The children watched him closely, especially interested in how he managed with the one hand. Viola and her mother went into the other room and shut the door. Lane could hear their voices but couldn't hear what they were saying.

There was a soft knock at the door. Isaiah went to answer it, and Lane whispered, "No, lad, don't answer the door. Let's have your mother do that." Lane got up quietly and tapped on the bedroom door. When Viola opened it, he pointed to the door and made a knocking motion with his good hand. Viola pushed him into the bedroom and pulled the door closed, but it didn't latch, remaining slightly ajar.

Lane watched through the crack as Viola opened the front door. She stuck her head outside, looked from side to side, then pulled two people into the house. A Black man and a Black woman, probably in their twenties, bundled against the cold.

"You're safe here," he heard Viola say.

DAVIS

Washington, DC
December 1863

General Longstreet had met President and Mrs. Davis at the Alexandria train depot with a carriage. Longstreet smiled as he helped Varina into the vehicle. "There are a lot of good bargains to be had on carriages this morning. On real estate as well, I imagine."

Longstreet rode with them into the city, across the Long Bridge, the half-finished monument to George Washington visible ahead. The Capitol and its half-finished dome lay two miles farther along. A city of magnificent distances and unfinished buildings.

"I've set myself up in the War Department. Seemed appropriate. Stanton left in a hurry and the telegraph lines still work. You can stay at the President's House, of course. Or at Willard's Hotel."

Varina shuddered. "We're not going to stay in the President's House. That woman speaks to the dead, hears voices. It was just as bad in Jane Pierce's time. Like the morgue. Willard's Hotel will suit us just fine, General."

"We could have burned it down. The Executive Mansion. Still can if we want to. Let's go to the War Department first."

They drove along in silence. Davis and Varina knew the city very well, having lived there during his time as a congressman, senator, and secretary of war.

"Tell us about it, Pete."

Longstreet made a noise deep in his throat, what passed for a laugh. "Jackson's plan worked like a clock. When his lead elements got to Bladensburg Road, Fitz Lee and his troopers were already there. Stuart had made such a ruckus across the bridges that Meade had concentrated his forces there, waiting for the attack. Fitz and Jackson rode in like a parade. When Meade sniffed it, it was too late. He skedaddled north, to Philadelphia, I imagine. Fitz has some Virginia cavalry dogging them and we'll know soon where they reform."

"Stuart's men are now in the city as well?"

"Yes, though he left Kershaw and his South Carolinians in Virginia, guarding the approaches to the bridges."

"I see more people on the streets than I expected."

Longstreet was looking out the window. "That's the funny thing, sir. A lot of people stayed. You know as well as anyone that this may be, may have been, the Northern capital, but it's a Southern city. I expect a lot of people are just fine with the change of ownership."

They pulled up to the War Department, next door to the President's House. Outside, there were staff officers coming and going, and guards had been posted. Longstreet led the way, and Davis and Varina followed.

"This was Stanton's office."

Davis smiled. "And before it was Stanton's, it was mine. For four years." He looked at the papers, piled everywhere. Newspapers, telegrams, reports, God knows what. "I ran a tighter and neater ship. But we weren't at war then. I'd like to see Jackson. Stuart and Fitz Lee as well if they're here."

"Colonel Sorrell, will you see if General Jackson is in the building?"

Five minutes later, Jackson appeared, Generals Stuart and Lee in tow. Jackson bowed to Varina and shook President Davis' hand.

"Congratulations on a famous victory, gentlemen. You have all but guaranteed Southern independence."

"We are but humble vessels for His will, sir. Divine Providence has shown us the way."

Lee looked at the floor. Stuart smiled.

"You entered the city unopposed?"

"Not quite, sir. There was a battery supported by some infantry deployed across the road, but General Lee's cavalry got around behind them, and my foot cavalry gave them the bayonet, sir. We didn't see another Union soldier until we approached the Capitol, and they did not stay around to greet us."

Well. General Jackson still has a sense of humor, thought Davis. *He once enjoyed a joke as much as the next man. Perhaps not in Pickett's league, or Stuart's. But not outright taciturn like Old Pete.*

"General Lee, I understand you've sent cavalry to pursue Meade to determine where he alights?"

Lee looked uneasy, glancing from Jackson to Longstreet, then back to Davis.

"Yes sir. Colonel Beale is following them with the 9th and 10th Virginia. With orders not to engage."

Jackson looked straight at Davis. "General Meade's force was woefully inadequate to defend the city. McClellan left him with a couple of corps. I believe we could have followed Meade out of the city and destroyed him."

Longstreet gazed out the window behind Davis and said nothing.

"Thank you, gentlemen. Congratulations on your grand victory. General Meade will be back with General McClellan, and we shall be well entrenched here when they do."

Longstreet perked up. "George did us a favor. The forts and batteries surrounding the city are first-rate. He designed them. He'll have the devil's own time getting past them."

BURGOYNE

Near Saratoga, New York
December 1863

The fortunes of war, mused Burgoyne. *Sometimes the perfect plan unravels before your eyes. Sometimes it works to perfection. Today was such a day. We nearly destroyed McLellan's army. Campbell struck him like a hammer.* Burgoyne rode over the battlefield. As far as he could see in every direction, it was dotted with corpses, some in blue, some wearing red. Perhaps more blue than red. Soldiers were digging large graves and stacking bodies of both stripes. Surgeons and orderlies from both armies were tending to the wounded, and Burgoyne heard men moaning or crying for help as he rode past. He had seen countless battlefields, but he never got used to the cries of the wounded. The debris of battle, rifles, caps, knapsacks, dead horses, and dead men were everywhere.

As was often the case, his mood was dark despite having won the day. Warfare unleashed animal spirits to be sure, and he never felt more alive than during the heat of battle. But afterwards, when it was over, sadness and anger in equal measure descended upon him.

General Gordon rode up. "I give you joy, sir. A right thumping you've given them. They're in full retreat, and the only question is if they'll stop in New York or run all the way to Philadelphia."

Burgoyne nodded in agreement. "Your men did all I could ask of them today, General. You nearly pushed them into the river."

"Aye, and if they hadn't broken and headed south, we may well have done so, sir."

Burgoyne rode on with Gordon, sensing the mood and silence beside him. *I've never seen anything like it,* Burgoyne thought. *McClellan must have outnumbered us two to one. But he never committed his men. I'll wager half his troops never fired a shot. When Campbell hit them from the west, it broke their spirit. I've seldom seen an army so completely mismanaged. It's no wonder Mr. Lincoln fired him twice. He should fire him again, but he needs him so desperately now.*

Gordon spoke up. "Shall we follow them, sir, unleash the dragoons on their rear?"

Burgoyne rode on in silence. *Saratoga. A famous victory. John Fox Burgoyne, the son.* It had taken eighty-six years, but the stain was gone for good. "General?"

"No," Burgoyne finally answered. "General, we shall let Mr. McClellan run and lick his wounds. He and Mr. Lincoln have a decision to make. Do they stand and fight us somewhere south of here? Or do they try to dislodge General Longstreet from Washington City. Either way, as long as General Grant is engaged on the Mississippi, McClellan is caught between two fires."

Gordon's blood was up. His Scotsmen had attacked at dawn and forced McClellan to concentrate his forces to repel the attack. It was a sharp fight, but neither army gained ground. The Union forces didn't even know General Campbell and his 30,000 men existed, and when they struck from the west at about ten o'clock, the red wave carried over Union defenses and put the Federal Army to flight. Every instinct told him to pursue, not to let McClellan get away, to end it here. But Burgoyne had let him go. It seemed to Gordon that Burgoyne cared more about Saratoga than he did about McClellan.

Returning to camp, Burgoyne dismounted and handed his horse off to an aide. "Major Packenham, I want to know as soon as General Gordon's dragoons return. I want to know where McClellan makes camp tonight. And Major. I dare say I may need you to carry a message south again. But you may not have to travel quite so far this time."

McCLELLAN

South of Saratoga, New York
December 1863

There was no time to organize transportation by rail or boat.
The Army of the Potomac was moving south on its feet. Besides,
it wouldn't look good, the army boarding trains or boats and
abandoning New York. No, this was a fighting retreat, a strategic
redeployment. No need for alarm or panic. The army was intact, in
the field, and well led.

McClellan, on horseback, hadn't spoken to anyone for an hour.
Some of his corps commanders, Warren, Sykes, wanted orders.
Where were they headed? Would they stand at Albany? New
York City? Or would they retreat to Philadelphia, where Lincoln,
the Cabinet, and the Congress had set up temporary shop. Sykes,
especially, wanted to turn and fight.

"Sir, let my regulars set up a rear guard, and the rest of the army
can form on them. They barely fired a shot in anger this morning.
Never got in the fight."

McClellan looked over at Sykes. "We'll camp tonight near

Waterford. Set up your rear guard. Burgoyne may send cavalry to harass our retreat. But he won't offer battle again so soon. He'll take his time, follow us south, and try to squeeze us between his army and Longstreet in Washington City. If we move quickly enough, we can dispose of Longstreet, then re-engage with Burgoyne. That is what we shall do."

Sykes wouldn't let go. "We're going to leave New York unprotected?"

McClellan was tired, exhausted, and now he was angry. "We're not leaving anything unprotected. This army is moving in good order, to reform and fight again. We shall make our way to Philadelphia, the current seat of the national government." He had wired Nelly to take the first train from New York to Philadelphia and stay with his family there.

Lincoln had also wired. *Request we meet earliest convenience. A. Lincoln.*

McClellan mumbled aloud. "I'm not going to make it so easy for him this time. He gave me his word I could finish the job this time, and by God I will."

What to do about Seymour? McClellan intended to march right past Albany. He couldn't spare men to protect it. Seymour would be apoplectic. He would have to deal with that later. The damned Peace Democrats would have a field day.

McClellan had sounded certain about Burgoyne's plans, but in truth he didn't know what the British would do. They might well try to pursue and exploit the situation and destroy the Army of the Potomac in the coming days.

"Captain Wilson."

Wilson rode up beside the general.

In a whisper, McClellan said, "I need to see the woman."

"Yes sir. Her house is a few miles ahead, between here and Albany. I'll bring her to you after we make camp."

McClellan went over the battle again in his head. For the

twentieth time. There is nothing he could have done differently. His plan was as sound as a nut. Gordon had attacked, and Warren had held him at bay for a couple of hours. A few more hours and McClellan would have unleashed an enormous counterattack. Sykes and two corps, held in reserve, would have overwhelmed Gordon and they would have driven him from the field. Then the surprise attack came from the west. They appeared out of nowhere. Troops he wasn't aware of. *They almost drove us into the river.* Custer had assured him that Burgoyne had no other reinforcements. It had all gone to pieces in twenty minutes. *They'll say I didn't commit my forces. Just like Antietam. Lincoln will say I didn't commit my forces.*

The sun was down, and the army had covered twenty miles after four hours of hard fighting. Men were starting to fall out of the ranks and sleep by the side of the road.

"Captain, we'll make camp here. Get the word to the corps commanders. And Captain, don't forget to bring the woman here."

LANE

North of Albany, New York
December 1863

Viola's mother was in the other room, putting the children to bed. The newcomers had been fed quickly, then taken to the cellar. Lane, watching through the crack in the door from the other room, had seen Viola move the eating table, pull back the rug, and pull open a door in the floor. With a lighted candle, the couple had made their way down the ladder into the cellar. Once the door was closed and the table and rug replaced, Viola had fetched Lane from the other room and seated him before the fire. They sat beside each other in identical handcrafted wooden chairs. A long silence ensued, both staring into the fire. Finally, Viola spoke.

"You can't ever mention what you saw tonight. To anyone. It would mean my arrest and my children would probably starve to death. And it would disrupt something very important."

Lane considered. "You're hiding runaway slaves."

"I'm helping human beings achieve the freedom that all God's children deserve."

"You're part of a network?"

"You ever hear of the Underground Railroad?"

"No. Is it in Albany?"

"It's here. This is it. People like Sarah and Michael slip away from their masters, and a long line of people like me help them make their way north, to Canada."

Lane had heard of such a thing, in Boston. Churches were involved. Not his church. "Sarah and Michael are the people in the cellar?"

"Yes."

"What does this have to do with selling potatoes to the British, and the Union soldier who visited last week?"

"Nothing. The British don't know anything about this. The Union soldiers neither. I have other business with them. Information."

"With both sides, is it? I don't understand. On the one hand, you're helping slaves escape. On the other hand, you're feeding the British Army, which helps the Southern cause. If they win the war, slavery will continue in the southern states. I don't understand which side you're on."

"You don't need to understand. And as for contradictions, what about you? I thought the Irish hated the British. You seem to have a lot to say to General Burgoyne."

"It's complicated. But I want the same thing for my people that you want for yours. Freedom."

"You're comparing your people to my people? You have no idea what you're talking about."

"Sure, my people have been virtual slaves for seven hundred years. They stole our land, and now we pay them rent for the right to make a miserable living off it. They exclude us from the professions. Make it difficult to educate our children. We're second-class citizens in our own country."

Viola stared at Lane, her hands gripping the seat of her chair, and her eyes blazing like the fire. "Virtual slaves? You left Ireland. Was that against the law? Can they hunt you down and whip you for that, and make you go back?"

"No, but—"

"It's hard to educate your children? Is it illegal to teach them to read and write?"

"No."

"Can one landlord sell your children to another landlord?"

"No. All I was saying is that I'm also working to free my people. I wasn't saying that the circumstances were the same."

"Working to free your people? By conspiring with the British?"

How much should he tell her? Lane was about to speak when Viola's mother came out of the other room and quietly closed the door.

"They're asleep." She looked at her daughter and at Lane, then at the fire, which was burning down. "I'll go to the barn and get some firewood." She opened the door and stepped outside, but was back in an instant, shutting and locking the door.

"What is it?"

"Blue soldiers."

"How many?"

A pause. "Maybe a million. Looks like they're setting up camp."

DAVIS

Washington City
December 1863

Jefferson Davis should have returned on the train to Richmond with his wife, but had remained in Washington. He again read the note she'd left for him when she departed.

You have a country to run. You're not the Secretary of War. Nor should you play the conquering hero. You've told me countless times. This isn't a war to conquer territory. It's a war to preserve the southern way of life, whatever that might be. You should come home and leave the soldiering to Longstreet and the others.

Varina was right, as was generally the case. But Davis was going to stay another day or two, ride out with Longstreet and survey the defenses that McClellan had built and that Confederate troops were now manning. He hadn't decided if they would fight to hold Washington City when the time came, or just slow the Northern troops and fall back on Richmond.

The news that Burgoyne had defeated McClellan at Saratoga had changed things. A week ago, Davis was frustrated at Longstreet's lack of action and because Custer had given Burgoyne a bloody nose in New York. Now everything had changed. Lincoln had few options. Asking for a negotiated settlement, which would guarantee Southern independence, seemed the most likely.

Davis was sitting in his old War Department office reading reports and looking at maps. He was hoping to hear directly from Burgoyne, and perhaps now, unless Meade had cut all the wires heading north, they could communicate by telegraph.

Longstreet, trailed by Moxley Sorrell, his senior staff officer, entered the office without knocking.

"Sir, you'll want to see this. Discouraging news indeed." He handed Davis a sheet of paper. "From General Pemberton in Vicksburg."

Davis read the message, then read it again. *Out of food and ammunition. Disease rampant among civilians and troops. This day surrendered army to Genl Grant. Terms unconditional. Pemberton.*

Davis stared at the paper, then placed it carefully on the desk. He smoothed it with his hand, as if that might change the content. He looked up at Longstreet.

Old Pete never seemed to change expression. "They held out longer than anyone thought they could. Seven months. Bought us a lot of time. Better now than a month ago."

Davis looked at the map. The loss of Vicksburg meant the loss of all navigation on the Mississippi River.

Longstreet watched Davis, knew he was plotting lines on the map, measuring distances in his head, working through possible courses of action. He waited, then said, "This will free up troops to come east. I'll wager that Lincoln will want either Grant or Sherman to replace McClellan."

Davis nodded, still studying the map. They had time, but not a lot. It was probably a thousand miles from Vicksburg to Washington. *They could fight their way here, through Tennessee and Virginia,* he mused. But if he were Grant, Davis would put troops on the cars to St. Louis, then Ohio, maybe on to Pittsburgh. Then he would come overland, hit the Confederacy from the west. *Or Grant could threaten Richmond as well from the west. It all depends on Burgoyne. Could he finish McClellan off?*

"General, we may want General Bragg to fall back into southwest Virginia, within striking distance of Richmond. Or send a couple of divisions . . . General Johnston at least. We will have to look to the western approaches to Richmond."

"Yes sir. The sooner we can finish this business, the better. Sam Grant proved he has a very long attention span. A seven-month siege for God's sake. Better to win this in the field where we have room to maneuver."

Davis was still staring at the map. "General, it suits us to hold Washington City for the time being. The pressure on Lincoln to end the war is enormous. Squeezing McClellan between here and the British forces is sound strategy. But if Grant or Sherman come east, we'll fall back to defend Richmond. Defending what's ours is how we win."

BURGOYNE

Near Saratoga, New York
December 1863

Burgoyne sat by the fire between Gordon and Campbell. Their staff officers stood around a similar fire, twenty feet away and out of earshot, occasionally shooting glances over to make sure that the generals didn't need anything. It was cold and clear, and Burgoyne inched his stool closer to the fire.

He had said little to anyone since the battle had ended. Campbell, who knew him better, sensed a calm and serenity that was different. Gordon, anxious to pursue McClellan, saw indecision, inaction, lack of will.

Campbell broke the long silence. "Sir, how does General Grant's victory in the west change the calculus for us here?"

Burgoyne pondered the question and answered in a quiet voice. "Time. Grant, or at least some of his army, will no doubt come east to try to retake Washington City. It will take them some time to get there. A couple of weeks probably. So, we need to be done with McClellan by then so we can help our Southern friends."

Gordon couldn't believe his ears. If time was their enemy, why were they not even now pursuing McClellan, destroying his army? "Sir, the dragoons report that McClellan stopped for the night this side of Albany. Will we truly let him get away, and he beaten badly, and his army demoralized? Might we not finish him off, sir?"

Burgoyne looked up from the fire. *Bordering on impudent,* he thought. *If we weren't three thousand miles from home, I'd relieve him. The Scots are bloody great fighters but find it hard to keep their mouths shut.*

"General, I believe we will see Mr. McClellan again. I've been turning it over in my head. Lincoln has lost Washington City. He can't afford to give up the northern half of the country as well. His government has fled, the newspapers are calling for McClellan's head and for peace negotiations. Lincoln needs McClellan, and he needs him to hold the line where he is. I believe he will have no choice but to turn and attack us. That's why we're staying here. At Saratoga."

Gordon looked at the fire and stole a glance at Campbell, who was watching Burgoyne.

Burgoyne stood. "Gentlemen, it has been a long day. Your men performed splendidly today. They will have another opportunity, and soon enough. And gentlemen." He paused, looking directly at Gordon. "You may think that I'm wedded to this place. Banishing ghosts. Making things right. Call it what you will. That is not the case. We will fight Mr. McClellan on the ground that most suits us. For now, this ground suits us. Goodnight gentlemen."

Burgoyne walked to his tent, closed the flap, and sat on the cot. He had thought about this day for sixty years, and mostly thought this day would never come. Perhaps he had banished ghosts, or at least put them to rest. His own ghosts in any case. *Burgoyne? The chap who won the great battle at Saratoga? That's the fellow.* He pulled off his boots and was suddenly too exhausted to take off his uniform. He lay on the cot and was asleep in seconds.

McCLELLAN

Rosendale, New York
December 1863

Outside the American Hotel in Rosendale, New York, fifty staff officers, guards, and hostlers waited for the meeting inside to end. Young boys stood by, delighted with the activity and the presence of so many soldiers. Townspeople peered out through their windows or found an excuse to walk by the hotel before being shooed away by the guards. It had been two hours since George McClellan had arrived on horseback, dismounted, waved off his staff, and entered the hotel alone. President Lincoln had arrived by overnight train earlier from Philadelphia, accompanied by Secretary of War Stanton and John Hay, his personal secretary. Hay had met McClellan at the entryway to the hotel and led him to what was normally the dining room but which for today at least served as the seat of the government of the United States of America. Hay could see that the general was fuming. He'd had a train ride of his own from Albany to work himself into a lather, and he had done so.

Lincoln was dressed in his trademark dark suit, a black cravat at his throat. The ubiquitous stovepipe hat sat on a chair near the door. Stanton was seated, poker-faced, silent. A witness? Lincoln had been standing the whole time, and was animated, gesturing, talking too much. McClellan tuned him in and out, decided to sit, and went over again in his mind what he wanted to say to the president.

"General, it won't do. I need you to stay here, up there, and keep General Burgoyne at bay. If you don't want to do that, I'll find a general who will."

McClellan, red in the face, looked at the floor. "Mr. President, you gave me your word that this time I'd be allowed to finish the job. We were on the very cusp of victory twice previously when—"

Lincoln waved a bony hand and cut him off. "We are not on the very cusp of victory at this moment, sir. Washington City is in rebel hands and your army is in retreat. We are indeed on the cusp, but not of victory, sir. If not for the news from General Grant I'd be sitting down with Jefferson Davis to negotiate terms instead of imploring you to stay in the field. Sir."

Grant. It had taken him seven months to subdue a ragtag, half-starved rabble at Vicksburg, and now he's being dangled in front of me as the savior of the Republic. A drunk and a butcher. "Will General Grant be coming east?"

Lincoln stopped his pacing, turned, glanced at Stanton, then looked at McClellan squarely in the eye. "Yes. I've asked General Grant to come east. He will leave General Sherman in charge of the Western Army. Grant will come east by train with a couple of corps. He shall work in concert with General Meade and the rump of your army to retake Washington City. And then he will look toward Richmond. I don't believe that the rebels will try to hold Washington City; it serves them no real purpose beyond inflaming public opinion and the press."

McClellan said nothing. Grant would be the savior of Washington City, would restore the government to its seat of power.

"General, there is no doubt the situation is dire. But if General

Grant can restore Washington to its rightful ownership, and if you can deal a blow to General Burgoyne, we shall regain the momentum and the strategic initiative. If not, I fear the Democrats will nominate a peace candidate next year." He glared at McClellan. "And I believe they will probably prevail. Everything depends on you whipping Burgoyne. So that is an end to it. You will keep your position. You will not bring your army south. You will turn and take the fight to General Burgoyne."

No stories. No jokes. No reminiscing about the circuit riding days in Illinois, or about his soldiering days during the Black Hawk War. At least that. *I'm still in command of the Army of the Potomac. And I need to deal with Burgoyne before Grant has time to come east.*

McClellan stood, looked at the president, nodded in the direction of Stanton, paused, then saluted, wheeled, and walked out of the room without a word. He nearly bowled John Hay over as Hay offered to show him out. Outside, McClellan stood in the doorway as staff officers scrambled to mount their horses, and a soldier led McClellan's own horse over to where he stood.

Once mounted, Captain Wilson rode up alongside McClellan, looked over at the general, and asked, "All well, sir?"

"Very well, Captain. We have a train to catch. And an enemy to crush."

Relieved, Wilson spurred his horse to keep pace with the general, who had moved ahead at a brisk canter.

LANE

North of Albany, New York
December 1863

John Lane waited outside General Burgoyne's tent, staff
officers and guards eyeing him suspiciously.

He had arrived at the British camp with a wagonload of potatoes.
Sentries had pointed him toward the quartermaster, but Lane had
insisted on seeing Burgoyne. It had taken an hour, couriers running
back and forth between the sentry outpost and the headquarters
tent, but finally Major Packenham rode up with two dragoons, one
of whom was leading a horse with no rider. Packenham remained
mounted and said, "Mr. Lane, you'll come with me, please. Can you
sit a horse?" Packenham eyed Lane's empty sleeve.

"Sure, wasn't I in the army?"

"That wasn't my question."

"If the horse is gentle in nature, I believe I can."

Packenham laughed. "We'd best walk then." He jumped down,
and said, "It's not far. Sergeant, take my horse back if you will. And
see that the wagon gets to the quartermaster."

Lane hesitated, watching as the sergeant climbed aboard the wagon and prepared to drive off.

Packenham laughed again. "You'll get the wagon back. Where's Miss Viola? Your, em, business associate?"

Lane had rehearsed the answer with Viola, but still felt himself stumble. "She's, em, engaged in the purchase of additional potatoes. She asked me to make this delivery." Packenham seemed satisfied with the answer.

Walking through the camp, Lane could see that the mood of the army had changed. Soldiers were standing in groups, laughing. He remembered his first weeks in the Army of the Potomac, the feeling of invincibility. Before Fredericksburg.

After half an hour of waiting, an aide emerged from Burgoyne's tent and motioned to Lane to enter. Inside, Burgoyne sat between Generals Gordon and Campbell, a map, as always, spread before them.

"Mr. Lane. I didn't expect to see you so soon. I've no news from London as yet. It's too soon."

"Yes sir. I wanted you to know that I met with John O'Mahony in New York."

"With whom do you say?"

"John O'Mahony, head of the Fenian Brotherhood. He's ready to send the word to every Irish soldier in the Union Army, through their—through our—network. He's enlisting the help of powerful men, generals and the like. He's just waiting, we're just waiting, for the word from you that London has approved the deal."

"Yes. Mr. Lane, as you know the Union Army sits scarce ten miles from here. If you're correct, fully a quarter of those soldiers are Irishmen. Entire regiments are made up of Irish. It would be a sign of good faith if you, em, unleashed your men now, rather than waiting for official approval from the crown. It would be a sign of good faith, would it not?"

The other generals nodded, Gordon adding, "Just so. Good faith."

Caught off guard, Lane had mumbled that he would take the message to O'Mahony and see what could be done.

Outside the tent, Packenham was waiting and took Lane back the way they had come. His wagon, empty sacks in the back, was waiting for him at the sentry post.

On the ride back, Lane found himself worrying about Viola, her family, and the people hiding in her cellar. Lane had slept on the floor in front of the fire, and in the morning, he and Viola had discussed, in whispers, how to proceed.

"I need to stay here. I don't trust these soldiers with my family. Or with my visitors. You take the wagon and deliver another load of potatoes to the British. When you come back, I'll want to know exactly where they are camped."

"Why do you want to know that?"

"Why do you want to talk to General Burgoyne?"

"Are you a spy?"

"Are you?"

Lane had pondered the question for a full minute. "In a manner of speaking. I'm working with the British to gain freedom for my people."

"Your people?"

"In Ireland."

Viola stared at him. "You're helping the British so that they'll free your people?"

"Yes."

"So, you're helping the British support Southern independence which will guarantee the survival of slavery in the South."

Lane thought back to his boyhood, attending the hedge school in County Cork. He and other likely lads receiving instruction from a former priest. Harsh discipline but high standards for country boys. Latin. The classics. Logic. Viola reminded him of his teacher, Mr. Flaherty, a failed priest. All Socratic method.

"I suppose I am. But it's for a higher cause."

Viola stood ramrod straight, fists clenched at her side, and eyes blazing. "A higher cause? Higher than freeing human beings from slavery?"

Lane didn't answer. Soon after, he'd left the house, loaded the potatoes into the wagon, and set off. A Union sentry asked, "Do you live in that house?"

"No," he'd answered. "It belongs to my business associate."

DAVIS

Richmond, Virginia
December 1863

Jefferson and Varina Davis sat in their chairs before the fire,
Varina knitting socks for soldiers, as always, and her husband
uncharacteristically reading the Richmond newspapers.

"Do you recall two years ago we thought the war would be over
by that first Christmas? And yet here we are."

Davis looked up from the *Dispatch*. "It's a happier Christmas
than it might have been. A month ago, I thought all was lost."

"You never told me that."

"Longstreet bogged down in front of Washington, and by all
appearances happily so."

Varina smiled.

"And Custer having his way with Burgoyne in New York. I admit
I did not see a path to independence."

"Are you worried about General Grant? The papers say that he
will come east and march on Richmond."

Davis saw Grant in his mind. A bad reputation. A poor student at West Point. The drinking. Didn't look the part of an officer and a gentleman. But in Mexico, he'd shone. Pickett, Longstreet, Grant. Poor students, bottom of their class, and all heroes now in their own way.

"Sam Grant will come east, and he'll come to fight. He'll be relentless. He'll use all the resources that the North can provide him with. He'll use up his men and he'll keep coming. So yes, I'm worried about General Grant."

"Will you defend Washington City?"

"No. Ours is a war of survival, not conquest. If the British want to attack and burn it, again, so be it. There's hardly a building worth saving anyway. Half-built buildings and monuments and dirt avenues. In due course, once we know what Grant plans, I'll pull Pete back to defend Richmond. And hope that Burgoyne can deal with McClellan once and for all."

"Are you surprised that Lincoln has kept McClellan?"

Davis smiled. He was long used to the game. Varina already knew the answers to the questions. She knew that it helped Davis process his thoughts. What might she have accomplished under other circumstances?

"No. And yes. The well is about dry for Lincoln. McDowell, Pope, Burnside, Hooker, Meade. He's out of options. George is a fine organizer and drillmaster. He's a superior engineer. But that's why Lincoln is bringing Grant east. Those western generals, Grant, Sherman, Sheridan, they're tigers. He needs some of that fight in the east."

"And how about our fight?"

Davis did a quick analysis. "We still have the advantage in leadership, especially with Jackson back. Pete is steady and dependable. Stuart is a tactical genius and fearless. Fitz Lee shows all the signs of being a capable cavalry commander. And Jackson does seem to benefit from his Divine Providence. Our problem isn't *fight*. It's *things*. Like rifles, boots, cannon, food. It's not just your Richmond shops that are empty this Christmas."

"I see you've taken to reading the Richmond papers again. I find that you are a fair-weather reader of the news."

"I find that I am as well. It turns out that Mr. Cowardin now believes I am a wartime leader on the plane of Caesar and Alexander. A latter-day Washington. To be lionized. So yes, I currently read the *Dispatch*."

Varina smiled. "Yes, Mr. Cowardin's paper has indeed changed its tune. I advise you not to grow accustomed to it. He will print what he can sell. The weather changes with the season."

"Have you seen Mary Lee?"

"Yes, the general is poorly. His heart, she says. The two of them must keep all the doctors of Richmond employed."

"Mmm. I was thinking of paying a call on the general."

BURGOYNE

Near Saratoga, New York
December 1863

John Fox Burgoyne stood in his tent. He was tired of sitting, tired of waiting for McClellan, tired of making the rounds to visit the officers and regiments of his command. In fact, he was just tired. Sixty years a soldier. And now, with his victory at Saratoga behind him, he just wanted to get on with it, get it over with, and go home.

Home. He'd finally had a letter. It came with the same dispatch as the message from Palmerston. He'd put it aside to read later. First things first.

The message from the Prime Minister had arrived earlier than Burgoyne had anticipated. Palmerston had not dawdled, had taken the request seriously and acted on it. The reply, however, was not what he expected.

London
December 1863
General:

I am in receipt of your letter. Your proposal to accept assistance from the Fenian Brotherhood in exchange for Irish Home Rule has provoked discussion at the highest levels of Her Majesty's Government. As an Irish peer and landowner, I myself have grave misgivings. However, Her Majesty has advised that she wishes to see the North American venture succeed at all costs. She therefore has agreed that you may use your discretion in soliciting Fenian assistance. Promises such as that of Home Rule shall be ratified as political circumstances permit. Her Majesty urges the utmost caution that any arrangements not be made public.
Palmerston.

I suppose this is why Palmerston is a politician and I'm a soldier. My discretion, is it? And as circumstances permit? Does that mean Home Rule would be delivered at the proper political moment, or that it would be delivered if the proper political moment presented itself? Either way, the nuance will no doubt be lost on my one-armed Irish rebel and his mysterious legion of revolutionaries. It's rather lost on me.

Burgoyne put the paper back in the leather case in which it had arrived. He picked up the letter from his wife, started to read it, got halfway through the first of two sheets, and put it down. About as much warmth in the one letter as the other. *I'm less concerned about the need to replace the carriage and much more interested in the family. I wonder if Hugh is at sea. It is time he had his own ship. And the girls. At sea in their own way.* He picked up his wife's letter, intending to finish it. He began again, then returned it to his field desk.

He put on his cloak and hat and walked out through the tent flap. The staff, as always, were gathered around the fire doing their best to stay warm.

"What word, Major?"

Packenham rubbed his hands together for warmth and said,

"No change, sir. The Union forces remain in camp north of Albany. They've taken no pains to dig defensive positions and look in no hurry to head south. It seems you were right, sir. I'll wager they head back our way."

"Aren't I always right, Packenham?"

"Indeed, sir, that is my experience to this point." Looking at his comrades gathered around the fire, he added, "In fact, we're all in agreement."

The other staff officers smiled and watched, jealous of Packenham's easy repartee with the general. Burgoyne looked at the faces of his staff officers, young men in their twenties. A few years younger than Hugh. Just as eager for glory and action. What made some men seek a life of ease and pleasure, and others to seek adventure? It had never crossed his own mind to be a London gentleman, to work in the City, to run an estate. All he'd ever wanted was to be a soldier. And to erase the original sin of Saratoga from his soul.

"Thomas."

Packenham looked up, startled. Had the general used his Christian name?

"Sir?"

"Walk with me a moment. You've been idle too long. I should like to see Mr. Lane, the, em, Fenian. Would you be so kind as to fetch him here?"

"But he was just here a day or so ago, sir, was he not?"

"Indeed he was, Thomas. I need to see him again. Things are afoot, do you see?"

Packenham smiled. "Right away, sir."

McCLELLAN

South of Saratoga, New York
December 1863

McClellan sat in his tent, going over in his head the meeting with Lincoln earlier in the day. As much as he despised the man, he could now see clearly the way forward.

Nelly sat beside him. He had asked her to visit, unsure when he might have the chance to see her next. She had taken the train up from New York City.

"I don't expect you to lay out your grand strategy, but the fact that you invited me to camp means you'll soon be going into action."

"Indeed, it may."

They sat quietly, McClellan's wheels turning, Nelly pretending to read a book. There was nothing awkward in the silence.

"You've said nothing about your meeting with Mr. Lincoln. Imagine. Did you ever think that meetings with the president would be commonplace and unworthy of comment?"

"All too commonplace. For all his homespun manner, he is a superior politician, I'll grant him that. He as much as said he expects me to run against him in the fall. Yet I suspect he is setting up General Grant to supersede me. It is Grant who will come east and take Richmond, saving the Union, while I spar with Burgoyne in the frozen north. Lincoln knows that Grant has no political ambitions, doesn't have a political bone in his body. His success poses no threat to re-election."

"I see. So, Grant's success will be Lincoln's success, assuring his re-election. Your own victory against the British will be a sideshow. An important sideshow, but not enough to defeat him."

"There may be a way."

Nelly looked up from her book. "You'll beat Sam Grant to the punch."

McClellan smiled. "Let me see if we have a uniform that might fit you. Our hats have no feathers, though some of the Southern officers are partial to them."

Nelly returned the smile. "I prefer to offer my services as a civilian strategist. That way I can sleep in my own bed and eschew the marching aspects of military life. You may keep your uniform. I should like a look at the hat and feathers."

"Beat him to the punch indeed. If we can deal with the British quickly, we can threaten Washington before Grant can transport his army east. I don't believe Davis will defend Washington. We might take it back without firing a shot, though a few shots fired will please the newspapers."

"Where will you fight the British?"

McClellan picked the map up from his field desk and spread it between them. "Here. Saratoga. Burgoyne seems determined to stay there and fight there. No doubt he feels a need to erase the stain on his father's name. That is fine with me. I appreciate an enemy who is immobile and wedded to a particular place. It makes the planning and execution that much easier."

"The father seemed such a jolly sort. I've read *The Heiress*. It's quite amusing. And after he returned to England he became an advocate for the French Revolution. Your General Burgoyne seems much less interesting."

"He's interesting enough. He makes few mistakes. My dear, I believe I shall ask Wilson to escort you to the train station. I believe the atmosphere will soon be less conducive to reading and polite conversation."

Nelly looked at him. "George, you are correct. If ever there were a moment for fast and decisive action, this is it. I shall look forward to joining you in Washington."

McClellan smiled. "I'm going to order the uniform in case you change your mind."

LANE

Between Albany and Saratoga, New York
December 1863

It had been a dizzying couple of days for John Lane.

Fetched by Major Packenham, he had gone to see General Burgoyne for the second time in as many days. Burgoyne had told him that Lord Palmerston and the crown had agreed to the Fenian proposal of Home Rule for Ireland, after the war, in exchange for Irish soldiers in the Union Army switching sides now.

"Is there a piece of paper to sign? Is there a date certain for Irish Home Rule, say sixty days following the end of the war?"

Burgoyne had brushed aside the questions. "Surely, Corporal Lane, you don't expect that Her Majesty is going to sign an agreement with the Fenian Brotherhood? And as for a date certain, I should think that Her Majesty's word would be sufficient."

Lane had wondered, *how far do I push him?* "Surely, General, accustomed as we Irish are to accepting the word of a benevolent crown in all things, I'd prefer to have something to hang my hat on."

Burgoyne paused, looking sharply at Lane. "I suggest you hang your hat on the following. That upon the successful conclusion of the war, assisted by the Fenian Brotherhood, the crown will grant Irish Home Rule as soon as political circumstances permit."

"You'll understand, General. I need more than that. We'll be asking Irish soldiers to commit treason against their adopted country. We'll need a guarantee that it's worth the risk for them."

Burgoyne had expected no less. He thought about his long career. The swamps of Louisiana. Chasing Boney through Spain. Long years away from his family, barely knowing his children. Crimea. And now this independent command, and so far from home. Lane was right, of course. He couldn't ask men to commit treason for anything less than a guarantee.

"You have my word, Mr. Lane. Within ninety days of a successful termination of this war, in which your Irish soldiers have supported our cause, you will have your Home Rule."

Lane knew he was out of his depth. What proof would he have that Burgoyne had given his word? And what weight would Burgoyne's word carry in London? Burgoyne was rolling the dice. Lane decided that he would as well.

"Fair enough." He reached out with his good hand.

Burgoyne looked puzzled, then seemed to suppress a smile. "Yes, of course." He grasped Lane's hand and shook it.

"I'll inform Mr. O'Mahony and we'll get cracking."

"Please see that you do. I expect General McClellan to attack soon, and it would be convenient indeed if his Irish troops had other plans for the day."

After meeting with Burgoyne, Lane had driven the wagon to Albany where he had wired O'Mahony. Knowing that he couldn't be explicit, Lane puzzled over how to inform the Fenian. He finally wrote, *Permission received to rouse the Fianna. Meet me in Albany today if possible.* Lane smiled. O'Mahony the scholar would get the reference to the Fianna, the legendary Irish warriors from mythology.

O'Mahony hadn't wasted any time, and he had arrived in the

afternoon with General Thomas Francis Meagher in tow, the most famous Irish soldier in America.

In the wagon ride from Albany, Lane had tried to answer their questions about his meeting with Burgoyne.

"Palmerston gave his word then?"

"In a manner of speaking, sir. It was General Burgoyne who gave his word, based on his correspondence with Palmerston. I believe the term was something like 'as soon as political circumstances permit.'"

O'Mahony and Meagher were silent.

"What do you make of that, lad?"

Lane had prepared for the question. "I believe it's the best chance we've ever had or will ever have. I believe that if we deliver, General Burgoyne will ensure that the crown does as well."

"We need to see Colonel Kelly, commander of the Irish Brigade. What's left of it. The poor bastards. The fellas who weren't slaughtered on Marye's Heights . . . sorry John."

"It's fine, sir."

"The rest were slaughtered at Chancellorsville. The brigade is more of a regiment now. But if we can convince Kelly and those lads, others will follow."

O'Mahony looked at Lane. "Can you find Colonel Kelly and the Irish Brigade? Do you know where they are?"

"I do, sir. They're camped in my front garden. Well, the garden of my, em, business associate. We'll be there in two hours."

DAVIS

Richmond, Virginia
December 1863

Jefferson Davis expected Robert E. Lee to look ill. His wife had said he was suffering from an undisclosed heart ailment. In fact, Lee looked years younger than the last time Davis had seen him, when Lee took his leave of the Army of Northern Virginia. He had put on weight, his face had color, and his hair and beard were neatly trimmed. *Perhaps there's something to be said for retirement,* thought Davis.

"Mr. President, it is an honor. By rights I should be calling on you."

"Not at all, General. I have need of your counsel so am delighted that you were able to see me today."

Lee nodded, the nod of the aristocrat. As if to say, *Of course you do.*

They were seated in the small parlor of Lee's home in Richmond. Arlington, the estate that had come to Lee through Mary, and to her through her relation to Martha Washington's grandson, George

Washington Parke Custis, had been in Federal hands until Longstreet had re-occupied northern Virginia. Davis wondered why the Lees hadn't moved back. Perhaps he didn't trust Pete to hold Washington City. *And that's why I'm here.*

"General, you have heard the news that Lincoln will bring General Grant east with part of his army. They will no doubt try to liberate Washington City, then march on Richmond."

"Indeed. I wonder, Mr. President, if you will defend two capitals at once? I might think that Washington City is not worth the effort."

Davis smiled. "You've read my mind, General, as you read Meade's and McClellan's and Hooker's and Burnside's."

"Are we forgetting Mr. Pope, Mr. President?"

Davis wondered if he had ever heard Robert E. Lee attempt a joke. *Retirement surely does agree with him.*

"Not for a moment. Perhaps General Pope most of all. I too believe Washington City not worth defending. We gain nothing through conquest, everything by defending what is ours. I am leaning toward abandoning Washington City when Grant advances and falling back to defend Richmond. Do you have any thoughts on how General Grant might proceed?"

Lee was silent, far away. "I barely knew him in Mexico. One of the rougher sort. He was a quartermaster, not the usual path to glory. But he found a way to get into the war and behaved credibly. Then the accusations out west. Some men are born soldiers, excelling at every aspect of the military life. Others are warriors. Killers, I would venture to say. Grant is a poor soldier but a superior warrior. He will be relentless."

That word again.

"We are counting on the British being of some help. I believe McClellan will have no choice but to attack Burgoyne, and this time I expect the British to deliver a blow. If not, if McClellan is able to return south and threaten Richmond from the north, and Grant from the west, we will be in a difficult situation altogether."

Lee's eyes grew brighter, and he sat straighter in his chair. "If I were General Burgoyne, I would not wait for General McClellan to complete his endless preparations. I would take the fight to him. General McClellan excels at preparation but does not enjoy the fight. He is the opposite of General Grant in that respect. An exemplary soldier but a middling warrior."

"General, how do you recommend we prepare to defend Richmond from General Grant?"

Lee did not hesitate. "Grant will have more men, more guns, and all the equipment he needs. He will hit like a hammer. But we will be defending our homes, and we will have the advantage of interior lines. We will be able to move faster over shorter distances."

"Will that be enough?"

"No. Mr. President, you will need audacity. You cannot let it end in a siege. We just saw at Vicksburg how that will end. You will need audacity and you will need to take risks. You will need Jackson and Stuart."

"And General Longstreet, General?"

Lee thought a moment. "Of course. General Longstreet is the best defensive fighter in the army. Only think of Fredericksburg. But to defeat Grant, it will not be enough to defend, because he will never stop coming. You will need to outmaneuver and outsmart him. And for that you will need Jackson and Stuart."

An opening, perhaps. Delicately. "General, have you given thought to returning to the field? I believe General Longstreet would welcome your return, as I would."

Lee rose from his chair. "Mr. President, I have always found it difficult to refuse service to my country. If the time comes when you shall see a need for me, do not hesitate to call."

They shook hands and Lee walked Davis to the door. "Unseasonably warm. Just a couple of weeks ago I was worried about an early winter. It's so hard on the soldiers. But this? This is fine weather for warfare. Good day, Mr. President."

Davis started to walk the short distance to his office. *"If the time comes?" I thought I made myself clear that the time has indeed come. Well, we shall see.*

BURGOYNE

Near Saratoga, New York

January 1864

On the eve of battle, Burgoyne sat alone in his tent in dim lantern light, maps spread before him. But he wasn't looking at the maps and wasn't reading the reports of preparations and readiness brought to him throughout the evening by his staff. The work was done. McClellan would attack. The Union general had no choice.

Burgoyne was far away, remembering the eve of battles half a century ago. As a young soldier it was all excitement and glory, a lark, really. Dashing through black swamps, avoiding capture. The thought of killing men or being killed barely crossed his mind. King, in those days, and country.

Back then the noise, the smoke, and even the screams and the blood were all part of it. But rank begat distance. Now, if he could see a battle at all it was from atop a hill at a distance, movements of red or blue, the sounds of cannon distant, the screams of the wounded and dying not heard at all.

Burgoyne found himself thinking about the infamous piece of

American real estate on which he was camped. He had won a great victory at Saratoga, just days before, and now he had a chance to win another. The stain on the family name had been erased, the ghosts banished, and his reputation made. He found himself unwilling to leave the spot that had ruined one Burgoynes reputation and made another's. Perhaps he should have pursued McClellan, followed up on his victory, destroyed the Union Army.

But to what end? In what cause? Southern independence? Arrogant aristocrats, who'd taken the worst habits of their British forbearers and added their own prickliness, litigiousness, and parochialism. Breaking up the United States of America because they were a rival economic power to Britain? His father, after returning home, impressed by what he'd seen in America, had become an advocate of independence, and even of revolution in France. And for the first time, the son Burgoyne heard himself say the word, though not out loud. "Slavery."

He had known Wilberforce, though not particularly well. They'd traveled in different social circles. Too convinced of his own moral superiority, yet the arguments were powerful, and in his heart, Burgoyne knew—everyone knew—that he was right. Slavery was an abomination, yet the British pretended that this war was about something else.

Burgoyne sipped at the wine that Packenham had brought him earlier in the evening. Young, potent, slightly abrasive on the tongue. *Like this country. I could extend this metaphor forever,* he smiled.

He picked up the letter from his wife, still half-read. It was curious that he would so long to hear from her, then so dread to read. But not so curious at all. It had always been that way. The soldier's life suited them both. The marriage had lasted so long precisely because of the absences.

Burgoyne drained the glass and considered pouring another. It wouldn't do. He would leave that to General Grant. Lincoln, when told of Grant's drinking, had apparently said he'd send a case of whiskey to all his generals. *I should like to meet Mr. Lincoln. He'd be at home in one of father's plays. The country bumpkin as political genius.*

The attack should come tomorrow, or perhaps the next day. Grant was advancing and McClellan couldn't afford to let Grant win his war for him. *McClellan.* Burgoyne had half a dozen regimental commanders who could take his measure. *I wonder. Will he return the engraved sword we gave him in Crimea at the surrender? The great circle of life. Probably not. I should probably count on a standard issue dress sword.*

"Thomas?"

"Sir?" The answer was instantaneous, Packenham standing just outside the tent flap, awaiting final orders.

"Major, I should like to be awakened at four this morning. We may have business to attend to."

"Yes sir." In the dim light, Burgoyne couldn't tell, but he was certain that Packenham was smiling.

McCLELLAN

North of Albany, New York
January 1864

McClellan sat alone in his tent in dim lantern light, poring over the maps, noting in his head where each regiment was formed and where each was expected to be in place before first light. It was an intricate choreography that needed to unfold just so. Throughout the daylight hours he had ridden to each division, spoken to each corps and division commander in turn, talked to ordinary soldiers, gauged their readiness. He had written out the orders, but had gone over them in person as well, leaving nothing to chance. Staff officers came and went. McClellan would quickly read the notes they brought in, then dictate a response.

He had done everything possible to get the army ready for this moment. Nobody, he assured himself, could prepare an army for battle as he could. It was why the men loved him, had welcomed his return, and why they would fight for him. They were well-equipped, well-drilled, and mostly well-led.

Everything rode on a decisive victory, one that would allow him to leave a rump command to watch Burgoyne's battered force, and rush south to liberate Washington City. Before Grant could. Those victories, in New York and in Washington, would cement his place at the head of the army—and in history. But only the final defeat of the Confederacy, finally taking Richmond, would earn him the ultimate prize.

Grant. According to McClellan's agreement with Lincoln, McClellan was commander in chief of all Union armies in the field, so Grant was technically his subordinate. But in fact, Grant acted as an independent commander, reporting only to Lincoln himself. How would Grant respond to a direct order to stand down, to wait for McClellan to arrive on the field? To so order him was to risk him saying no. Better to let conditions on the ground dictate events. *Get there first.*

McClellan remembered Grant from Mexico. An officer but barely a gentleman. He took little care with his appearance. After Mexico, there was the talk. Drinking, and actions bordering on dereliction of duty. Grant had resigned before he could be court martialed. Or so it was said.

But nobody could argue with success, least of all Lincoln. Grant had won at Shiloh, though only after almost being driven into the Tennessee River. Forts Donelson and Henry. Victories for the navy, really. Then Vicksburg. A long, drawn-out, and costly siege against an undermanned and incompetent foe. The great eastern newspapers made much of him. *Wait until they meet him,* thought McClellan.

Everything is done. There is no more I can do. Tomorrow, it is up to the men and their officers. The plan is impeccable. But once in motion, it is out of my hands entirely.

He took pen in hand, and as he did before every battle, wrote a short note to Nelly. He didn't send them. He wrote them just in case.

"Captain."

"Sir."

"You'll see that this is delivered should anything happen to me tomorrow."

"Yes sir." Captain Wilson accepted the letter awkwardly, thought of stuffing it in his tunic, thought better, saluted, and repaired to his own tent to put the letter with his own belongings. *Odd,* he thought. *Does the general intend to be near the fighting?*

McClellan placed his boots next to each other, just so, next to the tent flap. His tunic and trousers he folded and placed on a camp stool. He hung his coat on a hangar, which hung from a rope stretched across the roof of the tent. He folded the map and straightened the pens and paper on the camp desk, then lay on the cot. He was asleep as his head hit the small pillow.

LANE

North of Albany, New York
January 1864

John Lane was in Viola's farmhouse, sitting in the wooden chair before the fire. Viola and her mother were in the other room, putting the children to bed. Below, in the cellar, Lane could hear the occasional muffled conversation or scrape of a chair or table on the stone floor. They wouldn't be able to leave anytime soon.

Lane went over in his mind the events of the day and wondered if the plan, his plan, would really begin to unfold in the morning.

Colonel Kelly had been easy to find. What was left of the Irish Brigade was indeed camped near Viola's farmhouse. O'Mahony was the first to spot the Brigade flag, a harp and shamrocks on a green field with a motto in Irish. He stopped at the sight of it, and muttered aloud, "'Who has never retreated from the clash of spears.' My own suggestion."

Meagher, in his peculiarly accented English, said, "Aye, and true enough. The lads were demons in front of the sunken road at Fredericksburg, eh John? But they mowed us down like hay. Chancellorsville was worse if anything."

Colonel Kelly was seated on a cracker box around a campfire, surrounded by other officers. Meagher said, louder than necessary, "God save all here," and the men shot to their feet. Meagher shook hands all around, smiled at the familiar faces, and introduced the others.

Kelly smiled. "Look what the fine weather brought. General, it's a pleasure. Couldn't bear to be away, is it? And you've brought your friends, I see."

O'Mahony spoke up. "Colonel Kelly, would you have a moment to walk with us?"

"I do, though I have a feeling from the look of ye that I might regret it."

Lane had lagged behind and watched. By agreement, Meagher would explain the situation to Kelly. *Meagher,* he thought. The hero of the 1848 rising, disastrous as it was. Exile in Tasmania. Escape to America. Then commander of the Irish Brigade, by any measure one of the bravest and most gallant units in the army. Lane had fought alongside them on Marye's Heights and had seen their mettle firsthand. Meagher was the kind of man others followed to their deaths.

Lane had watched as they went back and forth, though Meagher was doing most of the talking. Kelly looked stunned at first, then nervous, then sad. They rejoined O'Mahony and Lane.

"John, tell the colonel what Burgoyne told you."

"That ninety days after the war ends, assuming that the Irish have supported the British to a successful end, Ireland will be granted Home Rule."

All eyes had been on Kelly. O'Mahony spoke. "Paddy, it's the best chance we'll ever have. And your men hold the key. If the Brigade refuses to fight, the other Irish units will follow. Sure the lads run a great risk if things go poorly. But if we win, their place in Irish history is assured. And your own, for all that."

Kelly had looked at each of them in turn and smiled, though

there was little humor in it. "Sure the easiest way to enter Irish history has always been feet first, as a martyr. But I'll do my best. I'll talk to the lads."

Meagher's friendly face had grown dark and hard, the eyes burning, the body tensed and coiled. "See that you do, Paddy. Irish freedom rests on your shoulders. They'll write songs about you, lad."

Kelly no longer smiled. "That's what I'm bloody afraid of."

Lane's thoughts returned to the present as Viola came out of the room and latched the door quietly. She pulled another chair from the table to the fire, and said, "Who were those men with you today?"

"There's going to be a big battle tomorrow."

"Here?"

"Close enough. I believe McClellan will attack the British in the morning. You might want to take your children and your mother and go to Albany."

"I'm not going anywhere. And besides, I can't leave . . . I can't go. And you didn't answer my question. You generally never answer my questions."

"The leaders of the Fenian Brotherhood."

"Fenian Brotherhood? Irish?"

"Yes."

"You went and did it, didn't you? You're going to sell out the Union for *your* people."

"I'm not selling out anyone. I'm striking a blow for oppressed people everywhere, and especially in Ireland."

Viola stared at the fire, then turned back to Lane. "You're not striking a blow for your people. You're guaranteeing the enslavement of *my* people, like Michael and Sarah in the cellar. Like millions of others. And you're committing treason while you're at it."

Lane was silent. He felt sick to his stomach.

DAVIS

Washington City
January 1864

Varina Davis was seated in the parlor of their suite at Willard's Hotel in Washington. A fire burned in the fireplace, though it produced little heat. It seemed to draw warmth up the chimney rather than radiate it. Her husband paced, an annoying habit in a small room.

"Why don't you sit down and read the Washington papers. It will do you good to learn that you're a military genius."

"We'll see if they still call me a genius when they learn I'm withdrawing Longstreet's troops to defend Richmond."

"How did the general take the news?"

"With his usual display of emotion and prattle."

Varina smiled. "I see. In other words, he grunted?"

"Something akin to that. I believe he's pleased. He's no more comfortable than I playing the conqueror. He's not worried about McClellan. He's thinking about Grant. We'll all feel better if our army is protecting Richmond. And having to supply two capitals is stretching our resources thin indeed."

"And General Bragg?" Varina asked.

Davis sighed. "I believe he was surprised that I accepted his resignation. But he wasted a grand opportunity in Tennessee. General Johnston wired that he believed he could spare Bragg and some of his men to help us defend Richmond. I believe he just wants Bragg out of Tennessee. In any case, he should be arriving on the cars within a week, with about 10,000 men. They'll be a big help. That army has fought well, but always poorly led. Longstreet will have to deal with Bragg . . . but I speak too freely."

"It's nothing that everyone doesn't already know," she said. "How did the Army of Northern Virginia acquire such talent while the Western Army suffered its lack?"

"I have to admit that our retired general had something to do with it. He recognized leadership when he saw it. Jackson, Stuart, Longstreet, Hill, the rest. He understood the particular qualities of each and used them accordingly. And recognized those with, uh, other qualities as well. Beauregard."

Varina smiled. "You were not unhappy to see General Lee go. And now you want him back. Like a romance novel."

Davis frowned. "I have complete faith in Old Pete to manage the defense of Richmond. He's the devil to dislodge once he's dug in. But a siege is a numbers game that we will never win. We can't just defend Richmond once Grant arrives. We will need to defeat him. And that is a different kind of warfare altogether. That is Lee's kind of war."

"What news from the north?"

Davis' frown deepened. "Nothing. I expect McClellan to attack Burgoyne at any moment. He must. It is no secret that George despises Lincoln and wants to be president. If he can whip Burgoyne, then march into Washington City before Grant, he just might pull it off. As you see in the northern papers, the public is sick and tired of the war, and Lincoln's re-election is no foregone conclusion. Especially as he sits in Philadelphia, having been chased out of the capital."

"So, you do read the Northern papers."

Davis smiled. "Selected articles that suit my frame of mind."

After a comfortable silence, Varina said, "It's true, you know. This is truly a Southern city. The people, at least those who didn't leave, seem delighted that we're here. The White people, I should say."

"Yes. It was always an anomaly that the Northern capital permitted slavery. It confused their war aims and I believe that's why Lincoln finally decreed an end to it. A lot of people here would be happy to go back to the old ways." He looked at his wife. "White people, as you say."

Davis continued his pacing. "We should return to Richmond tomorrow. Pete and the army will follow. These next weeks will seal our fate." A long pause, then, "Burgoyne must crush McClellan so we can concentrate our efforts on Grant."

BURGOYNE

Saratoga, New York
January 1864

Burgoyne had been up since four and in the saddle since five.
The first attack had come in darkness, beginning with artillery. Most
of the shots had been long, as they always were. In sixty years of
soldiering, he'd seldom seen gunners fire short.

By six, still in darkness, infantry was on the move and the British
general could follow first contact all along the line by the sound of
rifle fire. Shortly after six, staff officers started arriving, the men as
high strung as their horses, some in battle for the first time, all alive at
least for now with excitement. Standing in their stirrups, breathless
from the ride and from the thrill, they delivered the first reports
from the regimental commanders, like this from the 92nd of Foot:
*Regt engaged all along the line. Enemy attacking in force. Will need
ammunition later in the morning.*

From all the reports it was clear that his army was holding
its position for the time being. *Let McClellan keep coming, throw
everything he has at us,* thought Burgoyne. *Play himself out, then,*

perhaps by late afternoon, I'll hit him with the reserve, and we shall truly test his mettle.

At seven o'clock, a staff officer rode up, saluted Burgoyne, and said, "Sir, General Gordon's compliments, and he wishes to report that Union infantry in his front have surrendered. In brigade strength or more."

"Thank you, Major. My compliments to General Gordon, and he should await my order before advancing. We shall move forward all along the line at the proper time."

"Sir, em, there's more. The Union troops. They've surrendered."

"So you reported, Major."

"Yes, but they've asked to switch sides."

"Have they indeed? An intriguing turn of events."

Just then Packenham, who had carried a message to General Campbell, rode up, a Union colonel in tow.

"Sir, may I present Colonel Kelly? The colonel commands the Irish brigade, which led the attack in General Gordon's front."

"A pleasure, Colonel. Have you anything to tell me?"

Even in the low light it was clear that Kelly was red faced and in a dark mood. "As agreed, General, my men are now under your command. God help us."

"Colonel, have other Irish soldiers followed your brigade's lead?"

Kelly looked at the ground. "I believe so. I spoke to a half-dozen commanders of mostly Irish regiments last night. I was very convincing. I believe most of them will do as I did."

"Thank you, Colonel. Thomas, please escort Colonel Kelly back to General Gordon. My orders for the general are that the colonel's men be deployed where and how they will be of the most use to him."

"General, we have your word that Home Rule for Ireland will be implemented as soon as the war ends, do we not?"

Burgoyne looked at him. "Yes. You have my word." *For whatever it may be worth,* he added to himself.

Packenham wheeled his horse. "Follow me if you please, Colonel."
He touched his hat to Burgoyne, and they were off at a gallop.

Astonishing, thought Burgoyne. *They've placed their faith and their very lives in my hands. Committed treason to their adopted country on my word and a handshake. I wonder if the crown has any intention whatsoever of honoring the agreement. God help them.*

McCLELLAN

Saratoga, New York
January 1864

McClellan had been up since four and had gathered his corps and division commanders one last time. They all had written orders, but leaving nothing to chance, he had gone over the orders again. Custer, whose cavalry had been out in force for the last twenty-four hours, reported that nothing had changed. Burgoyne's forces had not moved, and there were no signs that he was preparing to attack. All was ready.

"Gentlemen, I don't have to tell you that the very fate of the Union rides on our success today. Our country has been invaded and only this army stands between survival and ruin. Today we shall deliver a blow that will be felt not just in Richmond, but in London and throughout the world." The other officers were serious, hands clasped behind backs, nodding, filled with the import of McClellan's words and weighted with responsibility. Custer, apart, smiled and rubbed his hands together in anticipation.

The orders explained, the speech delivered, each man rode off into the darkness to return to his command. McClellan stood beside the fire, then paced. Turning to Captain Wilson he said, "We shall monitor events from here. I want all communications from the line brought to me immediately."

Wilson, hiding his disappointment, could only say, "Yes sir."

Entering his tent, McClellan sat at his field desk, took his watch from its pocket and marked the time. *Five-thirty.* In a few minutes, the big guns would commence their bombardment of the British positions. At six, the infantry would go in all along the front. Rising again, he went back outside, pacing nervously. This is always the worst of it, the waiting.

This time it would be different. McClellan would fully commit the entire army. There will be no room for criticism. And he would follow up the victory. *Once we've won the day, I'll unleash Custer with orders to make their retreat hell. Destroy their supply train. Harass their rear and flanks. And I'll wheel the rest of the army south, toward Washington City.* In a month, it would be over, and then he would deal with the other business. Politics.

At the first sound of the cannon, booming out in the pre-dawn darkness, McClellan went back outside and sat on a camp stool. At six o'clock, right on schedule, he heard musket fire ripple steadily up and down the line.

Now, at a little after eight o'clock, a staff officer rode pell-mell toward McClellan and jumped off his horse as he reined it to a halt. Staff officers had been riding in and out of camp since first light, bringing the first reports of the action. This one saluted and said, "Sir, I'm Captain O'Neill. General Gibbon sends his compliments and, uh, something has happened in the general's front."

"What the devil are you talking about, Captain?"

"Sir. A brigade, the Irish Brigade, surrendered. Other regiments have as well." The man had begun to weep, first quietly, then uncontrollably.

McClellan stood. "Was General Gibbon under attack at the time?"

"No sir. He was attacking. He was fully engaged, sir. Then the Irish Brigade surrendered. But sir—" Captain O'Neill was choking on his words.

"What are you saying, Captain, for the love of God?"

"The Irish, sir. They've taken up arms with the British. With the British, sir. They're shooting our boys." With that, O'Neill put his hands over his face and turned away.

"Captain Wilson! My horse. Take me to General Gibbon!"

LANE

Near Saratoga, New York
January 1864

Low clouds made the late afternoon sky seem later than it was on an already gray day. In the early afternoon, Union troops, who had begun the day in darkness, marching from their camp on Viola's farm north to Saratoga, streamed by her farm again, this time headed south. First the supply wagons, a long lumbering column guarded by anxious cavalrymen, urging them to keep going, step lively. Then ambulance wagons, filled with the wounded, the groans audible as the wagons bounced along the dirt road. Now, as the light began to fade, infantry units, the soldiers dirty and grim-faced with the mark of defeat on them.

Lane stood next to Viola, watching the Army of the Potomac retreat, another stain on their record, perhaps this time a fatal one. Their presence, a White man and a Black woman, drew hardly a glance from the passing soldiers, their eyes downcast at the road or far away.

Lane thought about his own war, and his own foolish anticipation about seeing combat. Then the grim reality of terror and defeat, and in his own case, a permanent reminder of what he'd lost.

Up the road, Lane could see a group of men on horseback, officers obviously, parting the foot soldiers as they rode at a trot. He heard one of them shout, "Make way for General McClellan, make way there." Exhausted soldiers moved to the side of the road. The general sat tall in his saddle, looking straight ahead, saying nothing. Lane recognized Captain Wilson, the soldier who had come to Viola's house late one night while Lane watched from the barn. Wilson spotted Viola and reined his horse.

"British dragoons are right behind us ma'am. You might want to come with us. No telling what their plans are for the civilian population."

"I have my family. I'll be fine here."

Wilson touched the brim of his blue felt hat, glanced for a moment at Lane, and was gone, cantering ahead to catch up with McClellan.

Viola turned from the road and began walking back to the house. Lane followed.

"You seem to know him pretty well."

She stopped. "I suppose I do. I've been providing him with information about the British camp, their defenses."

Lane walked quickly to keep up with her. "You really are a spy."

She stopped and looked Lane squarely in the eye. "I'm just someone who doesn't support slavery. Or put her own romantic dreams ahead of doing the right thing. So yes, I risked everything to help the only way I knew how. Can you say the same thing? What was your role in what happened today?"

"You'd have done the same thing. You're working to free your people. I'm working to free mine." It sounded hollow, and Lane knew it. *What in God's name have I done?*

"John. You told me yourself that in your country children can go to school. You can leave the country if you want to, like you did.

You can work for wages. You can own land. It's not against the law to teach someone to read. Do you really think it's like for like?"

Lane was silent as they entered the house.

"You can't stay here any longer. I can't have you under this roof."

"Why don't I help you move Michael and Sarah to the next stop? On your railroad. I'll attract less attention than you will."

"You think that will cleanse your soul? Your sins will be forgiven?"

"Tell me where they need to go. We can leave immediately. It will be safer if I move them."

DAVIS

Richmond, Virginia
January 1864

Jefferson Davis was uncharacteristically calm, reading from a stack of newspapers arranged neatly on the floor next to his chair. His wife looked up from the socks she was knitting by the fire.

"You've become a voracious reader of newspapers, Northern and Southern."

Davis didn't look up. "Good news has its salubrious effects on the mind."

"I see. Have you heard directly from General Burgoyne?"

"Yes. The newspaper reports are generally true. He routed McClellan at Saratoga. *Routed* is my word. I believe the general's message mentioned a 'providential outcome.' Perhaps I should introduce him to General Jackson."

"What of these rumors about Irish soldiers?"

"Burgoyne didn't mention them, but it seems to be true. Longstreet reports that Irish regiments didn't simply stack arms. They came over to our side and actually fought with the British. Took up arms against their former comrades. Welcome news, I'm sure. But frightening at the same time."

Varina pondered his words. "You refer to our slaves."

Davis finally looked up from his newspaper, frowning. He disliked the word. "Perhaps I am. If Irish soldiers can so easily turn on a promise of future freedom, what's to stop our people from doing the same?"

"There are those in your government who favor the arming of slaves. Forming Black regiments as Lincoln has done. To counter the manpower advantage of the North."

Davis shuddered. "The sooner we can put an end to this war, the sooner we can go back to living our lives as before. General Burgoyne has done his part for now. It will not be George McClellan who drives a stake through the cause of Southern independence. Sam Grant is another matter."

"When will you recall General Longstreet and his troops from Washington City?"

Davis looked at his wife. She has the logical mind of an engineering officer. "Pete has his orders. He'll begin sending troops south later this week. We'll leave Fitz Lee and his cavalry there for a time to delay McClellan's entry into the city. What I fear most is Grant and McClellan uniting their forces and marching on Richmond."

Davis paused and smiled. "But that's probably what George fears the most as well."

"My understanding is that General McClellan is commander of all Union armies, and therefore outranks General Grant."

"As always you are well informed my dear. That is indeed the case. How that will sort itself out on the ground may be a different matter, however. I'm certain that keeps Mr. Lincoln pacing the floor of his Philadelphia hotel room, as if he needed more reasons. He will surely look for a way to promote the interests of General Grant."

Varina laughed. "Jefferson Davis, are you taking pleasure in Mr.

Lincoln's discomfort? If not for the victory at Gettysburg that could be you, us, pacing a hotel room floor, in Nashville or Birmingham."

"It may yet be us."

"When might we expect General Grant to pay us a call?"

"If it were any other man, I'd say he would take his time, let the magnitude of McClellan's humiliation sink in. Let the newspapers and the public beg for him to hasten to save the Union. Grant is different. He will come when he's ready to fight. I should expect to hear from him in a couple of weeks. Possibly sooner."

"And what can we expect from General Burgoyne?"

"That, my dear, is the question on my mind as well. The British interest is in a divided and weakened union, and Southern independence directly serves that interest. I expect General Burgoyne to do what's in his power to bring a negotiated end to the war. He will press McClellan. But will he help us defend Richmond from Grant? Possibly subject his army to a prolonged siege? He will have studied his Cornwallis."

"You believe that General McClellan will re-occupy Washington when General Longstreet abandons it. Could General Burgoyne not then retake it from McClellan?"

"Quite probably. But it may serve our interests for Burgoyne to occupy McClellan and the entire Army of the Potomac while we deal with General Grant." Davis paused and looked at his wife. "You have an opinion so by all means let us hear it."

"Far be it from me to opine on military strategy. But as you once said, Longstreet is the very devil when defending ground. It is only common sense to keep McClellan's and Grant's armies separated."

"I shall inform Longstreet that you are in agreement. He will sleep better at night."

BURGOYNE

Between Saratoga and Albany, New York
January 1864

Sixty years of soldiering had taught John Burgoyne many things. Among them, that there was a time for decisive action, moments to be seized, opportunities that would not present themselves again. Another, that sometimes—not often, but sometimes—it was best to let your defeated enemy get away. This was one of those times. Burgoyne was certain he could have pursued McClellan's army, its troops beaten and demoralized, and destroyed it. His officers were anxious to do exactly that. Burgoyne thought of the hunt back home, that moment when men and horses all sensed it was time for the kill. It was like telling the hunters to let the fox go.

Burgoyne rode south at the head of his long column, surrounded by staff officers. He had sent Gordon and Campbell back to be with their troops, tired of their entreaties to let them finish the job. Bloody great fighters, they'd proven that again, but not grand strategists, and not given to silent acceptance.

Packenham rode next to Burgoyne, occasionally looking over as if to ask, though aware that he should not ask, "Explain this to me, please." Very well. "Thomas, you're wondering why we're taking our time, following General McClellan but a half day behind him."

Burgoyne watched. Obviously conflicted, Packenham was struggling for words. Finally, "Yes sir, if you please. We won, you won, a great victory indeed, sir. But we could have finished them off, sir. And still could."

"Of course you're right, Thomas. But consider. General McClellan has created an enormous problem for Mr. Lincoln. Should he fire him, again? Force him to turn and fight us, again? Hurry him, if the man can be hurried, back to Washington City to face General Longstreet? Do you recall the Iron Duke's toast?" Silence. "Well, I recall the Iron Duke's toast, though I was but your age at the time: *'Confusion to Bonaparte.'* We have succeeded in confusing our enemies, and that may serve us as well as the destruction of their army."

Packenham rode along, considering. "If I may, sir. You believe you can achieve the same goal, recognition of Southern independence, while sparing your men. And prolonging the, em, crisis of leadership in the Union army."

Burgoyne smiled. "I don't give a jot for Southern independence, Thomas. Slaveholders and faux aristocrats. The crown and the empire will be well served if the United States sees its territory, population and economic power cut in half. And yes. Mr. Lincoln's leadership predicament serves that interest well."

"Will we follow General McClellan all the way back to Washington City?"

"We shall, at least for the time being. Mr. Lincoln may want to ask President Davis for terms, though I doubt it. My guess is that Lincoln is banking on his General Grant coming east and changing the current course of the war. He shall wager his future on Grant's ability to retake Washington and then capture Richmond. If Grant can accomplish those things, the North may still be able to subdue and defeat the South. Much will then depend on us, will it not?"

Ahead of them they could see a wagon on the road, coming toward them, with four people aboard. As it approached, the dragoons who were escorting the general rode forward to wave it off the road.

Burgoyne recognized John Lane, the Fenian, riding alongside the driver, the young woman who delivered provisions to his army. In the back of the wagon were a man and a woman, both Black.

Burgoyne reined his horse to a stop. "Mr. Lane, my compliments. You were as good as your word. Young lady, I see you have a cargo of people rather than potatoes today. This army still needs to eat."

McCLELLAN

George McClellan sat in the special rail car, the same one that had brought him north. Nelly was by his side, having boarded in New York. McClellan had ridden with the army as far as Albany. Though the city was emptying out in anticipation of the arrival of British troops, the trains to New York City were still running. McClellan had given Meade detailed orders on taking the army south, as far as Baltimore. By the time they regrouped there it should be clear whether Longstreet would defend Washington City or fall back toward Richmond. He suspected the latter.

As they parted ways in Albany, Meade asked, "You're going to see the old man in Philadelphia?" Meade was aware that McClellan had been summoned again by Lincoln.

After a silence, McClellan had said, "No. There's no time. I'll take the train directly to Baltimore. By the time you arrive we shall have detailed plans for retaking the Capital."

Meade was silent for a full minute. "And Burgoyne? He's a half day behind us, biding his time. What if he offers battle between here and Baltimore?"

"Refuse it. This is meaningless real estate. The capitals hold the key. We shall retake Washington City. We shall have General Grant hold it and defend it from Burgoyne. And the Army of the Potomac will capture Richmond and put an end to the war."

Meade nodded. "Fair enough." He hesitated. "George, you know if the weather cooperates and we can ford the rivers, it will take this army fifteen long marching days to reach Baltimore. We can be there in just a few days if we use the rails and boats."

"I need you to stay in contact with the British, in case Burgoyne moves on New York City or Philadelphia. By the time you arrive, Grant should be there with advance elements of his army, of our army, and we'll be able to affect my plan. Move as quickly as you can, General."

McClellan and Nelly had ridden silently for hours, the general's mood black and sullen. As they neared Baltimore, Nelly said, "George, your army is intact. You'll soon be reinforced by General Grant and his Western Army. My guess is that you will find Washington City lightly defended, or perhaps not defended at all, and you'll be hailed as the liberator. Things are not as dark as they may have seemed."

McClellan, who had been looking out the window for the entire trip, turned and looked at Nelly. Everyone is a field marshal. Meade. Lincoln. Now Nelly. "General Grant will have no intention of reinforcing me. He will understand the weakness of my position with Lincoln. No. General Grant will want no part of garrison duty in Washington City. He will want to attack Richmond."

"Then you will give him orders."

"And if he refuses my orders? Neither Lincoln nor Stanton will support me against Grant. The hero of Vicksburg."

"You yourself said that Sam Grant doesn't have a political bone in his body. His prize is Richmond. You have your eyes on a larger prize."

McClellan was quiet, brooding. Finally, he said, "That's just it. Sam isn't seeking the prize I'm seeking. My fear is that he'll win it without even trying. The rough-hewn man from the West, the man on horseback, wanting only to serve his country. Who can resist? God help us."

"What happened with the Irish soldiers? Are the stories in the newspapers true?"

McClellan scowled. "Yes. Damned traitors. Whole Irish units surrendered to the British, then took up arms against us. It cost us the battle. We were holding our own against their attacks, and I was preparing to send in our reserves, which would surely have carried the day for us. But the whole left flank of the line crumbled when the Irish surrendered. I've issued an order: Any soldier caught with Fenian literature, or caught plotting with the Fenians, will be shot."

Nelly considered. "It might be instructive to make an example. As a precaution to further traitorous behavior."

McClellan turned back to the window.

LANE

Between Albany and Saratoga, New York
January 1864

Riding in the wagon next to Viola, with Michael and Sarah in the rear, Lane first saw a vast dust cloud rising from the road, then red-coated soldiers on horseback. General Burgoyne and his staff reined to a halt.

"Mr. Lane, my compliments. You were as good as your word. Young lady, I see you have a cargo of people rather than potatoes today. This army still needs to eat."

"Just out to buy more provisions now," Viola said. "I'll come find you when I have goods to sell."

"Please see that you do. You've hired more helpers? Business must indeed be brisk."

"My brother and his wife. Visiting."

"Yes, of course. Well, we've an army to follow and perhaps more business to attend to. Mr. Lane, we shouldn't be hard to find when the time comes."

With that, Burgoyne spurred his horse and his staff followed.

Packenham touched the brim of his hat and smiled as he rode past. Behind, the red-coated host stretched farther than they could see. Viola pulled the wagon off the road, and they bumped along slowly through bare farm fields as the British army streamed past.

They rode silently, Viola picking her way along and the others holding on tightly.

Lane inquired, "How much farther?"

"I'll let you know when we get there. We turn off the main road in another half mile."

"Do you think they suspect what we're doing?"

"The fact that we're traveling in broad daylight makes them less suspicious rather than more. But they don't care. If they cared at all about slavery they'd be on the other side, wouldn't they?"

Lane thought about the events of the last few weeks. His quiet life in Boston, teaching Gaelic to boys who wanted nothing more than to be American, their parents clinging to the old ways. Long hours reading and thinking about Irish history, about the wrongs inflicted by the British over 700 years. Romantic stories of failed revolutions and his frustration, knowing how they ended, and how what Ireland needed was fewer poets and dreamers and more warriors. And finally, his big idea to use the Irish soldiers in the Union Army to bring about Home Rule in Ireland.

And now, sitting next to Viola, glancing back at Michael and Sarah, the reality. That the direct consequence of his actions was the continued enslavement of millions of people. That would also be his legacy.

They rode on in silence. Viola turned the wagon onto a narrow lane, and the ride was smoother again. After ten minutes, Viola said, "That's the house ahead. Tell me if you see anyone, anyone at all. If you do, we'll just keep on moving and not stop."

Lane looked back at the man and woman riding in the back. They had been silent for the entire ride. They were no doubt suspicious of the White man riding up front.

"It was a mistake. I understand. I can't undo what I've set in motion."

Viola looked over and frowned. "It's never too late to repent. You just need to decide that's what you're going to do. You let me know when you've made up your mind. I have some ideas. You won't like them. Coming along on this ride isn't going to save your soul or right any wrongs. But maybe there's a way."

Lane was about to respond, but Viola said, "I don't see anyone. I'll take Michael and Sarah inside. John, put the horse and the wagon in the barn for now. Quickly."

DAVIS

Richmond, Virginia
January 1864

Jefferson Davis sat beside General Longstreet in matched wooden chairs in his office, both staring at snow flurries out the window. General Braxton Bragg, recently arrived from Tennessee, sat in a third chair, this one upholstered in gaudy fashion, and judging by style and wear, sometime early in the last century.

"General Bragg, welcome to Richmond. General Longstreet, thank you for coming. Gentlemen, I'm delighted to have our armies back on Southern soil and defending what is ours. Taking and holding Washington sent a powerful message to the Union, but our future lies not in conquering territory but in protecting it. General Longstreet, has McClellan re-entered the city?"

As usual, Longstreet didn't answer immediately, and, as usual, it wasn't clear to Davis if he had been listening.

Finally, "Fitz Lee made sure that McClellan couldn't just march into the city. Made him earn it. Fitz hit him hard at Wheaton and again at Silver Spring, but just hit and run, no interest in a general engagement. So yes, McClellan is back in Washington City, and I understand from our friends in the city that Lincoln and the cabinet are due back from Philadelphia at any time."

"And our own army?"

"Just like old times. Right now, I'm holding the line of the Rappahannock, but I've a mind to pull back closer to Richmond. Maybe as far south as Ashland Mill. I want to keep my supply lines short but still have room to maneuver."

"General Bragg, what's the current disposition of your men?"

"Sir, I've got 10,000 men camped along the James River west of the city. These are veteran troops, hard men. They're anxious to show what western boys are made of."

Longstreet briefly turned to look at Bragg, then returned to the window. His Methuselah beard helped hide his facial expression.

Davis caught Longstreet's glance. "General, your boys will indeed get a chance to show what they're made of, and soon enough. I understand that General Grant is on his way to Washington City. The last report we have is that he was seen boarding a train in Pittsburgh earlier this week, which means he may already be in Washington."

Without turning from the window, Longstreet said, "I believe Mr. Lincoln will send General Grant our way. Keep McClellan in Washington City to defend it from Burgoyne. We'll need Burgoyne to keep McClellan occupied so that his army doesn't join up with Grant's."

Davis hesitated, then said, "General Longstreet. Pete. We all know what Grant is capable of. What we must avoid is a siege. The Union has endless supplies of men and material, and we have neither. Grant must be defeated in the field, or at the very least driven back north. If Grant is allowed to dig in around Richmond, sooner or later he'll strangle us."

The huge clock in the corner ticked audibly. Bragg stared at Longstreet, who was studying the snow flurries with scientific interest. Bragg, uncomfortable with the silence, broke it by saying,

"Mr. President, my men are anxious for a fight and prepared to take the offensive."

Longstreet turned to Davis. "Maybe I've spent too much time with Jackson lately. But I'm thinking the good Lord saved him for a purpose. I believe it's nigh time to introduce General Jackson to General Grant. Of course, they met at the Academy, and in Mexico." And with a look at Bragg, "But Grant has never had to deal with the likes of our Stonewall out West."

Davis let the last remark sit in the air for a full minute. "General Bragg, you'll place your fine troops at the disposition of General Longstreet. Gentlemen, I expect the coming battle to decide our fate. Southern independence is in your hands."

BURGOYNE

Montgomery County, Maryland
February 1864

John Burgoyne sat on a stool in his tent, alone. He could hear other officers talking, too loudly, around the campfire outside his tent. Burgoyne knew well the importance of being seen, of talking to his officers and men, but he was tired and preferred to be alone.

He had followed McClellan's army south through New York, New Jersey, and Delaware, and was now encamped in Maryland, not fifteen miles from the Federals' capital. McClellan's retreat, for such it was, had run like a clock, covering twenty to twenty-five miles a day, a relentless pace for a defeated army. Burgoyne had maintained a half-day's march between the two armies, confident that McClellan had no intention of offering to fight.

Now that McClellan had re-occupied the city, Lincoln and his cabinet had returned as well from their exile, arriving by boat to avoid Burgoyne's army. The Northern newspapers ran bold headlines predicting an epic clash to decide, again, the fate of the capital and perhaps of the entire war. Burgoyne laughed to himself. What had they said about McClellan on the Virginia peninsula? Something about being bottled up. Now the Union's commander was stuck in Washington City, preparing for an attack that, God willing, would never come.

This is their fight, not ours, he thought. *Let Mr. Davis and General Longstreet fight Grant, who will come after them soon enough. We've done our part and keeping McClellan busy up here is as much as they can ask.*

Each day Burgoyne would send artillery to various locations outside the city to lob a few shells in, and each day he would send dragoons to harass one of the sixty-eight forts that defended Washington. *Let them know we're here, make them think that we're planning a major assault.* He laughed to himself again.

For the truth was, the weight of his father's humiliation at Saratoga no longer hung over him like a shadow. The word *Saratoga* no longer stuck in his throat. Those ghosts, if they ever existed, had been banished, and Burgoyne felt as though his time as a soldier, sixty years, was ending. A life of service, of duty. But in the solitude of this Maryland winter evening, he realized that he cared not a jot for Southern independence. And more, he didn't care that he didn't care.

"Thomas?" Pakenham stuck his head in through the tent flap.

"Sir?"

"It has been some time since you've visited your friends in Richmond. Have you a mind to pay a call?"

Packenham's face was aglow in the dim lantern light, a smile stretching ear to ear. "Indeed I do, sir. I long for southern climes."

"Just so. See to a very good horse and provisions, and one of your ridiculous civilian disguises. I should like you to deliver a message to President Davis."

McCLELLAN

Washington, DC
February 1864

George McClellan arrived at the Executive Mansion ten minutes early for his meeting with President Lincoln. John Hay, the president's personal secretary, met the general at the Pennsylvania Avenue entrance. The soldiers standing guard stood at attention, arms at their sides, as Hay led McClellan in silence through the doors and down the long corridor to Lincoln's office. Hay tapped on the door, opened it without waiting for an answer, and stepped aside to let McClellan enter.

Lincoln was seated on a cushioned chair, with his back to the door. Across, on a small sofa, sat General Ulysses S. Grant. Grant's eyes met McClellan's and held the gaze.

Lincoln turned and rose to greet McClellan.

"General McClellan, thank you for coming this morning. I believe you know General Grant."

McClellan nodded. Grant hesitated, slowly stood, and said, "General McClellan was one of the cadets we looked up to at the

Academy, and we crossed paths in Mexico." He stuck out his hand, and McClellan had no choice but to grip it firmly.

It was clear that Lincoln and Grant had been meeting for some time, and McClellan could sense that things had been decided. He had arrived early to the meeting, but too late.

"General Grant was just telling me about the final days at Vicksburg."

"A great victory, General. Congratulations." Grant nodded but said nothing.

"General Grant arrived on the cars yesterday, along with his staff and a couple of regiments of infantry. The bulk of his army will arrive within ten days. How many, General?"

Grant was staring at McClellan. "All told, 50,000 men of all arms, give or take. Mostly infantry. The cavalry will take longer; they're coming overland. I've put Sheridan in charge of them. He's got some, uh, modern notions about the use of cavalry."

McClellan noted that Lincoln had said "his army," referring to Grant's men. *He means my army. They're all under my command, Grant included.*

McClellan stared back at Grant. "Fifty thousand men? I'd assumed you'd bring more."

Grant was slow to respond. "It's enough. I left the bulk of my army with Sherman to look after Joe Johnston."

"General McClellan, perhaps you can tell us about the Irish soldiers. What happened in New York?"

McClellan felt the anger rising in his throat. *He's doing it again. He's going to fire me or worse, demote me and put me under the command of Grant.*

"Traitors," McClellan said. "There's no other word for it. They didn't just surrender, they switched sides and actually fired on our troops. The battle was well in hand. We were on the cusp of total victory."

Lincoln and Grant were silent, until Lincoln spoke. "I was

shocked to hear that General Meagher was involved. I understand that a braver soldier never wore the uniform. We have to make an example of the leaders. Pinkerton wired—"

Lincoln searched among papers on the table in front of him and held up the one he was looking for.

"Pinkerton wired that he has arrested Meagher and an accomplice, a John O'Mahony, who says he's the leader of the Fenian Brotherhood. He found them in New York City, not even trying to hide. They'll be tried for treason."

Grant spoke quietly. "Shoot them."

"Beg your pardon, General?"

"Shoot them. No need for a trial, but if you need one, give them to me and I'll put them through a military tribunal. We'll get it done quickly. I've got thousands of Irish soldiers in my army. They need to know what happens to traitors."

McClellan looked at Grant, then at Lincoln. *"My army"* again. "They'll need lawyers."

Grant spoke louder this time, a man confident in himself and in his surroundings. "Fine. We'll shoot the lawyers as well."

Lincoln boomed a high-pitched laugh. *Inappropriate to the moment,* thought McClellan.

"That reminds me of the story of the lawyer, the debutante, and the devil."

McClellan interrupted. "Mr. President, I know your time is valuable. Now that General Grant has joined us, should we not discuss the chain of command, and plans to capture Richmond?"

The smile left Lincoln's face. He shot a quick glance at Grant, who was looking at his boots. "Indeed, we should, General. Indeed, we should."

LANE

Between Albany and Saratoga, New York
February 1864

John Lane shivered as he sat on the dirt floor of Viola's barn.
The blanket wrapped around his shoulders didn't stop the shaking.
It was more than the bitter cold that was making him shiver.

He read again the headlines of the *Albany Argus*, which Viola
had fairly thrust into his hands the evening previous. After their
return from delivering Michael and Sarah to the next stop on the
underground railroad, Viola had driven the wagon into town to
purchase more potatoes for Burgoyne's army, now a half-day's ride
south of her farm, following McClellan's retreat at a distance. The
newspaper had caught her eye in the store.

The headlines screamed:

Treason in the Ranks!
Irish Soldiers in Diabolical Fenian Plot!
Join Rebel Army, Fire on our Boys!
Leaders Caught, to be Hung!

Woodcuts of O'Mahony and Meagher accompanied the story. Meagher was dressed in his uniform as colonel of the Irish Brigade, Napoleonic hand inserted in his tunic. Lane read the story again, sick to his stomach. Pinkerton's men had arrested O'Mahony and Meagher without a struggle at O'Mahony's office in New York City. While the headline announced that they'd be hung, the article quoted General Grant's announcement that they would be shot as traitors. Grant also said that other leaders, including a one-armed Irish merchant, were still at large and would be hunted down and shot as well. Lane read no further.

The door to the barn opened and Viola entered, a tray of steaming food in hand. She placed the tray on the floor next to Lane and stood above him, hands on hips.

"You know you can't stay here. I have too much at stake. My family and my, uh, work."

Lane looked up, still shaking. "I have no place to go. I can't go home to Boston. They're looking for me. They'll shoot me. Or worse."

Viola looked angry but her voice was low and calm. "John, you knew what you were getting in to. Or you should have. I'll pack some food for you. I think you have two options. You can head south and seek protection from the British Army. Or you can head north to Canada. But you have to leave here. The Union soldiers know we were, um, business partners. They'll start looking for you here."

Lane was trying to think clearly. The easiest thing to do was head south, find the British Army, and ask Burgoyne for protection. But there was no guarantee that he would help, and then what? Better to get away from the war altogether. Canada.

"Can I use your network, your railroad, to get to Canada?"

Now Viola sounded as angry as she looked. "You hatch a plot to support Southern independence and slavery, and now you want to jeopardize a network that helps people escape from slavery? You've some nerve!"

Lane stood, letting the blanket fall to the ground. "Please. They'll shoot me. It's my only chance."

After a long silence, Viola said, "Eat that before it gets too cold. I'll bring you some food to pack. You should leave as soon as it gets dark. You've got a long trip ahead of you."

DAVIS

Between Richmond and Ashland Mill, Virginia
February 1864

Jefferson Davis had been in the saddle for almost three hours, and was nearing Ashland Mill, some twenty-five miles north of Richmond. Longstreet, good to his word, had brought his army south from the line of the Rappahannock to the line of the South Anna River. A less formidable natural barrier, to be sure, but that much closer to Richmond. Longstreet wanted short supply lines and easy communications for the coming battle.

Davis had read the papers searching for clues to Grant's intentions. But Davis knew that the best clue was the man himself. Grant had little nuance. He came at you with overpowering force, and the question wasn't if Grant would attack, but when and from whence.

Grant. If the Northern papers were to be believed, McClellan remained in overall command of the Union armies. But he would remain in Washington, defending the Northern capital from Burgoyne's army, camped barely fifteen miles from the city's ring of defenses. Grant would take the field. Davis imagined Lincoln threading that needle. He couldn't think of two people less inclined to entertain Lincoln's stories and jokes than Grant and McClellan, the one all business, the other all pride. *Serves Lincoln right. I'm not the only one who has to balance prickly egos.*

Davis found Longstreet sitting on a stump between his tent and a campfire, whittling with an oversized knife. *What is it about whittling?* Davis' upbringing hadn't included time for idle knife play. Off to the side, silently, stood Bragg with a gaggle of officers, some of whom Davis knew, others whom he didn't recognize. Westerners.

Longstreet stood up slowly, then tossed the knife point first into the dirt with a practiced motion. "Good morning, Mr. President. Here to see the fireworks?"

Longstreet's attempt at humor was weak but appreciated for its rarity.

"I plan to leave the fireworks to you, General. I'm here to ask if there is anything you need."

Longstreet smiled. "A hundred thousand more men and a million rations. And some cannon. And a new pair of boots."

Davis returned the smile. "Where is Grant?"

"Still camped on the Maryland side of the Potomac, last I heard. He has infantry arriving every day on the cars. Our friends tell us that Sheridan now has the cavalry and will be arriving in a week or so. Fitz Lee is watching the Potomac fords and we'll know when Grant moves south."

Davis listened intently and considered. *I can't ask Pete too many questions. But I need to know what he has in mind.*

"And when Grant crosses the Potomac, you'll wait for him here?"

It was Longstreet's turn to consider. *He needs to know what I'm up to. He has that right.*

"Yes and no. Sam Grant isn't Burnside or Hooker. We can't let him get a head of steam up. Fitz will contest the crossings. He'll harass Grant's supply trains. I'll be dug in here, waiting for him. But our Stonewall will have a surprise in store."

"A flanking movement?"

"That's right. Like Chancellorsville, only with twice as many men. We're counting on Grant being undermanned for once, and we're banking on his propensity to move in straight lines. McClellan will keep as many men as he can in Washington City and force Grant to travel light. That's our opportunity."

Propensity? Has the general been reading of late? Quietly, Davis asked, "And what about General Bragg and his frontier ruffians?"

Longstreet smiled again. "General Bragg's men are anxious to prove their western mettle. They'll be positioned between my men here and Grant. They'll take the first blow and take the measure of Grant's army for us. Their orders will be to engage in a fighting retreat, lure Grant here, and give Jackson time to mount his flanking movement."

Davis could see it all in his head. An ambitious plan. *Maybe my immovable rock finally understands the need for maneuver and aggressive action.*

Longstreet was positively voluble now. "What do you hear from Burgoyne?"

Davis frowned. "I had a visit from one of his officers. An extraordinary young man. Passes through enemy lines like an eel through your fingers. Burgoyne has no plans to go on the offensive. He's content to keep General McClellan bottled up behind the defenses he himself designed. There's some justice and satisfaction in that I suppose. Burgoyne does feint, posture and threaten, artillery shells and the like. A chip off the playwright father."

Longstreet could sense Davis' unspoken disappointment. "Hmmph. I'd be content with a little less playacting and a little more gunpowder. But this was always our fight and I suppose we'll have to deal with Grant on our own."

BURGOYNE

Montgomery County, Maryland

March 1864

Burgoyne was in his tent, poring over maps drawn by his topographical engineers. They showed Washington City and the ring of forts and batteries which surrounded it. Burgoyne was aware of the great irony, that George McClellan, now hunkered down behind those defenses, had in fact designed them.

As an engineer, Burgoyne had a keen interest in and understanding of military fortifications, and from a purely professional standpoint he liked what he saw. McClellan was clearly capable, and the placement of the defenses was quite sound.

But Burgoyne's interest in Washington's defenses was, at this point in the war, purely academic. He had no intention of attacking in force. Knowing McClellan as an opponent, as he now did, he was quite sure that it was enough to threaten and feint to keep the Union Army immobilized in the city. McClellan, and Lincoln, couldn't afford to let their capital fall once more.

Outside the tent, a horse's hooves pounded to a halt. A sentry poked his head through the tent flap.

"Major Packenham has returned, sir."

"I'll see him at once."

Burgoyne smiled at the sight of Packenham standing at attention and saluting, while dressed in the guise of a prosperous businessman.

"The hat is a particularly nice touch, Thomas."

Packenham snatched the bowler hat from his head. "Beg your pardon, sir. Thank you, sir."

"What news from President Davis?"

Packenham seemed to struggle for words in uncharacteristic fashion. "I should describe him as disappointed, sir."

"Well. So. Life is full of disappointments, is it not?"

"Just so, sir. I believe President Davis had some expectation that this army might either launch a full attack on Washington City, or perhaps even swing south and defend Richmond."

"I can assure you, Thomas, that no such promises were ever made. Our agreement was always that we would launch a northern front, which we have done."

"Yes sir."

"What else, Thomas?"

"President Davis expects that General McClellan is charged with the defense of Washington City and that General Grant will take the field and advance on Richmond. I believe that President Davis fears a siege above all things."

"As well he should. His challenge is to defeat Grant in the field, or at the very least drive him from Southern soil once he begins his advance. We shall do our part in keeping General McClellan behind his formidable defenses."

McCLELLAN

Washington, DC
March 1864

McClellan sat alone in his study at his home in Washington City. He had returned from his meeting with President Lincoln and General Grant and had gone upstairs without a word to Nelly. He'd been in the study with the door shut for some hours.

Nelly climbed the stairs quietly, entered the study without knocking, and gently closed the door behind her. Without looking at her husband, who was seated at his desk, hands folded on his lap, she walked over to the fireplace. While her husband had spent countless days and months in the field, he was a hopeless fire maker while Nelly excelled at this as at most things.

She carefully ensured that the chimney was drawing, then lit the kindling. Within minutes, the fire was blazing and the temperature in the room, and the mood, began to warm.

"Are you still in the employ of the United States Army?"

A long silence, then, "Yes. In fact, I'm still it's commanding general."

"Well then. God is in his heaven."

"God may be in heaven, but Sam Grant is in the field. I'm to be an armchair general, working out of the War Department."

"But Grant's superior officer?"

Another long pause. "Yes, and no. I asked the president specifically if Grant would be operating under my command and my orders, and he said yes."

"But?"

"But then the president was at pains to explain that General Grant should enjoy 'considerable latitude' in carrying out my orders. 'In the interests of speed,' he said. I took that to mean that Grant would run his own show."

Nelly still stood next to the fireplace, in quiet contemplation. McClellan watched her. *I'm not sure who will take this harder, Nelly or me.*

"And what orders did you leave with Grant?"

"None." A pause. "I was reluctant to give orders that he might choose not to follow."

Nelly walked over and placed her hands on McClellan's shoulders. "I should think general orders, such as 'march on the enemy and destroy him' would do nicely in a situation such as this one. If Grant defeats Longstreet under your orders, perhaps there will be glory enough to go 'round."

McClellan laughed, but there was no humor in it. "Yes, perhaps. But who would you vote for? The general who almost won the war three times, then sat in an office in Washington when the final victory was won? Or the homespun man of the West, the man of few words, the son of the frontier who crushed the enemy in the West then crushed him in the East? The man of the hour, and of destiny. The answer is plain."

"You yourself have said that Grant is not a political animal."

"And I believed it. But you should have seen him today in

Lincoln's office. Like he owned it. Measuring the curtains. I believe he senses his destiny."

"What will Grant do? How was it left?"

"That's the strangest part of this. It was left in the air. No talk of strategy, or even of the next move."

"Surely Grant will move on to Richmond?"

"Surely he should."

Nelly turned a log with the poker, and sparks flew up the chimney. "Come downstairs, George, and we'll have supper. The war isn't over, and the election campaign has yet to begin. You haven't lost either and may yet win both."

McClellan smiled in spite of his dark mood. He stood, looked around his study, straightened two of the maps on the wall, and followed Nelly downstairs.

LANE

Montgomery County, Maryland
March 1864

In the end Lane had opted for the protection of the British Army. He knew that Federal authorities were looking for him, and he knew that if caught he'd be hung or shot. Canada would have been closer and faster, but Viola had refused to let him use her network to try to get there.

Lane's trip south, in search of Burgoyne's army, had been faster and easier than expected. He had simply boarded a train in Albany, changed in New York City, and gotten off in Baltimore.

He had watched closely, certain that Pinkerton men would be out in force searching for him, but in fact he'd noticed nothing out of the ordinary at the train stations or on the cars themselves. He'd bought a newspaper in New York City, and learned, to his shock, that O'Mahony and Meagher had been convicted of treason by a military tribunal, then shot. Perhaps the authorities, and the public, would be satisfied with this very public punishment and lose interest in pursuing other conspirators.

In Baltimore, Lane had taken a day to try to learn the exact whereabouts of the British Army. He'd read the papers, but all they could tell him was that Burgoyne was encamped in Montgomery County, outside of Washington City. As always, he figured the best place to get good information was a tavern.

Taverns were easy to come by in Baltimore. He remembered that from his brief time there recovering from his war wound. He entered a likely establishment and was shocked to see three British soldiers seated at a table, obviously closer to the end than the beginning of their drinking. Bottles and glasses littered the table.

Lane hesitated, then approached. "Might I buy you gentlemen a drink?"

All three stopped short, turned, and looked up at Lane. After a pause and a professional sizing-up, which included a long gaze at his empty sleeve, one answered, "Well you might."

Lane went to the bar, bought a bottle of whiskey, got a glass for himself, and sat in the empty fourth chair at the table. He opened the bottle, poured what he considered a generous portion in three of them and a half-ration in his own, raised his glass and said, "Cheers." Two of the soldiers answered "*Slainte.*" The third mumbled something unintelligible.

Lane couldn't believe his luck. He considered asking in Irish, but instead said in English, "Where are you lads from?"

"Mayo."

"Kerry."

"Cork."

"Cork, is it? I'm a Kilcrumper man myself. Near Fermoy."

There followed a jumbled conversation, two of the soldiers far gone in their cups and aiming to fight each other or a willing third party, and the third, the Corkman, beside himself with his good fortune of finding a neighbor with ready money in a tavern in Baltimore.

Lane led his new friend gently around to the subject of the

whereabouts of his army. "What brings you to Baltimore at all, and your army camped near Washington?"

"Grub. We've eaten every chicken and suckling pig in the County of Montgomery and sure the sergeant sent us here to the city to buy food."

"And have you done so? Bought food?"

"And isn't the wagon out front full to the brim with potatoes and carrots and eggs and flour? We're just having a wee cup before heading back."

"I'm headed that way myself. Would you mind at all giving me a lift?"

The all-night wagon ride had been cold and bouncing, and at times Lane had to take the reins himself as the soldiers slept off their revelry. Morning found him at the edge of the British camp, talking his way past British guards, telling them that he had important information for General Burgoyne. It took the whole morning and numerous trips back and forth to headquarters for the guards to determine that Lane really did know Burgoyne, and that he might indeed have information of value. Eventually an officer appeared on horseback, jumped to the ground, smiled, and Major Packenham said, "Mr. Lane, I'm delighted to see you again. General Burgoyne will see you now."

DAVIS

Richmond, Virginia
March 1864

Jefferson Davis was unable to sit still as he awaited news.
He had spent his day pacing his office one end to the other, twenty-three steps, and reading the very occasional dispatches from his commanders in the field.

Now he was at home, pacing in the slightly smaller drawing room, seventeen steps in each direction.

Varina looked up from the wool socks she was knitting. "I suppose it would have little effect if I explained that your pacing does not hasten news from the front."

"None at all."

"Might you alight for a moment and explain the current situation?"

"I don't believe that I can."

"Alight, or explain?"

"Alight. And there's little to explain. Fitz Lee reported that Federal cavalry forced the Potomac crossings at first light. At multiple fords. There were sharp fights up and down the line."

"As expected."

Davis stopped in his tracks and stared at Varina for a moment, then continued his march. "Yes. As expected. Fitz and his boys are in constant contact with the Federal cavalry, which apparently came across in brigade strength. Maybe a couple of brigades." He looked at his wife. "A couple thousand troopers."

Varina continued knitting, a silent scolding, as if to say that the explanation of "brigade strength" was superfluous.

"Perhaps a couple of brigades, I say. They are raiding cattle, stealing horses, burning crops, and the like."

Varina, without looking up, said, "And you fear that it looks more like a cavalry raid than an invasion. You're wondering, where's the infantry?"

Davis stopped his pacing and sat in the chair next to his wife's. He placed the palms of his hands facing the fire. He was always cold, especially in that damn house. "That's precisely what I'm wondering. Fitz is watching the cavalry, and Bragg and his men are between Longstreet and the Potomac. Bragg reports no activity on his front." A long pause. "What is Grant up to?"

"Perhaps General Grant has no stomach for another Fredericksburg or Chancellorsville, and another 'On to Richmond' campaign that ends in mud and failure. Perhaps he's not the bumpkin butcher that they say he is."

Davis stared at the fire, and for the first time said aloud what he'd been thinking since midday. "You think he might be going after Burgoyne rather than Longstreet."

Varina laughed. "I'm hardly a military strategist, much less a mind reader. But if your General Grant isn't south of the Potomac, he must be north of it."

Davis could see it. The Federal cavalry was a diversion to keep our troops occupied. Grant could catch Burgoyne napping and, with luck, destroy his army or force him to retreat northward. Then Grant could wheel south, join forces with McClellan's troops, and come for Longstreet.

Davis rose from his chair and resumed pacing.

"Your first duty is to protect Richmond and our, uh, independence. I should think that the British Army can fend for itself. General Burgoyne was certainly in no hurry to attack Washington City, or to join forces with Longstreet. I don't believe you should send our boys running to help the British. You owe them nothing. They joined this war for their own purposes."

Davis was now practically running from one end of the drawing room to the other. "Yes, of course. But if Grant can defeat Burgoyne, or force him to retreat, then our path to independence narrows considerably. Perhaps fatally."

"What will you do?"

Davis thought about Robert E. Lee, puttering around his house in slippers, writing his memoirs. What would Lee do? Lee would do what he always did. Attack. "I'll go see Longstreet in the morning. We have some decisions to make."

BURGOYNE

Montgomery County, Maryland

March 1864

General Burgoyne was seated on a folding chair in his tent. John Lane stood before him, his hat in his good hand, looking tired and unshaven. And scared.

Major Packenham had led Lane from the guard outpost to the headquarters tent. Lane had spent enough time in army camps to see that in this one discipline was slack and the soldiers were relaxed. Anyone could see that this army was comfortable and not expecting to see action anytime soon. Lane deduced that Burgoyne would be content to threaten Washington City without actually attacking. *Hold McClellan in place and let Grant and Longstreet do the fighting.*

"Mr. Lane, I see that you've escaped capture. Thus far."

He apparently finds it amusing that I'm running for my life. "You know they've shot O'Mahony and Meagher. As traitors. And they're looking for me. I'm asking for your protection."

Burgoyne looked at Lane, the corners of his mouth upturned. "So, you'd like to join the British Army. Well, you'll find thousands of your compatriots in our ranks. You should feel at home."

Holding up the stump where his hand used to be, Lane said, "I'm not in a position to fight . . . I'm simply asking for protection."

Burgoyne tired of the game. "Major Packenham can take you to the Irish Brigade. Colonel—"

"Kelly."

"Just so. Colonel Kelly. I'm sure they can spare a shelter half and some potatoes. That will be all, Mr. Lane."

Lane didn't move. "You've every intention of keeping your promise, General? Regarding Home Rule for Ireland?"

Burgoyne, seemingly absorbed in looking at a map, did not look up. "I gave you my word, Mr. Lane. I'm a British officer and a gentleman. I am a man of my word." A pause. "Whether I am in a position to keep my word, that is a different question entirely. It will all depend on success in the field. You'll recall that our, em, arrangement was always contingent on success. On victory. On the Southern states winning their independence. No independence, no deal."

Lane felt sick as well as scared. He didn't know what he wanted anymore. Home Rule, certainly. But at the price of Southern independence and the maintenance of slavery? He thought of Viola.

Burgoyne finally looked up from his map. "I've no personal objection to Irish Home Rule, Mr. Lane. I've spent considerable time on your island and know many of your countrymen. In this army and in society. I would be pleased if our agreement were finally consummated. But as I say, it is out of my hands. Good luck to you, Mr. Lane."

As Lane turned to leave the tent, he heard a shrill whistle, rising in pitch, which he recognized immediately, followed by a tremendous explosion, followed by another, then another. In the distance, he heard the crack of a rifle, followed by the familiar ripple of rifled muskets discharging up and down a line.

Burgoyne pushed Lane out of the way, bursting through the tent flap to find chaos outside, men on foot and horseback shouting and charging in every direction.

Major Packenham rode up at a gallop, leapt from his horse as it stopped short, and yelled over the din. "The enemy is attacking in force, sir. From the west and the north, it would appear. Our men are falling back, and some are running. Sir, there is no time to lose. I suggest you mount and we find a place to make a stand."

Burgoyne stood motionless in apparent disbelief. He'd thought his war was over.

"Sir?"

"Yes, Thomas. We shall find a place to make a stand."

An orderly brought Burgoyne's horse on the run, and Packenham fairly threw the general up into his saddle.

"This way, sir."

Lane watched as red-coated soldiers came through the headquarters area in waves, some in small groups, stopping to fire. Others had dropped their weapons and were running as fast as they could. Lane joined the runners, knowing that he was literally running for his life.

McCLELLAN

Washington City
March 1864

Sitting in his office in the War Department in Washington, McClellan heard the distant boom of the big guns. He was accustomed to Burgoyne's hit and run tactics, sending a battery to a hill on the Maryland side of the Potomac and lobbing some shells into the city. This was different. These guns were much farther away, but from inside the building McClellan couldn't tell from which direction the sound was coming.

"Captain Wilson, if you please."

An officer appeared in the doorway before McClellan had finished speaking.

"Sir?"

"Captain, do we know what guns those are? Odd that Grant would force the Potomac crossings with artillery. Send the cavalry."

Wilson hesitated for an instant, and said, "Sir, the cannon fire is coming from north of us."

"North? Burgoyne's guns? Who would he be firing at so far a distance?"

At that instant another officer appeared at the door, one who looked like he'd just ridden a long distance very quickly. The officer, chest heaving and red in the face, looked at Wilson, then McClellan, saluted, and said, "Begging your pardon, sir. General Grant's compliments and he wishes to report that he has engaged the British Army in the vicinity of—" The officer pulled a paper from his pocket, glanced at it, replaced it, and continued. "He has engaged the enemy in the vicinity of Rockville. The enemy is in flight, and General Grant is in pursuit, sir."

McClellan stared at the officer in disbelief. "Have you come directly from General Grant, captain?"

The captain, at first believing he was the bearer of great tidings, began to understand that the commanding general might see things differently.

"Uh, I have, sir."

"When did General Grant begin his march toward Rockville?"

"That would have been yesterday evening, sir. A night march. We were in position by daybreak and attacked at midday. Many of the enemy soldiers were eating their lunch or sleeping. It was the most splendid surprise, sir." This last was said in a trailing voice, as if he no longer believed it.

"Indeed, captain. I shall have a message for you to take back to General Grant. Wilson, find the captain a change of horses and something warm to eat and drink."

After Wilson and the courier left together, McClellan slumped in his chair. So this was what Lincoln meant by *considerable latitude.* Undertaking a major attack within earshot of the Federal capital and the commanding general and sending notice only once the attack was underway. *It's exactly what I feared, but unacceptable nonetheless.*

McClellan took a sheet of writing paper from the desk, dipped his pen in the well, and began. *General: Your courier has informed me that a general action is underway against the British Army.*

McClellan stared at the paper, pen in hand, then carefully placed the pen back in the well. He crumbled the paper into a ball, stood up, and walked over to the fire, tossing the paper into the blaze.

Wilson returned, alone, and stood at the door at something resembling attention. McClellan put on his cloak and hat and walked past Wilson into the corridor.

Wilson scrambled to find his own cloak and ran behind the general. "Sir? Where are we going?"

"We're soldiers, Captain Wilson. To the sound of the guns."

LANE

Montgomery County, Maryland
April 1864

John Lane didn't stop running until the red-coated soldiers did. They had finally stopped, reluctantly, when their frantic officers fired in the air and hit them in the back with the flat of their swords. A line had begun to form, and some measure of order was restored. As more British soldiers arrived, the rabble became an army again.

Slowly the rout turned into a battle, lines of blue and red a couple hundred yards from each other, exchanging murderous fire. Lane found himself, almost unimaginably, with a company of Irish Brigade soldiers. Incongruous blue among the red. Someone said they were from the 28th Massachusetts Infantry. Lane remembered them from Fredericksburg. Among all the brave men trying to scale Marye's Heights, they had stood out.

The ground around Lane was littered with the dead and dying and their now unneeded weapons. He picked up a musket with his one hand and recognized it immediately as an old 1842 Springfield smoothbore, Meagher's weapon of choice when he commanded the

Irish Brigade. "Worthless against rifled muskets," he muttered. As soon as he picked up the weapon his arms and his one hand wanted to load and fire with that automatic precision that had been drilled into him, but it was no use with the one hand. He threw the weapon to the ground.

While his blood was up and he felt no fear, Lane realized it made no sense to stand on the line without a weapon. He turned and walked toward the rear, past officers, swords in hand, bellowing unheard orders over the din of the battle. Staff officers rode toward and away from the line, carrying desperate orders and requests for reinforcements, and supply wagons brought ammunition forward and wounded to the rear. It was all too familiar to Lane.

He had walked for ten minutes when he came to a small rise. A group of officers were seated on horseback, straining to see through the smoke. Lane recognized Burgoyne, with Major Packenham beside him.

Beyond the officers Lane came to a makeshift field hospital where surgeons performed their primitive triage and stacked discarded limbs like cordwood in the field next to the tent. A surgeon in a blood-soaked apron handed Lane an arm. Seeing Lane grab it with one hand, the surgeon seemed to briefly sense the irony, then returned to his desperate business. Lane gently added the arm to the pile.

In a moment of inspiration, Lane picked up a soldier's discarded red coat, which was lying on the floor of the field hospital. *I don't suppose the poor bastard will be needing this.* With his red coat and his one hand, Lane quickly blended into the ranks of the British wounded.

Lane turned to look as the noise of battle seemed to grow louder, and saw the human wave of red coats once again take flight. Officers were desperately urging their men to stand and fight, but one look at the rapidly approaching blue wave made clear that this day would belong to the Federal Army.

A line of wagons filled with the wounded was moving with the retreating soldiers, and Lane hopped into one. Nobody said a word. Twenty minutes later, Lane saw Burgoyne and his staff, escorted by dragoons, ride by at a respectable canter. *Careful not to look desperate or defeated,* thought Lane, *but in a hurry nonetheless.* Lines of British soldiers followed, defeated but still armed and under orders. They were all headed north.

DAVIS

Jefferson Davis had made the now familiar ride from Richmond to Ashland Mill a half dozen times in the past month. Each time the air had felt that much warmer, and he could follow Spring's progress as buds turned to leaves and the country roads became dustier with the warmer weather. While the weather was pleasant, the scars of war were everywhere. In deep thought, Davis barely noticed.

As he approached the rear of the Confederate lines, the sights and sounds were familiar. Soldiers supposedly on guard leaning lazily on their muskets, coming to something approaching attention as they realized who was in the saddle. Hostlers hitched and unhitched horses from wagons or watched as blacksmiths shoed them. A mostly empty field hospital served as a gathering point for idlers and staff officers.

Davis took it all in without really looking. He had decisions to make, decisions that could well determine the course of the war and the future of Southern independence.

As Davis and his small entourage entered the camp, he saw Longstreet approach on horseback, accompanied only by his ubiquitous staff officer, Moxley Sorrel.

Davis saw Longstreet pull a watch on a chain from his pocket and glance at it. *It must be about three o'clock,* thought Davis.

"I was tired of sitting in camp and was riding out to meet you. You're here sooner than I expected."

"I got an early start. Left Richmond at noon. A couple of hours in the saddle does an old soldier a world of good."

Longstreet turned and rode beside Davis the short distance to his headquarters tent. Longstreet dismounted slowly and looked up at Davis. *Does he do everything with purpose and care?*

"Pete, General, let's go for a ride."

Longstreet said nothing, but remounted his horse and followed Davis the way they had rode in. They rode side by side, the staff officers of each maintaining a distance behind though not ordered to do so.

"What do you know about Grant's attack?"

"Just that there was one, and that the latest information from Fitz Lee is that it's ongoing."

"What's he thinking?"

Longstreet pondered for a full minute. "I reckon Grant thinks he can defeat the British first, then come back for us."

"If he does defeat Burgoyne, there's no longer a reason for McClellan to stay bottled up in Washington City, defending the capital. Grant and McClellan could combine forces and send 200,000 men our way."

"We'd have no choice but to skedaddle. Even with Bragg's men, we can muster but half that number."

"Let's hope General Burgoyne is up to the task. He certainly dealt with McClellan in New York, but Grant's a different matter entirely." A pause. "And he hasn't seemed, uh, hell-bent on victory while camped in Maryland. Almost like he thinks the war is over."

"He'll have figured out it isn't over now that Sam Grant has punched him in the face."

They rode together in silence. Finally, Davis looked at Longstreet and asked, "What do you think of crossing the Potomac and helping the British?"

For once Longstreet answered immediately. He'd obviously been considering the idea as well. "Bad idea, sir. We have no idea what's happening, and it would take me the better part of a week to get there."

"I was thinking cavalry."

Longstreet again answered right away. "Yes, Fitz could cross the river and be there tomorrow, but I don't think 5,000 troopers are going to make a difference."

"Bragg?"

Longstreet made that sound in his throat. His version of a derisive laugh. "General Bragg is camped near the Great Falls, on the Virginia side, so yes, he's much closer to the action. I suppose he could cross the river and be on the field in thirty-six hours, but the battle will be long over by then. No. I think we have to wait for news, and trust Burgoyne will do what he came all this way to do. And maybe Divine Providence."

Davis' brow deeply furrowed, and he wore a dark frown. "I've never been particularly good at waiting, nor in trusting in Divine Providence."

Longstreet smiled. "You need to spend more time with our Stonewall. Most patient man I've ever known. When good things happen, it's Divine Providence. Bad things are generally God's will."

"When do you expect we'll know what happened?"

"I don't expect we'll get any reliable information until tomorrow. We'll hear from Fitz Lee first. He has people on the other side of the river."

Jefferson Davis was not happy that the fate of the Confederacy may have already been decided, and that he wouldn't know about it until tomorrow at the earliest. "I'll camp here with the army tonight, Pete. I'm three hours closer to the news."

"I can telegraph you in Richmond as soon as I hear."

"No. I want the news directly from the trooper who brings it."

Davis turned his horse and spurred him to a gentle canter. As if the increased speed would hurry the news. Longstreet followed, and they rode in silence back to camp.

BURGOYNE

Rockville, Maryland
April 1864

Burgoyne had recovered from his shock and was calmly giving orders to staff officers who rode off to deliver them to the line officers who were trying to stem the British retreat. He was seated on his horse, on a low hill north of Rockville, on the road to Gaithersburg. He turned to Generals Campbell and Gordon, who had ridden hard to find Burgoyne and get orders.

Always the engineer, Burgoyne gave a quick, professional look around. "This ground will do. We'll stand here. Tell your men we go no farther. They must stand and fight here."

Campbell nodded, and Gordon said, "Aye sir, it's as good a ground as any. My men will fight." With that, both spurred their horses and were off to find their troops.

Grant's initial attack had been overwhelming and a complete surprise. Burgoyne wondered how he'd gotten into position undetected. He'd been certain that Grant would head south, toward Richmond, and that his own war was all but over, nothing more than babysitting McClellan in Washington City.

Packenham rode up at a splendid gallop, reining his horse to a stop followed by two complete spins.

"What news, Thomas?"

"Sir, our line is stiffening. Order has been restored for the most part, and many of the men who ran have drifted back into the ranks. The enemy's attack seems to have run its course and now we're popping away at each other. It seems the worst has passed, sir."

"Just so, Thomas. We shall hold this line today and counterattack in the morning. I don't believe General Grant has a reserve, and we have thousands of men who barely fired their weapons today. With luck we'll drive them all the way back to Washington City."

Packenham was staring through field glasses toward the battle line, barely half a mile in their front.

"Thomas?"

"Sir, perhaps you might take a look at this."

Burgoyne took the field glasses and focused through the smoke on the blue line of soldiers. He saw a man on horseback, cantering back and forth in front of his troops, seemingly oblivious to the wall of lead pouring from the British troops.

"What is that man about? He's mad."

Packenham took the glasses from Burgoyne, and focused again on the Union officer, who had turned to face the British Army.

"Sir," said Packenham with uncharacteristic emotion. "Here they come!"

McCLELLAN

Rockville, Maryland
April 1864

McClellan and Captain Wilson, and a handful of staff officers
who had hastily saddled up and followed them out of the city, had
been riding hard for two hours, the noise of the guns growing louder
with the passing miles. As they neared the town of Rockville it was
clear that a general engagement was playing out just to the north.
They could feel the boom of the big guns, and the cracking of small
arms was constant and ever closer. Ahead, McClellan saw a squad
of Union cavalry in the road headed toward them. He reined up, his
horse snorting and pawing the ground, exhausted but, like its rider,
exhilarated.

Seeing the stripes on the sleeve of a cavalryman, McClellan
barked, "Sergeant, what soldiers are these?"

"Company I, Fifth U.S. Cavalry, General, sir."

"Do you know where I can find General Grant?"

"Sure, I know where he was an hour ago, sir. We're part of his
cavalry escort and he sent us to look for General Custer."

"Take me to him."

The sergeant hesitated.

"Now, sergeant!" McClellan spurred his horse forward and the trooper had no choice but to do the same.

"Follow me, sir!"

Not surprisingly, the troopers were fine horsemen on splendid animals, and it was all McClellan could do to keep up with them. *This is soldiering,* he thought. *To hell with a desk in the War Department.* Within minutes they rode up to a farmhouse, the sergeant and his troopers neatly clearing the fence before halting in the yard. McClellan and Wilson entered through the open gate, and McClellan dismounted.

Seated on the porch of the house, smoking a cigar and dressed in what appeared to be a common soldier's uniform, sat Ulysses S. Grant. He was alone, his staff officers huddled in the yard, now staring in disbelief at the sight of the commanding general walking briskly up the steps of the porch. Grant did not get up.

"General Grant, I received your message. Thank you for informing the commanding general that you were going into action."

Grant said nothing.

"What's the situation?"

Grant rose slowly, threw his cigar onto the porch, and stepped on it with his boot. "We made a night march last night. Left the campfires burning to make 'em think we were still there. Got ourselves into position to attack and did so in early afternoon. Seems we caught 'em completely by surprise. They ran like greyhounds at first, but sounds like they've regrouped north of here, just south of Gaithersburg. It's an old-fashioned standup fight now. That's what you're hearing."

Grant called for a map and placed it on the floor of the porch. With a stick, he pointed to a spot between Rockville and Gaithersburg. "Here. That's where the fight is."

McClellan stared hard at the map and seemed to be calculating something in his mind. "Thank you, General." Then, looking up, "I shall assume command in the field now."

Grant visibly stiffened. His ruddy face turned a brighter shade of red.

"Beg pardon, General?"

"I'm assuming command and shall ride to the front. Sergeant, you're with me. Take me to the skirmish line!"

The trooper, who had remained mounted, smiled and wheeled his horse. "Sure, it won't be hard to find General, sir."

"What's your name, Sergeant?"

"Tom Nealon, sir. County Mayo born and bred. Strong in the arm and weak in the head."

As they rode out the gate, McClellan asked, "You had no truck with the Fenian nonsense, Sergeant?"

Nealon spat to the side. "No sir. I've a gun and a horse and all the beans I can eat. I get to kill rebels, and now I get to kill bloody Englishmen. Shoot the bastards, I say. The Fenians, sir."

McClellan and his escort rode through the detritus of battle. Wounded splayed on the ground or walking to the rear, dead horses, overturned wagons, and all manner of military equipment—rucksacks, weapons, kepis, and Hardee hats—as the noise of battle grew deafening.

They pulled up their horses next to an officer on horseback at the rear of his regiment, which was shooting from a kneeling position at the red-coated army just 200 yards away. Smoke rolled back from the firing line. The captain, for a captain he was, recognized McClellan and saluted.

"Begging your pardon, General. What the hell are you doing here?"

"What regiment is this, Captain?"

"The 21st Wisconsin, sir. Captain Charles Walker, at your service. XIV Corps, First Division, Third Brigade."

McClellan nodded. "Late of the war in the west, Captain. Welcome to the east. I trust it's to your liking."

Walker looked hard at McClellan and shouted over the din. "Very much so, sir. Lovely weather."

"Does the Western Army generally put captains in charge of regiments?"

"No sir. Fortunes of war. I was next in line when the colonel and the other field officers were killed or wounded. Chickamauga. Chattanooga."

McClellan nodded again. "Speaking of the fortunes of war. Captain, I should like you and your fine soldiers to join me. We're going forward. We'll need to rally these regiments alongside you."

Walker didn't change expression. "Yes sir. Pennsylvanians and Wisconsin boys mostly. Good fighters. They'll follow my orders. Your orders, sir."

McClellan removed his sword from its scabbard and placed his hat on its tip. Raising it in the air, high over his head, he spurred his horse forward and forced his way through the line of soldiers. Reaching the front, he turned and faced the troops. He trotted up and down the line, a couple of hundred yards in each direction, still holding his sword in the air, speaking to the men who couldn't hear a word he said. But his intentions were clear. Returning to the front of the 21st Wisconsin, he reared his horse for effect, shouted, *"Charge!"* and set out toward the British lines at a slow canter.

At first incredulous and motionless, in an instant the Union troops moved forward like one man, screaming at the top of their lungs and running wildly after the man on horseback.

LANE

Harrisburg, Pennsylvania
May 1864

John Lane had alternated walking and riding in an ambulance as the British Army marched north. His red coat with the empty sleeve meant he attracted no undue attention. His Irish accent similarly seemed perfectly normal in an army that counted thousands of Irish soldiers among its ranks.

After Burgoyne's surrender, Lane had briefly contemplated heading south, crossing the Potomac into Confederate territory where he'd be safe. But he knew no one there, and now that the British defeat had ruled out Irish Home Rule, he had no plan. He figured it best to stay with the British Army as they made their slow but steady way back to Canada.

It had been a close call. Following the surrender, Pinkerton men, accompanied by hard men from the provost marshal, had gone through the British camp and removed Irish officers from the regiments that had turned coat. They were easy to find, with their blue uniforms and sullen, guilty-as-charged faces. There was no place to hide. Kelly of the Irish Brigade was among the first arrested, marched out of camp, and shot. Lane heard that a couple dozen officers had been dispatched in summary executions. The enlisted soldiers had been left alone. *Shrewd,* thought Lane. *Witnesses who could testify to the futility and deadly consequences of treason.*

Lane was sure they were looking for him, the one-armed merchant, but his split-second decision to don the British red coat had apparently saved him. No one gave him a second look.

Lane found it odd that the British Army was marching back to Canada, weapons and supplies in hand and leadership intact. Lane had imagined that surrender meant humiliation. At the very least he expected that the British fleet would come for them, in Baltimore or Philadelphia. Hadn't Cornwallis' men boarded ship for home after Yorktown? But rumor was that Lincoln himself had decided that the British would walk.

Lane wondered about the future of a one-armed fugitive tailor cum Gaelic scholar in Canada. Sure, there were Irish immigrants by the thousands there. He had relatives of his own, cousins, who lived south of Montreal in the so-called Eastern Townships. One thing was clear. The triumphant return to a free Ireland—the man who had brokered the deal for Home Rule with the Crown—would not happen in this lifetime. He wondered how many Canadian Irish would be willing to pay for their sons to learn the old language. *Not enough,* he mused.

DAVIS

Richmond, Virginia
May 1864

The enormous clock in the corner of Jefferson Davis' office struck the hour as the generals walked in, by design or coincidence Davis didn't know, but in descending order of rank. Longstreet, Jackson, Stuart, Bragg, and Fitzhugh Lee. They arranged themselves around the large wooden table with no fanfare, Longstreet seated to Davis' right. Despite his mood, dark as always, he smiled. One of the great things about soldiers is that there is no question who is who and who outranks whom.

"Gentlemen. Thank you for coming to Richmond. I'd prefer to meet you in the field, but this seemed the easiest place to bring you together."

The generals sat upright in their chairs, hands folded on the table, with the exception of Jackson. His good arm was elevated in the air, as if letting the blood flow out of it altogether. Davis caught himself staring, though Jackson seemed oblivious, or at least not to mind.

"General Longstreet, I should like to hear your account of where matters stand with the defeat of the British Army and their apparent retreat toward Canada."

For once Longstreet wasn't staring out the window. Perhaps the prospect of imminent attack by overwhelming numbers has focused his mind.

"Mr. President. Gentlemen. I'll speak for myself, but Grant's attack on the British Army caught me completely by surprise. And it seems General Burgoyne more so. From what I understand, the British Army broke under the first two attacks, but had made a stand near Gaithersburg and was holding its own. Grant was all in, no reserve, small force, no more than 50,000 men. I understand that the British had some hope of launching a counterattack the next day since many of their troops hadn't seen action for the running. Then, well, McClellan."

There was silence around the table, finally broken by Jackson, arm now resting by his side. "An astounding act of soldiering. Clearly deeply moved by the spirit."

There was more silence, though Stuart seemed to stifle a chuckle, pretending instead to cough.

Finally, Davis asked, "Does anyone know precisely what happened? Regarding General McClellan?"

Fitz Lee looked at Longstreet, who nodded. "Sir, it seems that McClellan, uh, rode to the battlefield from Washington City, assumed command, and then personally led a charge that spread all along the Federal front and which completely carried the day. The British were routed, and Burgoyne surrendered. To McClellan. I'm told Grant was not present at the surrender."

Davis looked at each of his generals in turn. Outstanding field commanders, Bragg excepted. But even he was a soldier and a man of unquestioned personal courage. They'd all been prepared to fight Grant. What did it mean that George McClellan had suddenly been reincarnated as Alexander the Great?

"General Longstreet, tell me what you have in mind."

Longstreet also looked around the table. "Stick to the plan. Let Grant, or McClellan, or Grant and McClellan, come south. Fitz will contest the crossings. General Bragg will engage and lure them south, a fighting retreat. The bulk of the army will await, dug in, at Ashland Mill. And General Jackson will execute a flanking movement in force. If possible, he'll work his way behind Grant, and we'll crush them between us."

All were leaning forward in their seats, imagining the scene as Longstreet described it. Only Jackson was leaning back in his chair, arm again raised above his head, eyes closed, and he seemed to be humming softly to himself.

Davis nodded in agreement at Longstreet's words. "Very good. And, forgive me gentlemen, if our bravest and best efforts are unable to stop the Federal advance?"

Longstreet looked directly at Davis and said softly, "I believe you know the answer to that question, Mr. President."

Davis had regretted the question even as he asked it. "Yes. I believe I do."

BURGOYNE

Near Allentown, Pennsylvania
May 1864

John Burgoyne insisted on riding his horse at the head of the long column of British soldiers and wagons, currently making its way through Pennsylvania en route to New York and, eventually, Canada. *I led the army into the United States, and I shall lead it back out,* he thought. It wouldn't do to ride in an ambulance or supply wagon.

While Burgoyne was not naturally curious about land and topography, except as it related to warfare and defenses, he had to admit it was beautiful country. Untouched by war, tidy and neat, like home, and so unlike the area around Washington. A clear delineation between north and south. *The south is ramshackle,* he mused. *A wonderfully descriptive word.*

Major Packenham rode up and settled in alongside the general. "Sir, General Campbell should like to know where you plan to make camp this evening."

Burgoyne smiled, a tired smile, and said, "General Campbell will know we're making camp when the column stops, and the men pitch their tents."

Packenham rode in silence for a minute, then replied, "Yes sir. When the column stops." He wheeled his horse and rode back toward Campbell somewhat slower than he had rode from him.

Burgoyne laughed to himself. *I should like to hear how Thomas phrases that to our Scots terrier.*

Half an hour later Packenham was back, looking none the worse for his encounter with Campbell. *He'll go far,* thought Burgoyne. *As well he should. The future of the Empire rests on the shoulders of such men. Perhaps Thomas will have the opportunity to lead an army on an adventure such as this someday. And perhaps he'll be up to the mark in a way that I was not.*

Burgoyne found himself thinking, yet again, about the Battle of Gaithersburg, as the Northern newspapers were calling it. Or, inevitably, the *Gaithersburg Races.* Had he let the army down? The queen? Or had it been one of those moments when a single man seized history by the scruff of the neck and bent it to his will. McClellan. *It will never do to underestimate your enemy.*

Burgoyne knew that, in fact, it was both. Yes, McClellan had perhaps changed the course of history through one incredible act of leadership and bravery. But Burgoyne knew, without saying the words, that he had let the army get lazy in the weeks encamped north of Washington City. They were unprepared for Grant's surprise attack, and it was his job to see that they were always prepared.

After sixty years in the field Burgoyne didn't need a watch to tell him the time of day. The sun was an hour from setting, and he turned his horse off the dirt road into a farm field and reined it to a halt. He looked around, saw open fields, nearby woods, and a small stream, and said with a smile, "Now Thomas, you can inform General Campbell that we shall camp here for the night."

Packenham watched as he slowly lowered himself from the saddle and handed the horse's reins to a staff officer. Then the general did the unthinkable. He lay down in the grass and was asleep in an instant. It had never occurred to Packenham before that General

Burgoyne was old, but now he saw before him a very old man taking a much-needed rest. Thomas shouted to the staff officers and dragoon escort, "We shall make camp here," then wheeled his horse and cantered off to find Campbell.

McCLELLAN

Washington, DC
May 1864

George McClellan was sitting in the drawing room of his home
in Washington City. He had been busy at his desk in his upstairs
office but had come down for the company. Nelly sat next to him,
reading from *The Atlantic*.

McClellan had papers on his lap, but what he really wanted was
to talk.

Nelly looked up and smiled, sensing his need.

"I don't mean to interrupt your reading. *The Atlantic*. Well, well."

Nelly frowned. "An interesting piece, though rather crudely
rendered, I should say. 'The Man Without a Country.' One gets the
point early on, but the writer doesn't let go. Mr. Hale. It's an allegory,
if that's the correct word. He's really writing about the war."

McClellan gazed at Nelly. "I saw Lincoln today. And Grant."

Nelly closed the magazine and placed it on the table beside her.

"I see. Did he fete you as the hero of Gaithersburg? Or keep you
at arm's length, like someone apt to take his job from him?"

McClellan considered. "A little of both now that you mention it. He was, of course, delighted that the British were defeated and are in retreat, though I sensed that he would have much preferred that Grant had performed the deed."

"Did you discuss your plans for attacking Longstreet and taking Richmond?"

"In the most general terms. I would say the president was with child to learn my intentions, but he was disappointed."

"George, he's the president."

"Yes, and I'm the commanding general. Shoemaker, look to your shoes."

"And General Grant?"

"A cypher, as always. Wearing his damned corporal's uniform to a meeting with the president. Said very little in front of Lincoln."

Nelly waited. Then, "Meaning he spoke to you after the meeting."

"Yes, asked for a word as we left the President's House. Congratulated me on the victory, my victory, and told me he was at my service and awaited orders. Said he hoped he could be in on the kill, his words, when the army marches on Richmond."

"What did you say?"

McClellan laughed. "I told him that he would receive orders in due course, and that in the meantime, this time, I expected his army to remain in camp."

"George, were you on time this time? For the meeting?"

"I arrived at precisely the time I wanted to arrive." A pause. "Twenty minutes late." He smiled at the memory.

"George, I know your mother taught you that good manners never go out of style."

"She did. She also taught me measure for measure. Keeping the president waiting on occasion can never erase the slights and insults that I've suffered under his hand." He smiled sheepishly. "But it helps."

Nelly returned the smile. "George, I've been thinking. I believe it's time to mend fences with Governor Seymour. His nose may have been somewhat out of joint when the army, uh, moved south following the Battle of Saratoga. Now that things have been set right militarily, it is time to look to politics as well."

McClellan stared at his wife. "Yes. It certainly can't hurt to remind the governor of our victory, and that the time is coming to take important political steps. But I have no time to travel to Albany."

"No, of course not, George. But I do."

LANE

North of Albany, New York
June 1864

John Lane came to the familiar turnoff. He hadn't been sure that he'd recognize it, but he did, immediately. He looked around. Red-coated soldiers marched, heads down, mostly in silence, though in some cases comrades chatted quietly. Assuming that the simplest plan was the best plan, he said aloud to no one in particular, "I'll have a piss." He walked off the road and into the field and did indeed have a piss. When he was done, he kept walking, waiting for someone to shout or for the flat of an officer's sword to land on his back. Nothing. He kept walking, and in ten minutes he could see Viola's house.

Lane had been with the army for more than two weeks as they marched, or more accurately trudged, northward. His presence had attracted little attention, another wounded soldier, this one an Irishman. He mostly kept to himself and spoke as little as possible. He had made up and memorized a variety of identities so that, when he found himself with one unit, he would say that he was with another. No one cared enough to ask more questions.

His plan, such as it was, had been simple. Stay with the British Army until they entered Canada, then look for an opportunity to run away. He'd go first to his cousins in the Eastern Townships south of Montreal, then try to figure out his future.

His plan had been interrupted that very morning. As Lane walked along the road, he heard horsemen approaching from the rear and shouts to "move aside, step lively there, move aside."

Lane stopped and moved to the side to let the horsemen pass. As they did, one of them happened to look at him and meet his gaze. A look of recognition came over the rider, who stopped his horse, wheeled around, and rode back for a second look at Lane. The horseman dismounted and motioned to Lane to step further aside into the field by the side of the road.

Major Thomas Packenham, for it was he, said, "Mr. Lane. Perhaps a fortuitous coincidence. General Burgoyne was visited last night in camp by agents of the Pinkerton Agency. Do you know who they are?"

Lane nodded. He did.

"They are looking for what they deem the ringleaders of the Fenian business."

A shiver ran down Lane's back. "I thought that the Union Army had already shot the ringleaders."

Packenham looked up the road. His comrades on horseback were riding ahead. "Indeed. Some of them. But they are looking for others. Yourself included. General Burgoyne was, em, not helpful to the Pinkerton men. He was shown a likeness, a decent likeness, I should say, of you, and said he didn't know you. They are looking for you specifically. By name."

Lane felt sick. "Did the general have a suggestion of what I might do?"

Packenham smiled, a humorless smile. "He did not. But I would suggest you, em, end your service with the British Army and find a very good place to hide. The Pinkerton men were serious indeed."

With that, Packenham mounted, tipped his cap, said, "Good luck, Mr. Lane," and was off.

Knowing that the Pinkerton men were in the area meant he had to be careful. Lane took off his red coat and shoved it into the branches of the hedgerow by the side of the road. He found a tree four hundred yards or so from Viola's house, where he could sit on the ground, out of sight, but with a view of who came or went. He would wait until evening to approach.

DAVIS

Richmond, Virginia
June 1864

As was their custom after dinner each evening, Jefferson and Varina Davis sat before the fire, Davis trying to warm himself and Varina knitting socks for the soldiers.

"Would you say you're more Penelope or Madame Defarge?"

Varina looked up with a start. "I wasn't aware that my politico husband had read the classics." A pause. "But I suppose I'm more surprised to learn after all these years that you have a sense of humor."

"You didn't answer my question."

Varina considered. "Certainly Madame Defarge is the more compelling character. Rage. Vengefulness. But Penelope was loyal, faithful, clever. I should be pleased to play either on the stage."

Davis was surprised to find himself smiling. "Any man would be lucky to marry a Penelope. But perhaps the president of an upstart country, engaged in war with a powerful nation, would prefer to have Defarge by his side."

"Is there anyone in particular that you'd like me to send to the guillotine?"

"I have a list. A long one."

"I note with satisfaction that you aren't pacing this evening. The carpet and I are grateful. Are you at peace, my dear?"

Davis looked at his wife and thought for a long minute. "Perhaps I am. Though I shouldn't be. We can expect the Federals to cross the Potomac at any time. With our British allies disposed of, they shall focus all of their might on defeating Longstreet and capturing Richmond."

Varina was back at her knitting. "You are looking for an ending. It is past time for this war to end. You are at peace because you believe that the next battle will be the last one, for good or ill."

"I add mind reader to your list of talents."

"Your mind has never been difficult to read. Not since the day we met."

Davis laughed.

"Jokes, laughter, literary allusions. Where has this man been all my life?"

Davis frowned, the rare moment of giddiness past. "Hmmph. Serving his country. Whatever it may have been called at the time."

Varina also frowned, sensing her husband's mood swing, and the reason for it. Not hard to read indeed.

In a soft tone, "You believe that if we lose, they'll brand you a traitor."

"We both know that is the case. Both their perception and the reality. Men who lead successful revolutions are heroes. Washington. Those who fail are traitors. That list is much longer."

Davis looked at his wife. Varina had feared this conversation, but she felt relief now that they were having it. "I should feel better if you were to travel to Mississippi until matters are, uh, decided."

"You wouldn't request such a thing of either Penelope or Madame Defarge, and neither would agree in any case. I shall remain here. And let us hope that this drama has more of Odysseus and less of Charles Darnay."

"Hmmph. He was prepared to face his end with dignity. Darnay. But he escaped in the end, did he not?"

Varina, for once, had nothing to say in response.

BURGOYNE

Near Mechanicsville, New York
June 1864

In the days since Burgoyne's unexpected nap in the road near Allentown, he had experienced good days and bad. There were days when he was twelve hours or more in the saddle and seemed himself. There were days when Packenham convinced him, with less urging on each occasion, to ride for a time in a wagon. On this day, Burgoyne had refused the wagon and seemed to be in complete command.

"What town is this, Thomas?"

"I dare say town is an exaggeration, sir, but the map calls this place Mechanicsville."

Burgoyne gave the name considerable thought. "Mechanicsville. Visions of yeomen about their trades, sturdy blacksmiths, red-faced publicans, stout butchers, wagonmakers, wheelwrights. They named their town after themselves. Another age. Like home."

"Just so, sir."

"How far to Saratoga, Thomas? To the Heights?"

"Bemis Heights?" Packenham paused, doing the numbers in his

head. "I shouldn't think more than five- or six-miles, sir. No more, surely. Shall we make camp there?"

Burgoyne glanced left toward the sun, lowering toward the western horizon, but with a good three hours of daylight left, and said, "Yes. We should just make it before nightfall."

They rode in silence for the next hour. Packenham mused that if they were not a defeated army this would be a glorious summer. The weather was perfect, the countryside beautiful, and he had seen war and survived it. Even enjoyed it. He had not dwelt on what lay in store when they returned to Canada. Plenty of time for that yet.

They reached Bemis Heights as the orange ball began to slip below the horizon. The Hudson stretched out before them north to south, and the patchwork neatness of the farm fields reminded all of them of home.

"It seems like yesterday that we fought here." Burgoyne's voice had broken the spell. The major turned, and for a brief moment, thought he was looking at a ghost.

"Yes sir. You won a great victory here."

"Did I? It certainly doesn't seem so now."

As red-coated soldiers began the practiced ritual of making camp, Burgoyne remained mounted, staring into the distance long after darkness had fallen. Finally, unsure what to do, Packenham asked, "Sir. Shall we make camp?"

Burgoyne looked at Packenham, at first quizzically, then said, "So we shall, Thomas. So we shall." Then, awkwardly, "Could I ask for your assistance in dismounting. I'm suddenly quite exhausted."

McCLELLAN

Washington, DC

June 1864

George McClellan was waiting, impatiently, at the B & O Railroad Station in Washington City. As the train from New York eased up to the platform, he scanned the windows. He and Nelly saw each other at the same time. She smiled and waved while the general did his best to look dignified. There were scores of people on the platform.

McClellan approached the train as Nelly alighted, and she kissed him on both cheeks.

"Did you miss me?"

"Yes, of course, though I've been busy."

Nelly linked her arm in his and they walked through the station, out the New Jersey Avenue doors, and into McClellan's waiting carriage. Six cavalrymen escorted the carriage, two in front and four behind.

McClellan leaned out the window and yelled "home," at the same time tapping on the roof of the carriage with the butt of his sword.

"So?"

"I'm fine, George, thank you for inquiring, and how are you?"

McClellan looked at his boots for a moment, collected himself, looked at Nelly, and said, "Sorry, my dear. How was your trip? Are you quite well? I've missed you."

Nelly laughed. "Very good indeed, George. Much better. So. Governor Seymour sends his regards. The visit went quite well. The governor believes all is in train. There is no need for you to be present in Chicago. He will place your name in nomination, and he believes there's some chance you'll be home free on the first ballot. If not, soon thereafter. He wonders, have you a preference for vice president? He sent a list of names, which I'll show you when we're home."

McClellan looked at his wife in astonishment.

"Did you think I went to Albany to pass the time with Mrs. Seymour?" She laughed so hard her chest heaved. "I shall spare you the details of my time spent with her."

"And that's that?"

"And that is apparently that. Though I've no doubt that defeating General Longstreet would increase the odds of a first-ballot nomination."

"As to that."

Nelly raised her eyebrows. "And as to that?"

McClellan pointed upwards, as if to indicate that the driver and escorts had ears.

"When we're home."

"Yes, of course. George, the governor wondered if you'll resign your commission or run as a uniformed officer? I was not comfortable answering the question for you."

"It is a question. General Scott did not resign his commission. I don't imagine that I shall either. What to do once elected is a different question altogether. As commander-in-chief it won't be necessary to wear the uniform."

"The governor also had questions about the platform. He supposed that you oppose the peace faction and favor fighting the war to a successful conclusion. I took the liberty of saying that was the case."

"Just so."

"And the issue of slavery. The party platform will almost surely call for its abolition."

McClellan did not answer immediately. Frowning, he said, "Slavery shall die of its own weight. It isn't necessary for the party or for me to take a political stand that will unnecessarily provoke the voters. It will die a gradual death and our victory will hasten its end."

Nelly was quiet. Finally, she said, "I believe you should accept the platform as it will be written. To include abolition. You won't provoke the voters. You shall guide them."

They rode the rest of the way home in silence.

Once inside the house, and Nelly's bags upstairs, they sat together in the drawing room, each deep in their thoughts.

"You said you'd tell me when we were home. About your plans."

"Yes. I shall lead the army south very soon. Meade will have the Army of the Potomac. Grant his Western ruffians. And I shall be in overall command of 200,000 men or perhaps a shade more. Double the size of Longstreet's army. It should all be settled long before the convention at the end of August."

"George. You should tell Mr. Lincoln of your plans. It's the right thing to do."

"Yes. I will deal with the one president just as soon as I've dealt with the other."

LANE

North of Albany, New York
June 1864

Lane had watched Viola's house from his hiding place until well after dark and hadn't seen another soul during all that time. He had finally stood, stretched his legs and back, walked up to the farmhouse, and knocked on the door.

He heard low voices, footsteps, and a door close before Viola's mother opened the door a crack and peered out into the darkness.

"What do you want?"

"Is Viola here? I need to see her."

"She's not here."

At that moment Viola herself appeared at the door. "It's alright, Mother." She grabbed Lane by his good arm and pulled him inside. "Get in before someone sees you."

Lane had eaten at the wooden table, mostly in silence, though occasionally answering the questions posed to him by the children, who had gotten out of their beds to talk to the visitor. Where had he been? Had he been in the war? Was he going to stay downstairs with the others?

The last question had prompted Viola's mother to hustle the children back into the other room, as Lane took a seat by the fire.

"The Pinkerton men have been here, twice. I can't have that. Sooner or later, they'll figure out what I'm up to. You need to find someplace to go. Why didn't you stay with the British? Surely they'd protect you."

Lane looked as miserable as he felt. "I've been with the army for weeks. But now the Pinkerton men are looking for me among the British soldiers. It wasn't safe."

Viola stared into the fire.

"You can help me get to Canada through your network. I can't pay you now, but once I get to safety, I can send you something."

Viola stood, hands on hips. "Do you think I do this for money? You don't understand anything."

"I didn't mean that. I just meant that I would be grateful for the help."

Viola sat again, and minutes passed without a word. Finally, Lane asked, "Do you have a husband?"

With a withering look, Viola said, "Do you think these children appeared out of nowhere? Of course I have a husband. Or did. He joined the army. Went to New York City to join up as soon as they sent out the call for Black soldiers." A pause. "I had two letters from New York City and then nothing until I got a letter. From one of his friends. He was killed at a place called Fort Wagner. In South Carolina."

"I'm sorry. A hero's death." Lane instantly regretted his comment. A stupid thing to say indeed.

Another silence, and Viola's mother came out of the other room and closed the door quietly behind her. She removed the dishes from the table and made a show of cleaning up from the meal.

"There's no guarantee that the others will help you. On the network. I don't know them. I just take people to the next stop, as you saw when we moved Michael and Sarah. They might take you for a spy. Which of course you are. Or were."

Lane straightened in his chair. "I'll take my chances. What do I do?"

"Mostly you do what you're told and stay quiet. I'm expecting visitors tonight. We'll put them downstairs and take them to the next stop tomorrow night. You'll need to spend the night down there as well. If the Pinkerton men come back, they'll search the barn."

Viola hadn't said yes or no to helping him escape. "There are blankets, water, and a lantern down there. If you hear a knock on the door or footsteps above, blow out the lantern and remain perfectly quiet. In the morning, don't come upstairs until I come down to get you."

"I understand."

Viola walked over to the large table, grabbed one end of it with her two hands, and looked at her mother. The mother put down the towel she was using to dry the dishes, grabbed the other end of the table, and without saying a word, the two women moved it six feet from its usual place. Viola folded back the rug which normally sat under the table, pulled on a metal handle, and lifted the floorboards to reveal a staircase, which led to the darkness below. Viola's mother handed him a lighted candle. "Watch your step."

As Lane stepped gingerly on to the stairs, there was a loud knock at the door. Lane whispered, "Your guests." Viola shook her head. "No, too loud. Hurry!"

Viola and her mother replaced the rug and table as quickly and silently as they could. Viola quickly looked around the room. Had Lane left anything upstairs? Another loud knock at the door just as Viola began to open it. Outside were two men with dark mustaches, bowler hats, and sidearms on their hips.

The shorter of the two men said, "Good evening, ma'am. We'd like to have a look around."

"You've searched here twice already. I haven't seen the man you're looking for."

The taller man said, "We've reason to believe he's in the area," as he pushed his way past Viola and into the house.

DAVIS

Between Richmond and Ashland Mill, Virginia
June 1864

Jefferson Davis had arrived at his desk at first light and had spent the early hours of the morning alternately staring at the huge clock in the corner and shouting for aides to bring him the latest from General Longstreet.

Each time the answer had been, "No news yet this morning, sir."

Davis was certain that the Federal forces would attack Longstreet today. They had crossed the Potomac five days ago, and aside from Sheridan's cavalry wreaking havoc on innocent civilians, had made a desultory advance southward. They had camped the night before in the vicinity of Chandler Crossing, and he expected the attack at any moment. Perhaps it was already under way.

Finally, at a little past nine in the morning, Davis couldn't take it any longer. He scrawled a quick note to Varina, picked his hat and riding gloves off the table by the door, handed the note to a clerk, and walked out of the office. Aides scrambled and followed Davis out the front door. To a staff officer, he said, "My horse." Other officers ran to find mounts, and in two minutes, Davis and his small entourage were headed north toward Ashland Mill.

As the miles passed, Davis strained, listening for the sound of the big guns, but he heard nothing. *I don't know for certain that the attack will come today, but I feel it in my bones.*

After a couple of hours, Davis thought he heard small arms fire, but he wasn't certain. As they approached Ashland Mill, it was clear something was afoot. Last time the rear of Longstreet's lines had been casual and relaxed. Now it was all motion and commotion.

Davis spurred his horse forward, and as his party passed a squadron of cavalry, he shouted at a startled lieutenant, "Take me to General Longstreet." The lieutenant wheeled and spurred his mount with Davis riding hard in his wake. In five minutes, they crested a small hill and found Longstreet in conversation with Fitzhugh Lee and Braxton Bragg. All three men looked over at the sound of the approaching horses.

"Gentlemen. What news, General?"

Longstreet smiled. Nothing put him in a better mood than imminent battle. "Fitz just came from the front. Sheridan is out in force this morning and probing our defenses." The pop of sporadic small arms fire could be heard to the north and west.

Fitz Lee looked in that direction. "That's them. Never seen so many Union cavalrymen in my life. All we can handle."

"General Lee, how many men would you estimate we'll be facing?"

"Sir, there's so much cavalry in our front that we can't get near the rest of their army. I just know I've never seen a dust cloud that size, or so many campfires."

Bragg jumped in. "My men have been in contact with the Federals since they crossed the river. They're engaged in a fighting retreat as ordered. I'd say we're facing fifteen corps. Grant and Meade plus Sheridan's cavalry."

All were silent as they contemplated the vast host advancing toward them.

"Do you expect McClellan will bring on a general engagement?"

Longstreet smiled. "I expect he will, and I hope he does. This is fine ground, and I feel like I could set up shop here for a long time. Jackson reported this morning that he's in position and awaiting word to spring the trap."

Davis was taking it all in, the sounds, the smell, the men running and galloping toward the front. *This is where I belong.*

"Then let it be so. General, gentlemen, I'll leave you to your business. I implore you to keep me up to the minute. General Longstreet, I shall be at home in Richmond."

McCLELLAN

Ashland Mill, Virginia
June 1864

George McClellan sat his horse atop a low hill north of Ashland Mill. His army had been on the move since before daybreak, and there had been cavalry clashes all morning as the two armies tried to determine each other's movements and intentions.

Along with a small army of staff officers, McClellan was accompanied by Generals Grant, Meade, and Sheridan. The two former had been with McClellan all morning, though both were itching to join their commands. Sheridan had joined them ten minutes previously, his horse lathered and snorting, Sheridan himself dripping with sweat from a morning in the saddle.

Sheridan was speaking. "I couldn't find the rebel left flank. Fitz Lee's cavalry was very aggressive." As he spoke, they heard the crackle of small arms off to their right. "As you can hear. But first reports from my fellas indicate that their right seems to be in the air. I need to be sure, but if that's the case, General, I'd hit 'em hard straight ahead, but send someone around their right. Who knows? The road to Richmond might be open."

McClellan looked at Grant. "General, your boys are holding our left flank. What do you think?"

Grant was chewing on an unlit cigar. "My men are ready when you give the word, General. But I'll feel better after Phil, uh, General Sheridan sends some cavalry over there again to be sure. I don't want to walk into something."

McClellan sniffed. "Now's the time, General. Send skirmishers out in force, but now's the time. General Meade, you may send the Army of the Potomac in, straight ahead. And General Grant, you will support that attack by hitting their right. General Meade, I shall ride with you. Let's be about our business, gentlemen."

Grant's only response was a poker-faced nod in McClellan's direction. He wheeled his horse and cantered off to the left, staff officers behind him. Meade was surrounded by his staff, barking out orders to each in turn, who shot off one by one to find the division commanders. Batteries of artillery galloped up and unlimbered on the hill, and in no time began lobbing the first shells toward the Confederate defenses less than a mile away. Soon Confederate shells answered, as the rebel gunners found the range. Staff officers held their nervous horses until Captain Wilson finally said, "Sir, we need to let the cannoneers do their work." McClellan and Meade rode to the rear, McClellan saying, "Fine, Captain. Find us another vantage from which to watch."

Half an hour later, the crack of small arms erupted all along the line in their front. Meade was engaged. Almost simultaneously they heard a similar noise far off to their left.

Meade cocked his head and looked at McClellan. "Too soon for Sam to be engaged. He'd need at least another hour to put himself in position."

McClellan tried to read the noise above the din of the battle in front of him, but it was impossible. "Captain Wilson, send someone to find General Grant and find out what he's about."

McClellan and Meade spent the next half hour riding behind

their lines, seeking a spot where they could follow the action in front of them. The battle lines were engulfed in black powder smoke, and it was impossible to determine exactly what was happening.

Meade, looking through field glasses, said, "I'll send someone up to have a look."

McClellan had been silent, staring at the smoke, and finally said, "I'm going. I want to see for myself. What happens in the next hour will determine the course of the war."

At that moment there was the sound of rifle fire immediately to their left. McClellan's party turned to see blue-clad soldiers running toward them in disorder, some turning occasionally to fire, others seemingly running for their lives. Behind them, a hundred yards distant, a butternut wave emerged from the woods, screaming and firing.

Meade didn't hesitate. He pulled his sword from its scabbard and rode into the mass of retreating Union soldiers, yelling, "Stop, form up. Goddam it, rally on me, form up!"

McClellan had pulled his sidearm from its holster, raised it in the air, and spurred his horse toward the attacking rebel line. Captain Wilson, more amazed than scared, hesitated for just an instant, then galloped after McClellan.

LANE

North of Albany, New York
June 1864

After the Pinkerton men had searched Viola's house even more thoroughly than before, but found nothing suspicious, Viola opened the trap door and let Lane back upstairs.

"You see how it is. They weren't satisfied when they left. They'll be back, and eventually they'll find the cellar. You have to leave."

"You said you have guests coming tonight."

"Yes. A husband and wife, I'm told, but that's all I know."

Lane was scared and exhausted, tears in his eyes. "Let me sleep in the cellar, then go with them to the next stop. Please."

Viola was tired as well. "I don't have the energy to argue or explain this to you again. You chose to throw your hat in with traitors and slaveholders. Now you're sorry. You want me to jeopardize my family and my freedom and jeopardize our network. You understand that what you're asking is selfish and unfair."

Lane began to weep. "Yes."

In fact, he did understand. He'd thought of little else on the long march north with the British Army. Intended or not, he was a traitor and a supporter of slavery.

Later, there was another knock at the door, this one softer, tentative.

Viola pointed to the guest room where the children were sleeping, and Lane entered quietly and latched the door behind him. Viola opened the door to allow a young couple and a baby to enter. Viola and her mother quickly exposed the trap door, and the newcomers and Lane were sent down the stairs.

Lane made a bed for himself in the corner of the cellar. He introduced himself awkwardly to the young couple, but beyond an exchange of names, they were not interested in conversation. Their baby was a marvel, seeming to understand the need for silence, and didn't make a sound the entire night.

In the morning, Viola's mother brought food for all of them and told them to be ready to move after dark. Lane tried to talk to her, suggesting that it would make more sense to move in daylight, like last time. He could drive the wagon and stick to the story that he and Viola were business partners. Viola's mother listened for a moment, then turned to go up the stairs.

"We'll do as Viola directs us," she said as her head disappeared above the ceiling. A moment later, the trap door closed again, and Lane sat down on his bedding, a long day of waiting ahead of him.

Lane dozed on and off during the day, and otherwise tried to think of the life that awaited him in Canada. He'd had enough of one-armed tailoring and doubted that there would be many takers for Irish language lessons in Quebec. Perhaps a writer, or schoolteacher. He wondered if he'd have to learn French.

After an eternity, the trap door opened again, and they climbed the stairs with their meager belongings, went outside, and boarded the wagon. Viola drove and the wife, Bethany, was seated beside her holding the baby, still quiet as a mouse. The husband, Solomon, sat in the back with Lane. There was little room as the wagon was packed with sacks full of potatoes.

"Why the potatoes?" asked Lane.

"Insurance."

They traveled in silence for an hour, the creaking of the wagon the only sound. The air was balmy, and the bright moon cast shadows. Each traveler was lost deep in thought, and the marvelous baby was asleep in her mother's arms.

Lane was jolted from his thoughts by the sound of hoofbeats coming up behind them, more than one rider from the sound of it.

Viola whispered, but loud enough for them all to hear. "My business partner and I are getting an early start to deliver potatoes to market. My sister and her family are visiting and along for the ride."

Two horsemen pulled up alongside the wagon, and Viola tugged on the reins, saying, "Whoa there."

DAVIS

Richmond, Virginia
June 1864

The knock on the door had come late in the evening, and Davis had answered himself. The servants, as Davis referred to the enslaved people who worked in his household, had disappeared over the course of the past two days.

Longstreet apologized for the late hour as Davis showed him into the parlor. "I thought it best to talk in person."

Davis pointed to the chair, his chair, by the fire, and Longstreet sat. Davis pulled Varina's chair around to face him.

Longstreet looked into the fire as if preparing for a difficult conversation.

Davis leaned forward. "I should like to hear everything, General. I'm not one to be mollycoddled."

Longstreet laughed despite the occasion. "Not my intention to mollycoddle, Mr. President. The situation is stable but dire if that makes sense. Our troops were driven back into the defenses of Richmond. If you climb a church spire, you'll see 'em."

"Yes, I took a ride this afternoon and inspected some of the defenses myself. They're strong. But a stone's throw from here."

"Mighty strong, Mr. President. We can hold out a long time in those trenches. But that's my point. Seems to me that a siege just prolongs the inevitable. If we're still determined to fight for independence—" He looked squarely at Davis. "If we're still determined to fight, we'd do well to get the army, and the government for that matter, out of Richmond while we can. Head south and west. Meet up with Joe Johnston, set up shop in Birmingham. Texas maybe. Maintain room to maneuver and campaign."

Now Davis was staring into the fire. Varina entered, carrying a tray with a bottle and two glasses. Longstreet stood. "Very sorry for the late hour, Mrs. Davis. I didn't mean to trouble you for refreshments."

"I heard you come in. You're always welcome in this house, General. Our people have run off, it seems."

Longstreet, still standing, nodded. "Seems every servant in Richmond has decided to find the Union Army. They've been streaming through our lines since yesterday. I gave orders to let them pass. We don't have the manpower to do anything about it."

"I shall leave you to your discussions. Good evening, General."

"Good evening, ma'am."

"Peter, what are the chances of getting out?"

"Hard to say, sir. Fitz Lee and his cavalry have been pushed back to the outskirts of Richmond as well. I've never seen so damn many Yankee cavalrymen. But Fitz thinks there's a small window. We'd have to decide now. The Federals will keep pushing west and south until they cut off the roads and railroads. Now or never, I'd say."

"Have you heard anything about McClellan's condition?"

"We hear he's still alive, though how, I don't know. He was carried from the field. I never thought I'd say that George McClellan is the bravest soldier I've ever seen, but damned if he isn't. Jackson's flank attack caught Grant completely by surprise and had them on the run.

McClellan stopped the rout almost single-handedly, and eventually Jackson ran out of steam and daylight. Grant's got the army for now. He knows a thing or two about a siege."

"If McClellan dies, he'll be a hero. If he lives, he'll be president. He's come a long way since the Seven Days and Antietam."

They sat in silence. Davis poured a couple of fingers of the brown liquid into the glasses, and they toasted without speaking.

"What are the chances of a counterattack? A breakout?"

Longstreet didn't hesitate, shaking his head. "Impossible. They outnumber us three to one, though I'm not sure they know that. McClellan was always given to exaggerating our numbers. Nope. We try to slide out to the west and south, to fight another day, or we hunker down in the trenches."

In his heart, if not in his head, Davis had always known it would come down to this. There would be a point at which he would have to decide whether to fight on or call it quits. It was hard to see a clear path to independence.

Davis swallowed the rest of the whiskey in a quick gulp. He stood and said, "Prepare the army to move south. The government will go with you. God help us."

BURGOYNE

Bemis Heights, near Saratoga, New York
June 1864

It was late, past midnight, but Burgoyne did not want to sleep.
He made a point of speaking to each of his generals in turn, and
stood, unsteadily at times, around the campfire and passed the time
with his staff officers. They, according to custom, would not retire
until the general did.

Packenham watched Burgoyne closely. He was at once animated
but at the same time had a ghostly pall. The young major had grown
accustomed to thinking of the general as old, and in the light of the
campfire, he looked every bit of his eighty-one years.

Finally, near one o'clock in the morning, Burgoyne wished
his staff a good night and walked slowly back to his tent. He said,
"Thomas, a word, if you please."

Packenham followed Burgoyne into the tent, lit the lantern, and
stood near the entrance, curious as to what the general wanted to
tell him.

Burgoyne bent over slowly and opened the wooden trunk which

sat at the foot of his camp bed. He lifted out a beautiful sword, an officer's sword that looked as if it belonged to the last century. He handed it to Packenham.

Puzzled, Packenham made a show of examining the sword in the lantern light, pulling it from its scabbard, examining the blade, the hilt, and admiring the craftsmanship.

"My father's. It's the sword he presented to General Gates here at Saratoga. Upon his surrender. Gates was a gentleman, as soldiers were in those days. He shook my father's hand, held the sword in his own hands to mark the surrender, then returned it to my father. I've carried it with me my whole career. To Louisiana, Spain, Ireland, the Crimea."

Packenham noted an inscription on the blade, impossible to read in the light of the lantern. Uncharacteristically at a loss for words, Packenham mumbled, "I've never seen it's like, sir. A relic of another age."

"You shall bury it with me, Thomas."

"Sir?"

"I should like to take it to my grave. A vanity, to be sure, but I won't be quite comfortable without it. I'm accustomed to having it nearby, don't you see?"

"I shall bear that in mind, sir. But no rush, I'm quite certain, sir."

Burgoyne took the sword back from Packenham and placed it carefully back in the trunk. "Now you know where it resides, Thomas. I shall be counting on you."

With that, Burgoyne began to unbutton his tunic, and Packenham turned to leave.

"Stay, Thomas. I should be grateful if you would take a seat and keep an old man company for a time."

Silently, Packenham pulled a camp stool in front of the tent flap and sat down. Burgoyne removed his tunic and boots and climbed into his bed. He extinguished the lantern, and Packenham, unclear if he should say anything, said, "Good night, sir."

Burgoyne responded, in a voice sleepy or weak, "Farewell, Thomas."

Packenham was unsure of the time, but it was still pitch-black outside. He had been dozing when he heard Burgoyne say, "Sarah . . . Sarah."

"Sir?" There was only silence.

Packenham knew at that moment that the general was gone. He approached the bed, closed Burgoyne's eyes, confirmed that there was no pulse, and walked out of the tent. He said to one of the guards, "Fetch the surgeon and the general officers. Urgently, if you please."

Ten minutes later, Generals Campbell, Gordon, Trevelyan, and Mountjoy, along with Burgoyne's chief surgeon, were at the general's bedside. Packenham stood behind them at the entrance to the tent.

"I can fairly say that his heart gave out. Nothing more or less than that, the passing of years, which none of us can escape."

Campbell looked back at Packenham. "You were with him, Major?"

"I was, sir."

"Did he give any last orders or have any last words, laddie?"

Packenham hesitated. "Yes sir. He said 'Sarah,' twice."

The surgeon grunted. "The wife?"

Campbell responded, "No. His wife is Charlotte."

The surgeon grunted again. "A mistress, perhaps."

Only Packenham understood that "Sarah" was indeed a mistress, a cruel mistress who had tormented Burgoyne since he'd first heard the word as a young boy.

EPILOGUE

Huntingdon, Quebec
March 1865

John Lane was sitting in the parlor of the small house he had rented in Huntingdon, Quebec. He was reading aloud from the *Montreal Gazette.*

Assisted by his wife and Vice President Seymour, General McClellan was able to stand before the Chief Justice to take the oath of office. With his right hand on a bible held by Mrs. McClellan, the general repeated the words in a soft voice, audible only to those nearest the podium.

"Do you hear?"

"Yes, I hear," was the response from the kitchen. "General McClellan is the president. It's a shame. Mr. Lincoln was much more devoted to abolition."

"The article says that Lincoln attended the inauguration. But not Mrs. Lincoln. She was feeling poorly. And it's the same in the end. The defeat of the Confederacy will mean the end of slavery."

Lane continued reading. *In spite of his injuries, incurred in the historic victory at Ashland Mill, the newly inaugurated President is expected to take the field to pursue General Longstreet's army, currently in camp near Birmingham, the temporary capital of the Confederacy. It is rumored that President Davis intends to flee with his cabinet to Texas and then possibly to Mexico.*

"What time are your students coming? Don't you need to prepare a lesson?"

Lane pulled his watch from its pocket. "I've half an hour. There isn't much to prepare. They've little interest in learning Gaelic, and frankly I'm losing interest in teaching it to them."

There was a long silence as Lane read, now quietly to himself. His eyes left the paper. He put it down and walked into the kitchen.

Viola wiped her hands on a dish towel and looked at him. "John, there's something I need to say. I need to go back. Home. To my house and my calling. Even if the end of the war means the end of slavery, as you say, it won't change people's hearts. I have unfinished business."

Lane stared at Viola for a long minute, then said, "Why don't we work together?"

"Because if you cross back into the United States, you run the risk of hanging. Are you prepared for that?"

Lane thought of his narrow escape from the Pinkerton men. The most unlikely abolitionists he could imagine. It hadn't taken them long to figure out what Viola was doing with a Black family in the back of her wagon, heading north. They'd let Lane go with the promise that he wouldn't stop until he reached Canada. Well, he'd kept the promise. But he hadn't promised not to come back.

"Yes. I'm prepared. I'll be ready to leave in the morning."

CPSIA information can be obtained
at www.ICGtesting.com
Printed in the USA
LVHW032250240122
709211LV00007B/411